WE ALL RAN
into the
SUNLIGHT

WE ALL RAN
into the
SUNLIGHT

NATALIE YOUNG

First published in 2011 by
Short Books
3A Exmouth House
Pine Street, EC1R 0JH

A CIP catalogue record for this book
is available from the British Library.

ISBN 978-1-907595-41-7

Printed in Great Britain by CPI Bookmarque, Croydon

For Aurea Carpenter

Je dis: ma Mère.
Et c'est à vous que je pense, ô Maison
Maison des beaux étés obscurs de mon enfance.

I say: Mother.
And my thoughts are of you, oh House
House of the lovely dark summers of my childhood.

Oscar Milosz

PROLOGUE

Canas, South-West France, 1985

From the middle of June that summer the heat went up into the high thirties and stayed there, so that nothing much happened in the village and nobody moved. People sat in their chairs with their mouths hanging open. Most of the time they slept. In the village shop, the water supplies and the ice creams ran out long before the delivery came on a Monday afternoon. Only right at the end of August, when the holidays were over and the motorways clogged with cars going home, did a wind pick up off the sea. It came in quite violently; clearing the heat out of the sky and making the sea go a deep blue far out. Then it rose over the sand dunes and the dry grasses on the floodplain. It moved through the swinging doors of the roadside cafés that lined the motorway on its final stretch to the Spanish border, until it came to where the vineyards were, some twenty miles from the coast, which was where the land began to rise into the hills.

The wind brought with it relief, and a kind of foreboding. In the village the children felt it. Even the cicadas might have felt it for it went very quiet all of a sudden as if, on the plane trees lining the main road, they had ceased their sucking of the sap and taken a pause, while the leaves turned in on each other with whispering relief and the rooks, startled out of their slumber, crashed around madly then stretched their wings and flew, croaking resentfully, at the sun.

There was only one road into Canas then, and you had to turn round in the square and drive out again with the church on your left this time and the east wall of the chateau rising up to your right. You could sit at the café, at a table under the lime trees, and that wall would dominate the square, blocking the afternoon sun. It was like a medieval fort, with only one window near the top. But if the shutters were open, which they often were in those days, and the light was right, you could look up through the balcony railings and see in through the old panes to the giant rose on the ceiling of Lucie Borja's bedroom.

Things changed that August day. Things changed in a way that no one would want to talk about in years to come. There was the heat, and then the air coming in like that, lifting the dust from the ground in the chateau courtyard, and nuzzling up to the front walls.

Lucie withdrew from the balcony and into the quiet of her bedroom. When her eyes had adjusted to the light she saw that Daniel was there – barefoot and silent; he was standing in the doorway.

'Come in,' she whispered and he stepped forward with the birthday present in his hand.

'It's not much,' he said. 'It's not as if there's any choice here though.' He stood beside her while she untied the ribbon and counted the almonds out on the bed. He'd tied them in a muslin cloth using a sprig of olive he'd got from the courtyard, and Lucie made a fuss of this, bending over with enthusiasm and attaching all kinds of importance to what was never really there.

'Chocolates would have melted,' said Daniel. He was nineteen. He was wiry, and dark-skinned and his eyes were a pale greeny blue, like pebbles of washed-up glass. His mother gazed up at him.

'Happy birthday,' he said, but his voice had no life in it. 'I've got to go because Sylvie's coming to help us prepare.'

'That's fine,' said Lucie, with her watery eyes. 'But will she stay for the party? And is Frederic coming?'

'Later,' Daniel said. 'He's up on the heath at the moment, with the flying club. They've got a sea plane coming in up there for fuel.'

'Are the fires still burning on the hills, Daniel?'

'Yes, Maman,' he said, quietly, 'there's an arsonist up there. He's setting fires on the hills, and now there's a wind picking up. It will only get worse through the afternoon.'

She reached for his hand and held it; rubbing the smooth skin with her thumb. 'It won't come for us though, Daniel. Nothing will come to disturb us on this night. Your poor Maman is getting old. But tonight we will eat all of your favourite things under the olive trees in the courtyard.'

'Me, Frederic and Sylvie won't stay for the whole meal,' said Daniel, backing away towards the door.

'Of course. I knew that. When does Frederic leave?'

'Monday,' said Daniel.

Two days, thought Lucie. 'I imagine that Sylvie will miss her brother when he goes,' she said. 'And you too.'

'Happy birthday,' he said.

15

'Thank you, my love.' Lucie smiled at her son's back as he turned to go.

And then he was gone, walking quickly in the corridor and down the wide stairs on the hard pads of his feet.

———

'Am I too early?' said Sylvie as she reached where Daniel was standing outside with one leg up against the wall. In the courtyard it was bright; intensely white, and Sylvie, in a floral dress, put her hand up to shield her eyes.

'It doesn't matter much,' he said. 'Early or late, it makes no difference to anyone.'

He shrugged and ground his cigarette into the step. Sylvie laughed. She had braces, which she did her best to hide, but her freckled face, in its corral of wild black hair, was almost pretty.

'I don't mean it doesn't matter much to me,' said Daniel, touching her on the shoulder to make her feel more at ease. 'I just mean it doesn't matter much to this place. Nothing makes any difference here.'

'Except this,' said Sylvie, taking the plastic wallet from the bag slung across her hip.

'You went to Béziers,' he said, excitedly.

'It's really good stuff. It was easy.'

'Same guy?'

'Same as always. Nice guy.'

'Did your dad notice you'd taken the car?'

Sylvie blushed, shook her hair forward, and then busied herself lighting a cigarette which she held out far from her body.

'It doesn't matter,' Daniel grinned.

'It doesn't matter at all,' she said. 'Nothing does. Right?'

He kissed her once, very quickly, on the cheek. Then he drew a green stem of marijuana from inside the wallet and held it under his nose.

'Mother of Christ,' he whispered, carefully putting it back into the pouch. It was how they'd got through this summer, he and his two friends from the village, smoking pot in the garden room across the courtyard from the chateau. Week after week, singing and laughing in there, rolling up smoke after smoke so the nights could go on, leading them on through the games and the psychedelic frogs towards the dry light of dawn.

'You ok, Daniel?'

'I'm fine,' he said, and he swallowed, his cheeks sucked right in as he put the wallet of grass in the pocket of his shorts. In his other pocket he flicked his lighter on and off and after a while Sylvie put her hand into his.

'You're going to miss him. We all are. It won't be the same.'

Daniel laughed coldly.

'You are going to miss him, Daniel?'

'Huh!' he muttered, taking his hand back and kicking the stones at his feet. 'He shouldn't be joining the bloody army. I wouldn't go, not for anything. I don't understand Frederic. Why he just takes these things lying down.'

'That's not how it was... he *wants* to go.'

'It's fine,' said Daniel, and he stuck his jaw forward and looked out across the vineyard. There was silence then. The heat came down. The cicadas were shrill in the grass. Sylvie was squinting as she looked at him.

'Is Arnaud here?'

'He went to town in the car.'

'Let's go see if your mother needs help,' she said, pulling the pocket of his shorts playfully, and then she walked ahead of him, grinning back at his solemn face.

———

By seven the light was pink-tinted and the midges were out and dancing around their heads. Lucie Borja stood on the steps with her ankles pressed together in little cream shoes. Daniel and Sylvie were carrying the dining-room table through the front doors and down to the olive trees, Daniel with his end of the table behind his back, Sylvie struggling as she came behind.

They bent beneath the trees and placed the table down. Sylvie flopped down over it. Lucie took in a breath of air between her teeth. It was right to bring the table outside. There was more air in the courtyard than round the back in the garden; it was a perfect fit between the four trees and soon they would hang the Chinese lanterns.

She watched Daniel standing back now, a little way off, looking up to the road that wound up through the pine trees onto the heath. On a grassy plateau up there was a runway, a turning field and a small hangar for the planes used by the flying club. The runway went from one end of the plateau to the other, and Frederic was up there cleaning the planes, helping out with the fuel. It was manly work and Lucie knew that Daniel wanted to be up there with him, not here with his mother. She wondered again about his restlessness and agitation. He was dreaming, perhaps plotting his own escape, and she felt the tears prick – always tears on a birthday; she was much too sentimental

– so she smoothed the linen on her hips and walked down the steps towards them.

'Oh, Daniel, Sylvie,' she croaked, 'how beautiful this looks. We should take a picture, no? Shall we light the lanterns, Daniel, *chéri*?'

'After dark,' he said, without looking at her, and Lucie felt the snub and that same old cold feeling, which was what propelled her from the edge of the table, walking towards him when her ankle gave on the bald patch of ground and the soft outer edge of her foot caved in. The fall wasn't a bad one, but Daniel didn't go to his mother, and the sound she made was a sound like no other sound he had heard. Only a child, only a baby, made a sound like that, thought Daniel, clapping his hands over his ears as he ran from his mother and across the courtyard into the garden room.

At three in the morning, Lucie's eyes flicked open. She lay very still. Then she flexed the ankle and felt to the end of the bed for her dressing gown.

In the room next door, her husband was snoring, his spirit sunk in the food and drink from the party. It would take an age to wake him. She kept close to the wall, clutching the handrail on the stairs. She couldn't smell the fire but she knew it was there, feeding like a lion in a corner of the kitchen. She moved quickly, talking to herself as she went. So they may have forgotten to check the gas rings; something might have been left on, some faulty electrical application. You could never trust the electrics; the place was wired in a haphazard way and the mice chewed through everything. But the fire wasn't in the kitchen, and Lucie had known that before she had even left her room. She came to the bottom of the stairs, and hobbled slightly across the hall, folding her dressing gown across her chest.

She slipped out of the kitchen door, along the front of the house, down the steps and through the keyhole archway, and down towards the garden room. The air was bitter. She stopped to breathe and she looked up at the stars and the white moon and there was nothing else – no wisps of cloud, no planes in the air – and it felt for a moment as if it was she alone standing on the earth right now, just Lucie Borja and all her stories, standing still under this big awful sky. She heard them singing as they had done earlier in the evening. *Bon an-ni-ver-saire...* like children singing from a colourful bank on the far side of her memory.

——

'*Fucking*!' her husband had said – just to take the wind right out of her mouth, just to take her fingertips off that napkin for a moment. Arnaud had been in high spirits at the dinner, better when the cheese and the pile of cherries dipped in chocolate arrived and everyone cooed and gathered around. The sugar went to their brains. The summer was killing them, it was true. Lucie stood up to make coffee.

There were four of them left at the table by then – the chef from the pizzeria had come and perched on the edge with his wine and cheese and Daniel, Sylvie and Frederic had gone to the garden room. Arnaud reckoned he'd have a fight on his hands to ask one of them to part with a cigarette but still he had gone off to find them, and the rest of the party had gone a bit quiet at the table.

He came back pale and lurching. 'I couldn't find anything to smoke,' he said. 'All the rooms in the chateau. Nothing, anywhere, to smoke.'

He was sweating.

'I thought they were *fighting*, Lucie. It was dark in there. They seemed to be fighting. Rolling over. Daniel was growling.'

'*Bon an-ni-ver-saire...*'

'Lucie!'

Her sixtieth birthday. The lanterns were pale pink and very still in the trees.

'They've always fought, those two – since childhood, Arnaud.'

'Sylvie was passed out on the floor by the sofa... It was just the boys. Lucie, listen to me!' But Arnaud stopped because he couldn't say what he'd seen. She wouldn't have let him, either.

'There is coffee. Could you bring the coffee cups, Arnaud?' she said and she went indoors then and straight up the staircase and up to the air on her balcony. The doctor, who had come for the supper, had lined her medicine cabinet with enough sedative to shush all the gossips in the village. She took one of these sedatives now and stood for a few moments breathing and then she sat on the edge of her bed and reflected on how the evening had gone, how well the food had been done; how subtle the cheese.

She took the air and she felt the softness in her head, and there was nothing to be thought about then, except sleep, which came and then went – like a coverlet being stripped away – to leave her with this fear that fluttered around her heart as she walked through the garden with the grass rasping around her ankles.

She kept walking, her face on the door to the garden room, her shoulders hunched forward. She opened the door and felt the thickness of air behind it; in her throat and eyes the smoke was bitter and she heard Daniel coughing, saw the flames licking yellow in the seat of the old horsehair sofa and leaping in the curtains above it. There was Sylvie on the floor by the sofa, drugged and sleeping, and Daniel was crawling towards her, shouting for her to wake up, fanning his arms over the sofa. Lucie's eyes glazed. She took in the chaos through the smoke in the room. She saw a chair broken and tipped over.

Daniel bent down to Sylvie with a towel over his head, his intention to move her outside to safety, but Lucie screamed and ran for her son, and the old paraffin lamp on the floor burst and flamed into Sylvie's hair.

Daniel's shoulders rounded over Sylvie's face; he batted the flames with his hands and screamed at his mother to get out as he stumbled with Sylvie down to the pool. Lucie tripped after him, out of the doorway, into the dark hiss of the garden.

'Do something!' he yelled, running back up the grass towards her. 'Get Frederic. He's in the fucking bathroom!'

His eyes were wide open, and red. Lucie knew that he was gone now; he was a million miles from where she was; Daniel, beloved, her little boy.

'I can't,' she whimpered. 'I...'

'You can't?'

The sweat was pouring from his face.

'Why can't you?' The muscle in his jaw was protruding

22

like a knuckle. 'What's wrong with you? What's wrong with *us*?' he rasped.

'I've done everything to protect you, Daniel,' she said. 'I've nothing left.'

Lucie felt her heart break then as her son ran back into the darkness. Arnaud was coming up behind her, running, his belly leaping from side to side. He was shouting, cursing God. He was waving something that looked like a piece of cloth.

'Frederic's in there, Lucie. Quick!'

He pointed to the bathroom, adjacent to the garden room. They had made it for Daniel. En suite. There was a door from the bathroom onto the courtyard and Arnaud had tried to get in that way to get some water to put out the fire. Now she turned after her husband and followed him in, running her hands on the wall in search of the light switch. But the light was already on in the bathroom. Light like at the circus. And the legs were hanging behind her head. She turned. She could hear Arnaud moaning, bending over, his head in his hands. The feet were there, like long brown rats dangling from the ceiling. He wasn't wearing shoes. And he wasn't wearing any socks. It was only his jeans torn around the ankles, and they were stained with oil and engine fuel.

The old couple backed out of the bathroom together and separated. Lucie's legs were moving beneath her nightdress to the outside tap to turn on the hose. She bent to collect up a handful of gravel, her thought to throw something at the fire; if she could find the strength, *Saint Perpetua*, to throw a handful of these little stones.

Then silence. A deep and total silence. And an odd numbing sensation, a fizz, like lemonade, up to the brain.

Lucie hit the ground, which smelt of dry limestone rock. She lay on the ground and the base stones of the chateau rose up like boulders on the overgrown grass.

THE ENGLISH COUPLE

1

Canas, South-West France, February 2006
It felt like a steal, this happiness. It felt like something only people much younger or much more in love were entitled to have.

Kate kicked her shoes off and pulled her jumper up over her head. In the bedroom of the village house they'd rented, Stephen was sitting up against the headboard, his eyes roving gladly as he watched his wife move with her hands on her hips. She was self-conscious; she looked down at herself and the shiny bob of her dark hair spilled forward revealing the back of her neck. She had found the string of beads at the market in town. Pink and purple, they were cheap and childish, and they released something in both of them.

It was a damp Friday afternoon. The rain had stopped but the sky hadn't cleared and now water spurted from the gutter and flicked against the window pane. Inside the house it was softly lit and cosy with the candles they'd dotted about. Kate was laughing, at Stephen trying to flatten himself on the small bed, and at herself now; she was trying to do a belly dance. She was a thousand miles from work and London; she was a thousand miles from her mother. Coming away had been her idea. It was Stephen who suggested the South-West of France. It had taken them two weeks to unwind. Kate had made a promise not to do anything, not to think, not to worry about anything. Let go, was her mantra, and simplify.

Stephen's neck was coloured from walking in the countryside, his jeans were stained with spitting wine. There was no mobile reception in the village; no television in the house, no radio. He did calculations in his head, stopped taking the fish oils and vitamin B. Kate kept saying how we need so little, and on his bedside table these days there was nothing at all.

Life in Canas was simple. It was perfect. It was waking late in an old wooden bed, cups of coffee, driving the 4x4 on the hills, their faces peering; just rocks and blue sky. The air chill in the evening, Stephen wrapped his wife in a sheepskin rug, made love to her in front of the fire.

They slept off London like dogs dreaming, reflexes shuddering, sounds being released.

From time to time they drove to the coast and walked together on the sand, their hands buried deep in the pockets of their jeans.

In the afternoons, they read yesterday's papers and the wine was poured. They took photographs, made films of the room, panning the camera round till they found each other, smiling, arms on the back of the sofa, heads tilted, serene.

On Saturday morning they went to market for the poussin and the vegetables. Kate said she could feel herself unravelling; her spirit coming loose. She gazed out of the window at the sunlight winking in the trees. Through a clearing there were glimpses of the canal running deep and indolent beside the road.

'Everything's so different here, Stephen.'

'Yes,' he said, 'it is.'

'Don't you love it?'

'Yes,' he said, and he pushed his finger to the compact disc he'd selected so that it slid into the player. Stephen loved his old French café music – just a man and his accordion rousing with the hope of postwar France.

'Please,' she said.

He inclined his head. 'Hmm?'

'I just want the quiet for a moment or two.'

'But the music's perfect,' he objected, and Kate looked to him but didn't say anything.

Then Stephen turned the music up a little with the remote control on his steering wheel. Kate couldn't bear that because it felt like a slight against her and so she turned to the window and bit her nail and after that she turned it down.

'I just love how quiet it is.'

He switched the music off. Kate carried on talking.

'After all the madness. All that rush. I feel like the city swallowed me,' she said. 'I barely remember being there.'

'I remember you there, darling.'

'Not all the time.'

'Yes, Kate. All the time.'

'But that's what I'm saying. It feels like a blur. To me. It feels like a blur.'

'I can hear what you're saying.'

She swivelled her eyes to his face. He was smiling and looking ahead at the road. He was a handsome man – tall and dignified, with a soft sweep of sandy hair.

'I'm tired,' she said.

'It's just different out here,' he replied, after a while. 'It's slower. That's all.'

'I like it slow. I love the roses all over the village. And I love the cross up there on the plateau. So black and thin and elegant. The way the sky changes colour around it. The sky is amazing up on the plateau.'

'Look, it's a heron,' he said, pointing.

Kate followed his finger to the bird perched on a sliver of rock where the succulent flies were dive-bombing the water so that when the car with the white faces looking out went past, the heron didn't see it but remained standing on its rock, perfectly fixed and still.

'You can hear but you don't listen,' said Kate, after a while. 'Nobody listens. Have you noticed that? We're all so busy talking. Don't you think?'

Stephen didn't respond. He smiled and put his foot down on the pedal so that the car roared through the silent countryside.

———

Stephen dropped her back in the village and then drove off into the hills to buy a new selection of wines. While he was out, Kate lost herself in the preparation of the food. She hummed her love of this little French kitchen, patiently tying the strings of her apron, lifting her hair at the back.

She unwrapped the cheese and washed the vegetables, running her fingers through the leaves. She peeled the potatoes and laid them out on the draining board. Then she stood for a while at the window, leaning out on her elbows, and she heard the bell in the clock tower and watched the tiny movement of air in the leaves on the fig tree.

It was a modest patch of garden; a square of rough soil in which someone had tried to grow some grass, and which was now overcome with dandelion, surrounded by a ring of gravel into which large thistles had driven their roots. The garden was wrapped by a high stone wall built of the same mixture of chalky limestone and black volcanic rock as the chateau.

It was what they had loved the most when they first saw the house and Kate thought of their reaction to it, which had been mutual and surprising and strange: to be standing in the window together when the Mayor's wife had moved on, and to blush simultaneously, as if the walled garden were a secret the two of them shared, something private and inevitable they had each already known about and would come to in time.

Kate and Stephen didn't have children, and one of the things they could do now that Stephen was ploughing his own furrow and Kate's business – an art gallery in Southwark – had really taken off, was rent out the London house and take a sabbatical, try something new. Kate was about to turn forty. They felt like they'd earned it – a sort of halfway break after twenty years of work.

'My husband's an economist,' Kate had said to the Mayor's wife. Stephen was fingering the oven towels with disdain. 'He's come here to work on a book.'

The Mayor's wife was standing very straight with her arms flat against her sides. Kate said she didn't know what she would be doing with her time here and the Mayor's wife shrugged because it didn't matter to her what anyone did with their time. It was only after the tour of the house, shaking hands at the door, that Kate said something complimentary about the roses and then made her little announcement. 'I'm just going to think rather than act!' she said, but it came out more aggressively than it needed to and it brought about a bit of a silence on the quaint little step.

———

Kate climbed up the stairs to the bedroom in the attic, which smelt still of the garlic she'd used on last night's lamb. She stood in front of the mirror and shook her hair out. She replaced the bra she'd been wearing with a sexier one and put on a long black cashmere sweater that was loose around the shoulders. On her legs she wore thick tights and sheepskin boots. She tousled her hair in the mirror, and pinched her lips a bit to make them look red and kissed. She drank the wine and looked at herself from the side. She didn't mind the way she looked out here. For the first time in a long time there were things she didn't really mind at all. Like her clothes spilling about the bedroom. And a cigarette smoked out of the bathroom window while staring out at the view of the chateau and the birds lifting off from the roof. And the fact that Stephen hadn't returned from his drive into the hills yet and wouldn't, in fact, be there, as they'd talked about, for sex at 4.30 (pick a time, any time, he'd said, laughing) on a Monday afternoon.

———

They sat in the kitchen where the lights were warm in the eaves. Kate put some candles out. Stephen opened the wine. At the table, they tore the legs from a warm, buttery chicken, and Stephen carved into the breast, releasing the steam from its ivory flesh. Outside the wind was picking up, swinging trestles of ivy across the window. They sucked cloves from a head of sweet garlic, dipped bread in the roasting tin to soak up the oil. Kate sprinkled salt on her greens and ate them with her fingers, picking them up, one by one, curling them luxuriantly into her mouth. Beside them the fire crackled quietly in the grate. They ate and drank. They didn't say much. There wasn't any need. Stephen wiped a drip of oil from her chin. Kate sat back and cradled her wine. She thought of the days spread out before her like drifting balloons and took another glug of wine. They held their glasses up.

'Another triumph,' said Stephen, leaning over to kiss her. Neither of them saw the white face that was pressed up against the window.

When the doorbell rang, it was Kate who got up to answer it. She opened the door and a burst of cool air came in.

It was late in the evening now; the streetlights flickered on and off in the square. A woman was standing out there holding a tray. She was small and shapely but her jeans and jumper were old and torn and her wild unkempt hair fell to the waist like the hair of a little girl. It looked as if it had never been cut.

'*Bonsoir*,' said Kate, warmly.

'My name is Sylvie Pépin.'

She nudged forward a little and tried to smile with her

head down towards the floor. She was childishly shy, and when she came into the light, Kate and Stephen could see that her freckly face was marked with thick cream scar tissue as if someone had gone at her cheeks with a compass, while behind the gold rims of her glasses the woman's eyes were shrunk as small as beads in the folds and creases of her skin.

'It's late, Madame, Monsieur, I apologise and wish you a good evening!'

On the tray Sylvie had a small glass of violets and a loaf of homemade bread. She put the flowers and the loaf on the table and said that she could clean for them, if they needed her. She could clean the house twice a week, or once, if that was better. Kate remembered now that the Mayor's wife had mentioned there was a woman in the village who could come and help around the house.

On the sofa, Stephen was staring. Sylvie blinked rapidly through her thick glasses and fixed her eyes on Kate's warm, animated face.

'You are chic, like a film star,' she said, quietly.

Kate spun away from the compliment and laughed loudly. Stephen smiled and moved himself slightly on the sofa. A silence fell on the room.

'I live there, over the other side of the church,' said Sylvie. 'My family house is there. It's only me though now. Me and my dog. Coco. He is my dog. My family moved away. My father is Lollo. He used to manage the village café. You may have heard of him. In those days it was busier than it is now. Especially in the tourist season.'

'Does it get very busy in the summer?' asked Kate.

'Seventy per cent increase in total population,' said Sylvie.

Kate nodded. 'What number are you?'

'Number 6 with the grey door. You don't need to worry about the dog. He's not vicious.'

Then she rounded her shoulders and cradled the tray against her jacket. She started to back away towards the door and made a couple of gestures towards her watch.

'There's a roof terrace,' she said, firmly. 'It'll need a sweep. There are books in the cupboard up the stairs. English books. And extra sheets. I've cleaned here for almost all the people who've rented this house. Germans, Swedes... I don't like Italians. They make no effort to speak French. I like English. Normally the accent is terrible though. So terrible. It can make us laugh. If I were you I would wash out the saucepans. There are scorpions here,' she said and she pushed the glasses up on her nose with a stiff little finger. 'Small brown ones. I expect you didn't think it would be hot enough. But it gets very hot here in the summer. When it gets that hot people go mad. There's a court case I heard about in Carcassonne where a man was cleared for killing his wife because of the wind. They lived on top of a hill. The wind whipped round all day, all night. It's the mistral. The tail end of it. It sweeps down the middle of France and sweeps off.'

Stephen sat with his legs bent, like an uncomfortable giraffe. These ceilings, this cramped dark little house, felt ridiculous. With the back of his hand he pushed a bit of fringe back and coughed impatiently.

Sylvie turned her head with a swish of hair. 'You come and see me if you need me.'

'Wait!' Kate called after her. 'Please don't go. Would you like some wine?'

Sylvie shook her head. 'I don't drink wine, Madame. Only on special occasions.'

'We've met no one since we arrived in the village, apart from the Mayor's wife who showed us the house.'

'She told me that you would come,' said Sylvie.

'I'm sorry.'

'The Mayor's wife told me someone had rented the house, number 17. We look out for each other. The Mayor's wife is kind. Most of the people in the village are. You'll find that everyone looks out for each other. It can become uncomfortable. Voyeuristic is not the right word – I don't know what is.'

'There's a lovely sense of community,' said Kate, smiling warmly at Sylvie, looking only through the glasses and into the eyes. It was an effort to avoid the scars.

'But it is relaxing. To know that one can lean on others when one is in distress.'

'Yes,' agreed Kate, eagerly, 'that's true. And it's so pretty here. It is very different from London.'

Sylvie nodded and continued to back out of the door. 'Goodbye,' she said quite firmly and then she lifted her hand from the doorframe and walked, half ran, into the square.

2

There was a point at which the serenity seemed to lift Kate up. In the stillness here she was weightless and free. It didn't seem to matter much, nothing mattered, and nothing was real.

For lunch they ate salad in the kitchen, picking it straight from the bowl. The tomatoes were enormous in their soft red skins.

'Where did you get this basil, Stephen?'

'In town. At the greengrocer's there. The man speaks English.'

'It's amazing.'

'We could mix it with olive oil, and garlic. We could have it with some angel hair pasta tonight. And that lovely new white I bought. The Viognier.'

'I love that wine, darling,' said Kate, chirpily.

'I'll put some more in the fridge,' he said, getting up at once to do it.

'It's so much nicer than I thought it would be. It's like everything I ever wanted, Stephen. I could stay here for ever, buy a place and do it up.'

'You'd get bored,' he said, gently. 'Trust me.'

'I can feel it, though. I can really feel it.'

'What's that?' he asked, absent-mindedly.

'This place, Stephen. This feeling.'

'Ah, but you felt that about the gallery, Kate. That place is your life. You put everything into that.'

'Meaning what?' she asked, slowly, and she leant forward across the table and fixed him with her eyes. She wanted him to see what was in there.

'Meaning nothing really, darling.'

Kate threw the remains of her meal in the bin. Stephen took a deep breath and leant back in his chair, switching his camera on and panning it slowly upwards so that it picked up the old wooden beams and the spiders' webs strung across the ceiling.

The sun came out. The air was clear. In the afternoon they drove to the coast.

Kate took a call from the gallery. She listened patiently, she laughed. Her assistant was panicking.

'It's tension,' Kate said. 'It's always like this before an opening.' She felt guilty not being there. It made her speak very softly, very brightly, as if to a child. She repeated the instructions. Then she rang off and she stared out at the vines. Stephen was trying to scratch his back. When she turned to look at him she saw that his hair was more dishevelled than usual. There was something not quite right about the set of his features; his cheeks were long-looking and grey. From time to time, she sensed him looking across at her. They were near the coast and the land was flat, there was nothing to see. Still, she was quite absorbed, losing herself in the swaying of rickety pines.

'Nearly there,' he said, then again, until she turned.

They parked on a road that ran along the coast. There

was no one around. The sea was rippling blue, but looked cold. They walked on the sand and sat for a while, watching a man curling a line on the shore.

Kate closed her eyes as she drove her fingertips into the sand. 'It's so quiet,' she said, dreamily. Then she felt the tightening feeling in her chest. 'What shall we have for dinner tonight?'

Beside her Stephen tried to put his hands in his pockets. He relaxed his knees and left his hands there, half tucked in. His hair was being swept flat across his head; his pale lashes tried their best to keep out the sand. He watched the man with the line. It was hopeless. The sand was blowing into his eyes, making him blink. He began to feel cold. He leant over and tried to kiss his wife but he did it badly and skimmed her ear. He looked at her slightly sallow complexion; she was tired again. He could feel a headache coming on.

They got back in the car and drove to the village in silence. Stephen kept the engine running in the car while his wife jumped out. Then he drove off into the hills to buy some more wine.

—

Kate drank deep of the wine he'd bought and went to bed early. In the morning she had no memory of the night before and she was up before he was awake. She taped sheets of thick watercolour paper to the bathroom mirror. She wanted to paint the birds she had photographed on the old chateau wall. She put Stephen's leather jacket on over her naked body. On the bed he was still asleep, one arm over his eyes.

In the bathroom window, the light was orange on the chateau. It looked calm and peaceful this morning and she bit her lip as the paper began to grey in thin, delicate lines. There was only this wonderful stretch of time before her, the distance of unmapped days to enjoy.

Stephen sat up on the bed, sweating. There was an empty wine bottle on the floor. He got up from the bed and walked towards the bathroom. She was standing there in his jacket, her hair loose around her shoulders. He stopped. Across his pale eyes, a film of the two of them holding each other, writhing... As long as it was like this. The endlessness. It was perfect. It had never been like this. They could, if they wanted, do anything.

'Ah,' he said, 'the painting demon. I knew it was coming, Kate. Just a question of time. '

Kate smiled.

'I had an awful dream,' he said.

'Oh, poor you.'

Stephen sat on the edge of the bath, a towel wrapped round his waist. He rubbed his face with his hands, looking around the space, the paint peeling off the window frames, thick white towels piled neatly in the corner. He had thought rustic was what he wanted. *Rustic French retreat* was how he had worded the search. But the oyster shell soap dish, the pale floral curtains, the cushions that were small and stiff and faded?

'Don't you wonder what happened there?' she said.

'Where?'

'In the chateau. The fire. Why it was left like that? And that woman, Sylvie. Wasn't she weird?'

He yawned. 'She was burnt.'

'In the same fire? Do you think she was there?'

42

'Ask her,' he said, and he scratched his head and wandered back into the bedroom.

———

Kate's mother rang from her house in Dulwich to say that she was dying. They had taken her three times to King's. Made her sleep the night in a ward with two other women who were also dying. Emphysema. They moaned about the food. Fits of talk, it was all they had. 'There is nothing left, Kate.' The women had talked about what was near to them, the male nurse who was black as night, the food, which wasn't what they ordered. One of them couldn't breathe. In the night, neither of them could breathe. There were blacks everywhere. Too many blacks. The women who were dying clung to their masks, their voices, husky, frightened; they called out for the nurse. One of them soiled herself. No one came. She nearly died. They took her away. It was Kate's fault. 'You have left me here,' she hissed down the phone. She was watching the racing on television. Can after can of coke. She was strong as a horse. Stephen moaned that Kate's mother would never die. Kate said they would have to do something.

'Don't be ridiculous,' Stephen mouthed. 'It's a ploy to make you come home.'

'We'll be home before too long, Mum. You'll be round for tea before you know it.'

Stephen shuddered. He stepped out onto the street to make a call to the office. Then he stood and waited for Kate beside the roses. In the square, the café was opening, the first of the old men wandering inside. Kate came out and joined him. They both looked up to the sky, which was cloudless: a deep brilliant blue. He slipped his hand into hers.

'Don't let her spoil it for you, darling. We earned this break.'

'Yes,' she said.

'She's fine.'

'She's not fine, Stephen. Anyone who puts herself into hospital three or four times a year for no real reason is not fine.'

'You know, sometimes I think it's your punishment, Kate.'

She looked up into his eyes that were pale and cold as fish.

'For marrying me,' he said, simply, and Kate couldn't fathom how he could have said this, which was why she smiled at him with her lips only, but Stephen didn't seem to see that and his eyes still looked into hers as if waiting for a reply.

'It's hard to believe your arrogance sometimes, Stephen. It's hard to believe I actually married a man who still thinks, after all this time, that I did it only to get back at my mother.'

'Well, a psychiatrist...'

'I'm not talking to a psychiatrist, I'm me, Kate, and I'm trying to talk to you,' she said, quietly, and then she turned with her shoulders hunched around her neck and walked off across the square.

By five o'clock she hadn't returned from her walk. Stephen shut the lid of his laptop and smeared pâté onto the end of a stale baguette. Then he threw the bread in the dustbin and went out, slamming the front door behind him. He hung around outside the café and looked in the shop. Then he crossed the square, slipping down behind the church and walking to the far end of the village and out towards the cemetery. He thought for a moment that she might have left the village by the main road and walked up onto the old airfield and the heath. But there was also one more place he hadn't checked in the village, the chateau itself, and the old gates Kate looked at when they pulled out of the square in the car.

He was certain now that this was where she might have gone, and so he walked quickly back into the village and forced a gap between the gates to find himself in a vast open courtyard, overrun with weeds.

Kate was at the top of the steps, bending over something. She picked it up and walked about. Stephen stood and watched her moving up there like a priestess in search of her senses. In her thin cotton dress and shawl she looked vulnerable. She had nothing on her feet. She was dwarfed by the vast, dreary walls. There were few windows, barely a roof; at the entrance were two huge double doors made of black oak, and studded with iron.

Kate stopped moving when she saw him and picked up her shoes. She walked down the steps and through the grass towards him; then she reached forward for his hand. 'I'm sorry,' she said, squeezing his hand. 'I got here and I found I couldn't leave.'

They went into the café for a drink and stood under the

television that was bolted to the ceiling. Stephen said that they might have made a mistake coming all the way out here. Six months was a long time.

'There's not much here, Kate.'

'There's us,' she said, smiling.

She was happy. Her face was flushed and more youthful with it. She said she thought that the chateau courtyard was lovely.

'All those birds flying about in the courtyard. And midges, like when I was young, dancing about above the weeds.'

Stephen went back to the bar and ordered a bottle of wine. He took it outside, to where the zinc tables were gathered around the fountain. He sat in the chair that was most in the square, making sure the dark lumps of the chateau wall were behind him. He watched the light flickering an acid green in the trees. The air was cool. After a while, Kate came out and sat down beside him. Stephen leant forward across the table.

'Don't you feel like we've come to the middle of fucking nowhere?'

'We have,' she said, quietly. 'That was the point.'

'Just look at these awful houses, Kate. Like a square full of old, rickety teeth. Don't you think? And the dog there, like a nasty little rat trying to crap by the fountain. Can you see that? Don't you think that's disgusting?'

'I don't know,' she replied, sadly.

'Bat country!'

'You're just cross that I had such a lovely afternoon, and you had a boring one, Stephen.'

'How can you have had such a lovely afternoon? You didn't do anything.'

46

'I remembered things,' she said, 'like how much fun I used to have before I started working. Maybe it's fine to just sit and think, and remember things. What's the point in dashing about? I'm worried about all the stuff we miss. I'm worried about the things that have been going on at the edges, Stephen. Like that lovely old man in the bar. You completely ignored him. You didn't even see him, let alone say hello. We hurry about. We miss so much. It scares me.'

'That man has tits on his playing cards, darling. You ok with that?'

She shrugged like a child. 'Who cares? We're so uptight.'

'Fuck's sake! I care!'

'I even like the wine here. Refreshingly unpretentious, I think. Un-up-its-own-arse.'

'It's rustic, Kate.'

'Yes, but why does it bother you?'

'Because we don't need to put each other through this. I need a shower, and a decent bed. I need to get back to the office.'

'Because you don't like the person you've become without it?'

'I had a team there. We were a team.'

'Instead of what?'

'Pardon?'

'Oh, Stephen, this is pointless. Go with it. We're here!'

'We could have taken a holiday, a normal one. Slept. Sat by the pool.'

'And then what?'

He was silent.

She stared at him with her glassy eyes, the brown so

dark it was almost black. They finished the wine and stepped under the plane trees, which rustled quietly in the night. They saw the flies spinning on the fetid fountain water. Then they stumbled quietly back into the house and tried to have sex in their bedroom in the loft.

In the morning, she was up and gone before he was awake. There was a note on the kitchen table. *Slept really well. Hope you're all right.*

Stephen fixed himself some coffee and ate the eggs that were left on the sideboard. The piece of toast he ate in two large mouthfuls.

This time he went straight for the chateau and he forced an entrance again through the gates.

Kate was there on the steps. She was wearing shorts and an old jumper of his. Her hair was still tousled with sleep, her face pale but calm. She smiled when she saw him and waved. Stephen ran forward; he was waving at her in a way that made him feel strange.

'Hello!' they said simultaneously, and he climbed up the front steps and walked round behind her.

He put his head to the chateau doors and tried to see in. There was a single keyhole, low down; no bigger than the one on an ordinary London door. He bent down over it and tried to see through the cracks in the planks.

'It's been abandoned years ago,' she said. 'Everything gone. You can feel that.'

'Can't see a bloody thing in there.'

'There's nothing to see, Stephen. It's empty.'

'What a disappointment.'

'A disappointment?'

'Look, are you done with sitting here?'

'No,' she said, very firmly, though she wouldn't look him in the eye. 'I'm not.'

'You're trespassing,' he said, coldly, and he turned and walked away from her then, his bright white trainers crunching loudly on the stones.

—

When Stephen got back from his run she was still there. She hadn't moved. The sky was fiercely blue by then, the pale stone on that altar of hers reflecting the sun in its glistening slivers of quartz. She didn't want to come back to the house for lunch. She was smiling, and thinking, she said. Quite happy. Stephen changed tactic. He wasn't going to let it wind him up. Whatever it was, she'd get over it soon enough. He felt sure of that. He got to the shop before it closed for the afternoon and he bought water for her, and fruit. He dropped off the bag. Then he went back to the house, pulled the shutters against the sun, and slept through the afternoon.

—

At dusk, he crossed the square and stopped in the bar for a drink. Emboldened and relaxed, he squeezed through the chateau gates and stood, pink-faced in the light, by the olive tree.

She was sitting up on the steps with her chin in her hand.

'Kate!' he shouted across the courtyard. She didn't

wave. She didn't even seem to hear him. 'Kate!' he shouted again and he heard the tremor in his voice.

She held onto his arm as they walked through the square, and when they arrived inside the house, she turned to him and put a hand on his cheek. She said she was feeling tired, a bit confused. She was sorry, she said.

Stephen watched her move about the kitchen in that sexy, effortless way she had with her limbs. He opened the wine and made a pasta sauce out of the tomatoes he'd bought at the market. The garlic was fresh and hard and sweet-smelling. Neatly, he chopped and chopped and piled it in, with the basil and a heap of fresh thyme. Kate was sitting at the table looking tired, and scratching her neck. The skin on her arms and legs was tanned now but she looked thinner, smaller around the neck and the chin. But she revived with the food and wine and they sat and talked for a while.

'Sometimes I sound like I'm a hundred,' she said. 'That whole conversation made me sound like a total bore.'

He told her that she was beautiful, more beautiful than anyone, with her dark hair and her neat little face with its white teeth and soulful eyes.

'Soulful?' she said, and the eyes that used to droop at the corners with all the disappointment for which she had found no one to blame were full of sadness now. There was a hole growing; she'd recognised that today. It was almost a relief. Letting go meant giving in.

The village outside was silent and peaceful, the candles flickered on the table. There was nothing she could do but try to be nice to Stephen, to listen to him talk through the book he was attempting to write.

They drank down the wine. Then the face appeared at

the window again and Stephen got out of his chair. He lurched a little drunkenly across the room. He had taken his shoes off, placed them neatly beside the door, facing, as always, into the room; ready for action. He bent down beside them and scooped up the note.

Chateau in a nice French village.
South-West France.
Very old. Very quiet.
For Sale.
Offers accepted in many currencies.

Kate took the message and passed it to Stephen. They smiled at the writing and read it again. Kate opened the front door but there was no sign of Sylvie or anyone at all.

Stephen turned his attention away from the note and towards coffee and they lay about for a while, reading books and magazines, and drinking the rest of the wine. The papers fell to the floor and one of the candles was knocked over and went out on the rug, singeing a small black hole in the fibres.

When at last they got up to go bed, Stephen took the message from the table and scrunched it up in his hand. He dropped it in the bin with the pasta sauce, the garlic peel and the wine corks, and when his wife came down in the night for a glass of water, she took the piece of paper out of the bin, and then sat for a while in the kitchen, looking out at the leaves on the fig tree in the garden.

3

'It's nothing,' said the boy who was working that morning in the café. In his right ear he had a large black rubber stud and a silver chain looping his hips. At Stephen's table beside the fountain he leant his weight against the back of the chair so that it made a small dragging noise, and inched closer to the table.

'Just a big old place with nothing in it. Big rooms. It's empty inside. See those windows? Last year the shutters came off in the storm. There's nothing there.'

Stephen followed the finger to the dark sheet of wall, fifty metres up, which was exposed to the square.

'When it rains you might see some snails in the courtyard. One year there were many snails. We tried to start a business, my dad and me. We tried to sell the snails in town. Took a whole load in.'

Stephen licked his finger and turned the page of his newspaper then folded it and laid his elbows over the fold. He was making some progress now on the book and the breakthrough had cheered him and levelled his tolerance towards the sleepy villagers.

'My wife loves it there,' he said. 'She seems terribly drawn to the place. It's a mystery to me. I'm lucky if I can get her to come out in the evening to eat!'

The boy's mouth was hanging open as if he struggled

to breathe through his nose.

'And I'm assuming it's a private property. I'm sure the owners wouldn't really welcome having her there...'

'Well, it's not exactly private,' said the boy. But who would know? It's hardly the village fun park. Like every year, we hold our annual summer party in there. Disco balls. Elephants. You name it. Fireworks flying off the roof. Duh!' The boy pulled the tea towel down from his shoulder and whacked himself on the hand.

'No, I'm sure not,' replied Stephen coldly, and returned to his newspaper.

The boy didn't move. He continued to stand with his mouth slightly open, gazing up at the window. 'Honestly?' he said, quietly. 'To some, I think it's more like a nightmare. And old Madame Borja keeps it on. She won't sell. We can't demolish it and so it sits there, looking down on the village like a monster, like King Kong. We can't move on.'

'Then my wife is in love with your nightmare,' said Stephen, which the boy didn't seem to hear.

'It doesn't matter. Who cares? The family left years ago. After the fire. Twenty years or so. Some of them died. Others just disappeared. Lucie Borja ran away to live in Paris with her nephew. I heard she died, though. Before Christmas. That's the rumour anyway. Even so, she'll never sell. Dead or alive, man. The Borjas keep it on. You can ask the Mayor if you want to go in.' He had pushed the chair as far as it would go. 'But don't get your hopes up. It's not a fun park. I think you'll find it completely empty. Sometimes, when we were kids, we went in with our bikes and stuff. It was open and we just rode on through and came out again. No one hangs around in there. I don't know why. Once, when I was a kid, like ten or eleven years old, I went in and I felt so weird. I had to come straight out again. It's cold. And draughty.'

'Where can I get the keys?' asked Stephen, and the boy seemed to wake out of his trance then. He smiled and lifted his hand up, poking a finger towards the Mayor's office, which was opposite the church on the other side of the square.

———

Up above them, in an overcast sky, the birds echoed each other, making loud throaty caws as they flew over the roof.

Kate, in a long baggy coat and flip-flops, had her camera slung around her neck. She climbed the steps slowly and stared down at the familiar dandelion grass that was growing quietly between the cracks. Where the top step met the wall there was a slick of grey concrete with a footprint left in it. Stephen was at the door already, bending over the key. She didn't like that he'd got there first. It made her feel depressed. She stood behind him with her arms folded and pulled in a deep, silent breath.

'Here we go,' he said gamely, and he smiled round at her while still holding the key. She felt infantilised and urged him to push at the door and go on in without her.

Stephen took her hand and left the door open behind them.

Inside there was dust and the air smelt of it.

The entrance hall was wide enough for fifteen men charging, the ceiling tall and arched. To the left, in the corner, tucked back behind the door, there was a small round table, incongruously small, and made of iron that had been painted a greeny grey.

'They would have had this out in the garden,' said Kate, keeping her voice very low. 'They would have taken it out into the courtyard for Madame to use for her cup and book, her platter of letters.'

Stephen rushed past her, the dimness and the silence making him uneasy. He tried to fight it like a man, his body language becoming erratic; he tipped his head forward and flicked the dust from his hair. Then he placed his hands on either side of the giant stone pillar supporting the ceiling at the bottom of the stairs. The plasterwork here was dirty white and old; it brushed off on his coat. Low down, the walls were damp and blackish, as if they had been sucking up some strange malevolence from the ground.

From the open door, winter sunlight stole across the floor. Kate stood and watched her husband backing away, brushing the plaster off his chest, half laughing, half coughing the dust out of his lungs. His enthusiasm seemed forced and unnatural, and she wanted to be away from him so that she could feel the breath of the place, and she went alone into the kitchen, which was long and thin with an enormous fireplace on the wall to her left.

On the outer wall, there were two sets of shutters and a large stone sink at the far end. There were gaps in the shutters and the light flickered on the floor. Kate's heart thumped as she tried to take it all in and she bent down to the floor, to feel the stone; it was smooth and shiny as marble. She felt the scratches left by furniture and she pictured a long kitchen table laid out with food, a cook busy working at one end of the table, sitting on a stool, sifting and kneading flour in her hands. She tried to people the place with children and artefacts; things that were simple, natural fibres, belongings passed down through the generations. Since the flight of the family the place had been looted.

Kate ran her fingers on the old floor, fingering grooves as smooth as bone. She thought about this man and his wife, tried to picture them, wondered who they had been and how they had loved each other right up to the end.

When Stephen came into the room, Kate stood up like someone caught doing something she shouldn't, and she smiled at him to disguise the emotion she was feeling.

Stephen turned to the earthenware pot that had fallen at an angle into the fireplace. There were hanging hooks. To the left and above the fireplace was a wooden platform enclosed by a large rickety wooden cage.

'They would have kept dogs in there,' he said loudly.

'Dogs?'

'To turn the spit.'

'Is that meant to put me off the place, Stephen?'

'Don't be ridiculous!' he replied, but she had gone out into the corridor now, and was using the blue light on her mobile phone to guide her to the end. She pushed at the door and found herself in an internal courtyard, which was dripping with damp.

The walls were sparsely trellised with a dry, yellowish ivy. In the centre of the courtyard three spectacularly tall and spindly pine trees reached up towards the light.

There was a wrought-iron balcony that ran round the entire square from the first floor.

'It's like something out of *Macbeth*,' said Stephen, following her, and he kicked at the stones that were cracked and mottled at their feet.

The air smelt damp and old. Up above, through strings of ivy that criss-crossed the air, birds were flying, cawing still. Kate perched on the bench and hugged her knees. She watched her husband standing there with his shoulders slumped forward. He was trying to understand what she felt about the place; he was having a shot at being here for her. She felt sorry for his seclusion.

'If I was the lady of the manor, Stephen, and you were the butler, would you bring me a cup of tea?' she asked, trying to be sweet and playful.

'Much obliged, Marm,' said Stephen, turning happily, and he bowed to her and presented the cup and saucer.

Kate sat bolt upright and pretended to sip at her tea. 'It's perfect,' she said, smiling, but she was making too much of it and she could feel the strain in her face. Stephen turned away and went on in then. He said he was going to look upstairs.

Halfway up, Kate looked out of the slit window and down onto the burnt-out storeroom so shrouded in dense green from the rain, so overgrown with weeds. The garden was stuffed full of ferns and poplars and huge oleander bushes that towered over the wall and over the roof of the store-house.

She went on up, running her hand up the wide, dusty banister. At the top of the stairs, she ran along the corridor. She went past doors opening onto rooms ransacked and left, paint peeling, to a door at the very end, which was locked. Kate stopped and pushed at the door. It gave onto a dark passageway and a circular room where Stephen was leaning out of the window.

Behind him the fields were a vivid green.

'It's the tower room,' said Kate and she stared down at the floor tiles that were cracked in the centre of the room, as if someone had been at them there with a sledgehammer. A mould clung to the damp on the grey outer wall like a white rash around the window.

'Christ, look at all the bird shit,' he said.

'But look at it!' she whispered. 'Look at these beautiful tiny little shutters opening onto the view, Stephen. Look at the vineyards, the light.'

'The light is lovely,' he conceded.

'People would think we had gone off our heads.'

'What did you say?'

It didn't matter, she told him. She'd been thinking aloud, trying to figure out what it would be like. Stephen bent to the only piece of furniture in the room, a narrow wooden bed bolted to the wall. He ran his fingers over something inscribed in the stone. Watching him, Kate felt something change. Some small adjustment in the air. She pulled in her stomach. It felt as if she ought to be sick.

———

Outside, in the courtyard, he sat down beside her on the highest of the steps. The sky was heavier now. Stephen felt his headache coming on.

'What is it?' he asked grimly.

'Not sure. Too much wine, I guess.'

'I don't mean in there, Kate. I mean you. What's going on with you?'

She looked away and felt embarrassed. She put a hand on his knee but couldn't bring herself to tell him about the restlessness she was feeling.

He put an arm around her shoulder and squeezed hard. 'You'll be all right,' he said firmly, and Kate agreed with that and she looked out across the courtyard and up to where the birds were flying about.

———

The nearest town was a twenty-minute drive from the village, and Stephen liked to go there on his own for a coffee in the morning, and a chance to get the paper. The greengrocer at the shop in town had a bald head and a broad, impish smile. His shop smelt of coffee and dried meat. He gave Stephen a paper bag for the oranges.

'Of course the chateau is haunted,' he said. He took his glasses off to polish them. 'Then again, it's all to do with perception. And imagination. I see a ghost, I think to myself, is this a ghost or is it something my eyes want me to see?' He shrugged. 'Who can know? The chateau is haunted? Maybe it is, maybe it isn't. But no more than you or I.'

He licked his thumb to pull a second paper bag from the string above his head. His thumbs were small, like a child's. Stephen could see through the curtain behind him to where a boy was lying down on the floor with his arms behind his head. The greengrocer laughed. He reached down into the trays of food in the counter, took a thick salami and began to slice it slowly, silently, each slice exactly the same, the width of a coin. He hooked a slice with the point of his knife and lifted it over the counter for Stephen to try.

'Yes, it was quite grand,' he said. 'Once upon a time. Old beauty, elegance. A beautiful courtyard. Plants such as you have never seen. You could drive into the courtyard and park beneath the trees. A mosaic of perfect white stones to the door.'

Stephen counted out the money he owed for the oranges. Above his head, the blades of a fan began slowly to rotate, though there was no heat in the room.

'My wife has been sitting on the steps outside the chateau for days, Monsieur. She seems to want to do little else.'

Stephen coughed; he could feel the colour banking on his cheeks.

Behind his glasses, the greengrocer's little eyelashes were blinking rapidly. He folded his hands on his apron. Beads of orange grease had appeared at the corners of his mouth.

'Is she waiting for the rain?' he said as a joke, though his face was without humour. 'It won't rain, you know. Not once the summer comes.'

'She's not waiting for rain.'

'Well for St Christopher then.'

'Who?'

'St Christopher,' said the greengrocer, and he collected up the coin from the counter then and slid it into his till.

Stephen turned to the window where the streamers were fluttering. He took the bag of oranges and made a knot of its neck in his fingers.

'She wants to know what happened there. Maybe if I can find out what happened there then the place will loosen its hold on her.'

'Well yes, Monsieur, but you are wasting your time trying to make friends with the villagers if all you want from them is the past. No one will tell you anything because they are French and proud and what happened is too sick to speak about.'

'Too?'

'Terrible.'

'Was the woman Sylvie Pépin in the fire? Was it she who was burnt?'

'And her brother died. He was found hanging in the bathroom.' The man shook his head. There was something green, a smudge of something; it looked like a pea above his ear. 'One of the villagers came down from Canas and came into the shop and said what had happened.'

'What did happen?'

'The Borja boy – freak boy – he killed the kid from the village, Frederic. Made it look like suicide. That's what people say. Then he set the fire.'

'Why?'

'Who knows? All it takes is one match. The doctor from here was called. He was a good friend of Madame Borja and he helped her remove the body. She was totally crazy. Everyone knew that. But Monsieur Borja was a good customer of ours. I believe he stayed on for some years after everyone else left. I think he tried to keep the place going. His wife returned to Paris on her own. She never came back. Some years later Monsieur Borja was found dead in the vineyard.'

Stephen nodded.

'The chateau simply went to ruin. He had cleared everything out by then. Sold it off, piece by piece.'

'Yes, we went in to have a look around on Saturday.

There was nothing in there. Nothing at all.'

The greengrocer shrugged his shoulders once more and wiped the sweat from his forehead with his apron. 'Most people down here, in these villages, they keep to themselves. Outsiders are not always taken in kindly. That was one of the Borjas' problems, of course, when they first came here. This is not like a metropolis; it is a peaceful part of the world. But that summer of the chateau fire there was something very strange in the air. It was so hot that summer. Things got out of hand.'

'Do you get many like it?'

'*My God, no*,' said the greengrocer and he shook his head and frowned. He disappeared through the beaded curtain into the darkness at the back of his shop.

Stephen drove back to the village in a mood and told Kate he was taking her out for dinner. They found a restaurant on the edge of town that was downmarket but warm enough inside. There were plastic flowers in baskets on the walls. Kate was wearing a black silk shirt that pulled tight across her breasts. Stephen ordered vodka cocktails to start. It was quiet as a tomb.

But they felt better after a glass of wine and Stephen said his *moules* were the best he had ever had. Kate leant over and dipped her bread into the garlic wine in his bowl. She sucked the pulp up, and couldn't seem to stop.

'I checked out that word on the internet, Kate. That word we saw engraved in the chateau?'

'In the wall?'

'It's Arabic. "Baseema". It's a name. It means "smiling".'

'Smiling?'

'Yes. Weird, isn't it?'

'Gorgeous,' she said and her eyes, when she looked at him, were bright and defiant. This was how she often looked at the moment and it made him feel afraid. She had messed up her hair so that it looked unkempt. Her lips were painted scarlet. More than anything, he wanted her to soften, to calm. He refilled her glass with wine.

The convivial owner with the black eyes was passionate about the wines. Stephen asked him questions. Everywhere, Kate thought, he did this; he made himself known. It was part of his charm, his warmth. To develop a relationship that would hold them all in the arms of the evening, and squeeze.

'We're keen to sample as much of the local stuff as we can.'

'The soil is very rough in the hills. For water, the roots of the vine have to work very hard; they have to go very deep. A beautiful wine.'

The owner swooned a little beside their table. He was Jewish, he told them, while making a joke. Stephen and Kate were nothing. Christians once, for a few months. Meetings with the vicar. Readings from the Bible and bridesmaid dresses. But the nativity scene got lost in a box, in the roof. They didn't have children to revive their religions and their lives were taken up: work, dinners, the gym, theatre, friends. And now, out here, she thought, they were busy trying to unlace themselves, trying to be free.

Kate lifted her glass to her lips. London was a blur. It was the mystery of her early life that she wanted to try to remember. Who she was before she started working and met Stephen and moved into his flat. She wanted to know why it was she had begun to feel excitement again, ripples of it, that travelled through her for no apparent reason. It felt inherently childish, something pure, to do with the joy of life and it made her want to kick free; she needed to figure that out now, what was doing it, why now.

She reached under the table for her handbag and the phone that had signalled a text from a friend. 'How's paradise?'

Kate showed the phone to Stephen and he lifted his glass high in the air. The light was shining on his forehead and when he laughed his nostrils flared, which made him look smug, and strange.

The waiter brought cognac. He spoke to them in English. Behind the bar, he had postcards of bullfighters, a woman with her hands folded on her pubis, her lips in an 'o'. Kate smiled patiently and tucked her hair behind her ears. She drank the cognac. At the gallery now, they would be running around hanging twenty-foot paper cages from the ceiling on thick iron chains. The cages would swing in the air and crash into each other, their hanging disturbed by the air from a turbine. But the cages would do well. The show would run and run. Even Kate's mother would make a point of coming up to see it. It would take the long-suffering Portuguese neighbour all morning to get them ready. Then the neighbour would be made to drive up to London, to push Kate's mother in and round. There would be a smear of bright pink lipstick and a grey chignon. She would sit in the corner and say nothing. She would sit in the corner and say nothing and stare at the cages though her large dark glasses.

Outside the restaurant the wind was picking up, fluttering the awning. Soon they would be back in their village, the bedroom in its loft, with the windows on the chateau. Kate decided that she would not return to the courtyard in the morning. She would stay with Stephen and sleep late. Let her body rest beside him. With a little more effort, she thought, she could make things lovely again between them. They would go into town, buy warm, fresh *pains au chocolat* from the baker and eat them out of paper bags as they strolled through the market. Stephen would choose the salami spiked with garlic. He would say the cheese was marvellous and she would enjoy his pleasure. She would buy some duck and cook up a meal so that they could eat together – husband and wife – in their walled garden, licking their greasy fingers and laughing together under the stars.

'Have you been to this part of France before, Madame, Monsieur?'

'We came here on our honeymoon. But by mistake, as a matter of fact,' said Stephen. 'We flew into Marseille. We were going east; the Côte d'Or, to Portefino. Kate was driving. She started west. We came here.'

'We were meant to,' she added, dreamily. 'We were pulled here.'

'Bollocks, darling,' scoffed Stephen. 'You were lost.'

The owner was laughing, holding his chin. His eyes were tired.

'More cognac, Madame, Monsieur?'

He filled their glasses. '*Santé*!'

'To the chateau,' said Kate, lifting her glass.

'The chateau, Madame?'

'My wife's fallen in love with an old wreck in the village we're staying in.'

'I think it's up for sale,' Kate told him, lifting her eyes up now, expectantly, almost coquettishly, as if this restaurant owner might be the one to help her buy the place.

'Ah but this is perfect!' he said. 'And now we can drink to you, and to your love of the real France. Where time really does stand still.'

Stephen laughed aggressively; he was getting bored of these people. They were stiff and dour and far too still. He snapped his credit card down on the table. They drank. Silence fell. The wind dropped a stone onto the roof of the restaurant.

On Tuesday, Stephen went on his own to the oyster bays to get a dozen oysters. Kate had been happier and more attentive the past few days and he had done some good work on his book. He wanted to reward them both with a picnic up at the lake.

As soon as he had gone, Kate rang the airline. They agreed that it would be a good thing if Kate went back to London on her own for a couple of days. Just to ensure that all was well at work. She would check on the house, and bring out their post. It would give her a chance to see her mother – and more than anything, they both felt, it would be good for her sense of perspective to be away from here. She booked a ticket for Friday morning. She would go for a long weekend. That gave her three more days, she thought, taking her camera and her sketchbook across the square to the chateau where Sylvie was standing dressed in a denim dress that flared on her hips and fell to mid-calf. Kate saw the long wild hair and the shapely figure and she waved as she got near.

'You have such beautiful hair,' she said.

Sylvie smiled and laughed and sniffed. She said she had never cut it. Not once. It had been growing for more than twenty years now. Since most of it went up in the fire.

'It was a paraffin lamp. It exploded beside me. Where I was sleeping.'

Kate had her hands over her mouth.

'My brother died here,' said Sylvie, tilting her head back, and then she followed Kate in through the gate and the two women stood and looked up at the front wall in silence.

'It's not a good place,' said Sylvie. 'My dog comes in but he won't stay.'

'Dogs are sensitive.'

'Yes.'

Sylvie's lip bunched when she smiled. From the pocket of her jacket, she took rolling papers and tobacco and she rolled herself a cigarette. Kate waited for Sylvie to make the next move. The woman had a hold on her, though she wasn't sure what it was.

Sylvie crunched forward in her dainty shoes.

'Did you get my note?' she said.

Kate smiled. 'Yes, I did. Of course. But God knows what made you think I have anything like the money to buy a place like this.'

'Someone does,' Sylvie said, and she squinted through the smoke escaping from her mouth. 'And when they do then Daniel will come back.'

'Who's Daniel?'

'Daniel Borja. He lived here. In the chateau.'

'The son?'

'That's right. Daniel Borja,' she said quietly, looking out over the vineyard and off towards the hills.

———

The next morning was hot, and the sky white, the car disappearing now and then in the avenues of trees.

They climbed into the hills; black rock formations leered up out of the slopes. They came into the town, which was just as they remembered it from their time there thirteen years before.

There were palm trees and a statue of a giant man in military dress pointing his finger down the boulevard towards the square as if the way was paved with gold to war.

'Algeria,' said Stephen.

'You remember this?'

'Of course.'

'How long has it been?'

'I remember this statue. It's for Algeria. Remember?'

Kate was holding her hair back; she was looking all around. Then she started off in the direction of the square. Stephen followed her. They both knew where they were going. They picked up speed and broke into a run and Kate said she felt afraid suddenly.

'The past is smaller than we remember it,' she whispered to herself as her feet carried her forward. 'We're blind, like dogs trying to break in, we cannot get back there.'

'He's there,' Stephen was shouting. 'He's there. Look!'

Kate saw the trestle table with the paper behind it. There was the basket man, his carrot-red hair, his huge

68

paunch, his square block of a head, and his vest which was grey and stained on the front with a slop of something that looked as if it had been slopped over a decade ago and the vest not washed in all that time. Kate shook her head. There he was before them now and there he was back then, and the two red-haired fat men with the stained vests came together in that moment and waved their hands for the English couple who were standing in the square, staring, lonely, astonishing themselves with this gift here in the sunlight.

'How long is it?'

Stephen was laughing.

'Thirteen years,' said Kate.

'Nothing has changed.'

And then to have laughed as they did, with such amazement, such relief, as they ran forward, and flung themselves on the table and began to pick up the baskets, grabbing them from the heap one at a time. The baskets were green, and blue and yellow. And this is her, my wife, thought Stephen, grabbing a basket with a white daisy on the front and handing it to her. She's back, my wife; this is how I remember her, he thought, and he laughed again. They could hardly carry them all; they were laughing so hard and with such relief they only partly heard the man's voice which wasn't French at all.

'We can't carry them,' Stephen was saying to his wife. 'We don't need them all.'

'It might not be him,' she replied quietly, but she was looking in her bag for her purse by now and he could barely hear what she said. Her face was shining, laughing. The sun was breaking out from behind a cloud, blinding them; it was much too warm suddenly.

'What are we doing, darling?'

'I...'

'Really,' said Stephen brightly, but kindly, 'what are we really doing?'

And the basket man coughed and came over, his hands in the back pockets of his shorts, his face wide open and amicable and blue.

'Please. Madame, Monsieur,' he said. 'Can I help you at all?'

———

They left the baskets and drove back to the village in silence. Stephen checked his emails and then climbed into the bedroom for a sleep.

Kate went back to the chateau. She felt calm here, that was all she knew. She spent time round the back of it, pulling through weeds in the garden. She sat on the steps, and the silence was almost unbearable. The size of its walls, the lack of windows, the crumbling tower. She felt it groaning around her, the ground moving beneath. She wanted to take the weight off, and go back in time.

———

'I've seen beetles,' she called down to Stephen when he came over later in the afternoon. 'Big black tremendous beetles scuttling on these stones.'

Stephen pulled his lips back in a wide, forced smile. His hands were folded behind his back. They were sleeping so well, eating delicious fresh food. They were light, inside and out. Even so, psychologically, he was treading water out here, and he felt listless, mentally soft as a result.

'Are you bored?' she said. 'Is that what it is?'

'We need to talk.'

'Is that why you come here each day to find me? Can't you look after yourself, Stephen?'

'Why are you here, Kate? What's the point?'

'I'm thinking!'

He laughed, picked up a pebble from the ground and slung it high, as far as he could.

'All day? For a whole fucking day? With your back up against a wall?'

He asked her if she couldn't smell the sewage, which came from a burst pipe in the village. She couldn't smell the rot, or the empty feeling of nothingness stretching from the pine tree across the vineyards into more nothingness.

She said she was confused. She was sorry. She didn't mean to exclude him. He sat beside her and said that he was feeling tired of it all. He thought that perhaps he should go back to London with her.

'Don't do that,' she said gently. 'Let's take a few days apart.'

Which was fine, he conceded. 'Absolutely fine.'

They sat on an old bench in the atrium under cover of spiders' webs and leaves, picnicked on bread and olives and cheese. Kate was hungry now and glad to eat. A breeze rustled the leaves in the trees but otherwise the garden was still. In a few days, Stephen said they could go to the coast, buy some oysters down in the oyster bays. There were flamingos there. He had seen them on the way in from the airport. She said she would like to see the flamingos, how pink they would be against all the blue; and that she would like to take a walk on the beach; throw some pebbles in at the sea.

'Good,' he said, feeling better at once for the shade and the food.

'Do you love me, Stephen?' she asked quietly.

He ripped a hunk of bread from the loaf and dragged it through the oil in the plastic container; tried to swallow it whole, like a snake with a small bird.

'I want to get back to our routine, Kate.'

'Then you should be going back. And I should be staying here.'

'But your mother.'

'Yes but you're the one who wants to be going back.'

'I think so, yes.'

'Can I stay?'

'I don't know, Kate. Can you?'

They wiped oil off their chins. Stephen pulled giant, glistening anchovies out of the jar and laid them across the bread. He cut a slice of blue Roquefort from the triangle sweating and shining in its paper on the bench. There was the drill of a woodpecker. In the village, a dog was barking.

He filled her glass for her and she leant forward to drink. She slopped more wine into her glass and tilted it up towards her mouth.

'I love this wine,' he said. 'So clean.'

'It's a nice wine,' she agreed. He turned and looked into her eyes, which were big and brown and suddenly full of love. How fickle it was; the way it came in and out, depending on the mood, on the sunlight and the quality of the wine. He watched the tears bead on her eyelashes and he put his finger there to flick them away.

'We were always going to go to Fiji. Do you remember that?' he asked, gently. 'That was our place. In the first year we moved into that house and we had no money and were always working just to keep it all going. We said to each other one night that we were doing it for a holiday – a great big holiday, one day, in Fiji. I can't stop thinking about that.'

'Why?'

'Because we never went there, Kate. We sort of lost it.'

'We got busy.'

'Things have changed a bit.'

'And I feel like I want a different life. I feel like I've paddled all the way out and dropped the oars and now the mist has come in and I can't find my way back to the shore.'

He was grinning as if he hadn't heard her, red-cheeked, insane. She looked at him then and her eyes neither moved him nor had any life in them at all. She was suddenly pale, and old-looking. He looked at the crow's feet around her eyes.

Behind her head, a spider was moving, its web a tremor of frailty in the shade. She told him she could hardly breathe. She bent down for her glass, and drank up the wine.

'That's it,' he said, and he could hear his voice; it was menacing and strange. 'Drink it up, darling,' he coaxed, and he placed a hand on the back of her neck, 'and then, when we have finished our food and finished our wine, we can drive up into the hills and buy ourselves some more. There's so much room in the car. We can buy as much as we need, darling. We can buy ourselves as much as we fucking need. We don't have to go back. We don't have to let anything change. Not if we don't want to. We had a plan. And there's all this time,' he said, standing up from the bench, holding his glass out at arm's length. 'All this time to drink and do what we came here for, here in the village with all the birds and the fucking insects and this rough awful heat-resistant grass...'

'Stop it,' she begged. 'Please.'

Stephen was silent. He had stopped eating. Kate was sitting on the bench, pale in her white dress and she felt small and exhausted. Her mind was still, but somewhere deep inside she felt a flutter of desperation for air, and she pulled in a deep and silent breath for herself, and she held it there.

LUCIE

1

Silence in the beginning. And the car moving on the lip of the valley like a fly on the rim of a bowl – pausing – engine rattling; Arnaud lifting his hands from the wheel and pointing down through the trees. They had come so far south. It didn't even feel like France any more but some other place of rock and whiteness and dryness over the mountains. Lucie sank into the neck of her coat. She couldn't conceive of Arnaud's pale, slightly chubby fingers working the vines on these hillsides, twisting and wrenching, digging this dry, rocky earth.

'Can you see it?'

He was pointing to the dark place in the valley. It was like a castle she had had as a child. She saw the towers rising up out of the village roofs that seemed to huddle in on each other in a nasty, conspiratorial fashion. It looked tatty down there, shabby, and old.

Arnaud wasn't trying to make his hands look like guns, and yet it seemed this way to her. She felt the point, two fingers stretched, one hanging limp near the trigger. *Bang*! She flinched and closed her eyes.

'Lucie?'

She turned her head away from him, looked out across the valley to where the hills paled in the distance. There was food on her lap. A soft cloth parcel of food. If only she had thought to get the blankets and wrap them around her legs and shoes. The nylon stockings did nothing to keep out the cold and her shoes were worn and thin. But the blankets were on the back seat with her suitcase and it was too late now. They were nearly there.

'Are you hungry?'

'Answer me. Can you see the chateau down there in the village?'

'There are eggs here. Two cooked eggs. A tin of meat.' She peeled back the cloth. 'A decent loaf.'

He turned the wheel a little, let the car crunch onto the grass beside the track. Lucie studied the food carefully, imagining the tastes of the egg and the bread in her mouth. It was an anxious kind of hunger. As if there were mice in her stomach, steadily gnawing away. The war put mice in everyone's stomach. She knew she was no exception.

Arnaud would most probably climb out now and take in the view. Either that or take her hand, whisper something about their future together and the fear. Whisper something about it all going to be all right. But that would be silly, foolish, of course. She wouldn't have the egg just yet. It was better to save it for later. The more she prepared herself the less anxious she would feel. And, of course, it was possible that he'd had enough of her moods already. She was guilty of these. Up and down. Like de Gaulle's million bouncing babies. He would tell her again that she needed to try to let go of the war. It was something they all had to live with. But it was in the past. He would tell her to think of the future. France had a future. There were babies to be born.

'You are always thinking of the food, Lucie. Nothing but the food.'

'It's important.'

'It's not all there is, though.'

Arnaud coughed with uncertainty rather than impatience. He was trying to make her happy and he had come here full of hope. She turned, *lift up your hearts women of France*! and shook her head quite prettily for him, her eyes going wide as she spoke.

'If you're not hungry, Arnaud?'

He reached forward for the handle and clicked it down. The door slammed behind him. Lucie watched his stocky legs plough through the long grass on the roadside and disappear into the trees.

In Paris, the girls said life would be good, much easier, down in the country. In the room above the hairdressers they had tried to imagine it. One of them stood up and staggered across the room with her arms out in front to mimic the weight of food. The others laughed. Lucie watched them all, smiling on the window ledge. Marie made gobbling movements in the air.

'And if the *land* is fruitful, girls?'

They were women thinking of bigger things. In their hearts they were fighting another war which was the war of women sent back to the hearth but still they knew how much she wanted to have a baby. Her sister was one of them. Marie wore black culottes with boots and thumped her heart when she went in and out of the printing room. She said there would be nothing else to do down in the south: baking and babies, baby baking, *my God, you could bake the fucking babies…*

A hawk circling for food above. The sound of dogs

barking in the valley. The Germans wouldn't have come this far south. No one would. The land was rough and barren and there was nothing for it to do but slough off now and slide all the way to the sea. She would not be able to do it here, to make a go of things and make it work.

There was bright green grass beside the road. Dandelion, wild fennel. There was rock on the other side of the road – a sheer wall of black basalt and a plateau that stretched all the way back to the town. They had driven through it in silence, he with his hands firm on the wheel, his brandy bottle in the leather pouch around his neck. They had driven almost all the way from Paris in silence, stopping only to rest a little in Lyon.

Lucie watched her husband walk back towards the car. He cut under low hanging foliage, pulling back branches of eucalyptus and fern. In his hand he carried a leaf, and he held it up for her to see. You could do worse than use the acorns of oak trees for coffee, she thought. Others had used chicory. Both would be bitter. But people had done worse.

In the village, the shutters were worn, colourless and closed. You got the feeling nobody came out, nobody dared. But the square was attractive; there were young cats in the roots of lime trees, a red winter rose bobbing on a balcony and a child folding itself over the fountain.

Arnaud turned the car into a passageway that looked too small for it and they twisted between houses made of crumbling stone. There were plant pots on narrow steps scrabbling up the sides of houses, a rustic wooden chair with a pair of polished shoes left out on its wicker seat. Lucie thought of the women standing behind these small bolted doors, whispering, holding pans of fish, boiling fish heads, wooden tables, bread.

Arnaud got out of the car and walked towards the tilt of gates, leaning in on each other, two withered sheets of green iron. Behind it, the walls rose up. They were high walls, the stone black as iron in places, windows few and far between.

In the courtyard, the car choked on the weeds. At the far end of it a pine tree soared high into the air. There was a low stone wall that marked the start of the vineyard. Lucie turned her head in the wide open space. The quiet was strangely calming and there was no one there but a huge solitary crow labouring down through the air and landing on the steps, wings rustling with the attitude of a businessman, or an old watchman paid to behave like one, its thick charcoal hook pointing at them, then back at the house, as if to say: *Come on then, come see it if you must; I've been waiting all this time.*

In the kitchen they stood with their suitcases, like two people who had found themselves in a different country.

Arnaud's cousin had said it would be like this. Empty for years, he said. The family were wine people and went to ruin. The only remaining son killed in the Great War. Arnaud bought the land because he believed it would make a wine everyone would care about – *See the shape of the valley, Lucie, just think of all the water, how it will collect in this basin.*

From her suitcase, Lucie took a photograph of her and Marie in Paris with their parents. She stood with the photograph in her hand, unsure where to put it, what to do first. Arnaud jiggled himself about to keep warm. He capered about, folding his hands into a funnel and shouting into the corners of the room, up at the ceiling.

'We can't see,' he said, pushing on the shutters. She looked at his thin little fingers and wondered again how they would manage, just the two of them, and this great old house, like an empty liner out on the ocean.

'You should go to the café if you need something to drink, Arnaud.'

He was grinning and he backed out into the hallway and through the big front doors, stumbling backwards down the steps and out into the sunlight. She saw his shadow and looked beyond to where the same enormous crow was strutting among the weeds in the courtyard, making for the car whose doors had been left open, exposing the food in their basket.

'Arnaud!'

But he had already got to the car and was bending down inside it making strange whooping noises. In a moment he was back, bounding up the steps, the basket in one hand, their suitcase of things in the other. He stood in the doorway and beamed at her. He was full of confidence, full of hope. Lucie smiled back at him. He took his cap off and threw it in the air, which was when she felt the tension in his recklessness – how clown-like it was – something staged to release or undermine her.

'There's no time for cafés, Lucie,' he said. 'We need warmth. We need a fire. The courtyard is full of sticks. I'm going to make us a mountain of sticks.'

'We don't need a mountain though. Just a few. For kindling. Then logs.'

Lucie pulled the air in and held it in her lungs until her eyes began to blur. It would have been easier to sit down now, to curl up and fold herself away. But the women of France had a duty to rebuild this country. There were babies to be born, families and homes to be repaired. The women had to rise up now – *women of France, lift up your hearts* – they had to make do, be strong. And the women of the village, what would they be like?

'I could start by making a cake, Arnaud. Inviting some women round?'

It was dusk of that first wintry day. They had pulled the shutters and they sat together staring into the fire. Lucie laid out the eggs, the bread and the cheese on the table.

'Tomorrow,' he said, 'I will look for a saw. There is a tree blown down in the garden. Have you seen it, Lucie?'

But she hadn't seen anything yet. It was Arnaud who went upstairs to look around. He laid the mattresses they brought on the roof of the car, in front of the fire, and covered them in the blankets. He said the rooms upstairs were not so big as these. They ate slowly and cradled cups of hot brandy and water. She felt the alcohol loosen her, set something free.

'This is a new beginning, Lucie.'

'But God knows where to begin.'

'What?'

In the night, she knew that the dreams would come; snow on the streets in Paris, people scavenging for food, the radio broadcasts, the terrible waste…

'God?'

'Yes. What can he do?'

'Who?'

'God.'

'God is everywhere, Lucie. You know that.'

'Yes, but what can he do?'

'Hm?'

'To help us.'

Arnaud said nothing. For a long time he sat chewing on a small piece of bread. Lucie didn't repeat her question. Her eyes had begun to glaze. She watched the fire blaze and hiss through a twisted olive branch and reach for the next one above it. It licked with a soft green flame then finally took hold.

———

We must help ourselves. These were the words she heard first in the morning, as if her question had been left hanging in the room, watching over her, waiting for her to rise, to the day, to the house, to this fact of married life. She stirred and felt the life come back into her limbs and she found she was not so cold beneath the blankets and the dust and dirt had not got into her lungs; she felt well slept, almost clean.

She pushed open the shutters. Marie wouldn't have cared about the blankets and the lungs. Marie would have slept in her boots, a cigarette tip dormant in her hand. A warm light stole into the room. Her eyes travelled slowly down the steps and out into the courtyard. Across the pale stripe of the sky there were small fingers of yellow cloud.

Arnaud got up from the mattress and took his brandy bottle from the table. He took a swig or two from what was left and then pulled on his trousers and coat.

'There is work to be done.'

'Arnaud, chéri, I....'

'I'm going out to the vineyard...'

'But what about breakfast?'

'What is there to eat?'

'Some bread. The jam.'

'We need more food. There is money in the wallet, not much. You will hopefully find an épicerie in the village.'

But the village gave up none of its secrets, not today, nor any morning that she walked quickly out of the chateau gates and through the square, peering in through the window of the café with its broken pane of glass, past the church and along the small passageways in search of a baker, a grocery store, even a stall selling fruit. She took each possible pathway through the village, down alleys reeking of urine, over cobbles worn smooth, past groups of cats licking their fur and sitting in groups in the first light of the sun.

The villagers themselves were suspicious. Doors were opened quietly; faces appeared and looked around in the air behind her, their sad eyes asking nothing nor giving anything away. Their doors were closed quietly, firmly; shutters on the upstairs balconies drawn in.

'Because the people here are afraid, Madame,' said the Mayor that afternoon, standing in the courtyard.

Arnaud walked towards them both slowly. He shook the Mayor's hand.

'Monsieur Borja, allow me to present myself...'

The Mayor pulled a bandaged hand from the pocket of his short brown trousers and held it out.

'He has brought us wine, Arnaud. Two casks. I've put them in the kitchen...'

Arnaud wiped the sweat from his forehead with the back of his arm. In this light, after his day outside, he looked ruddy and calm.

'Welcome.'

'Thank you.'

'My pleasure.'

Lucie smiled and looked at the ground.

'The Mayor was just explaining to me, Arnaud, why the villagers do not come out of their houses, and no one will help me with provisions.'

'We have all been disturbed by the war,' said the Mayor, addressing only Arnaud. 'Now people just want to get on with their lives.'

'But I was just asking if anyone might sell me something to eat, some clothes perhaps, some sheets for the mattresses, an old quilt.'

'Madame, have you come here with no clothes?'

'One suitcase. But I walked all the way to the town today, Monsieur, and I was able to buy some food.'

'You let me know if you have a problem with rats in the chateau. They are pests... they come in from the fields and eat everything.'

'I'm not scared of rats, Monsieur,' said Lucie, 'if that's what you're thinking. There were rats in Paris during the war. In the end we had to borrow our neighbour's cat to eat the rats. When we all got terribly hungry one week there was a suggestion we should eat the cat.'

The Mayor coloured. He had thought her prissy in her crepe and petticoat. Now she stood before him in slacks and a black round-neck jumper, small round-toed shoes; she was pluckier than he thought.

'I'd like to show you something,' said the Mayor, and

he led them across the courtyard to the gates.

'You won't have seen this; it's overgrown.'

The sun sank. Across the courtyard the heads of the thistles were painted orange.

'There is a plaque here, behind the post. It tells you when the house was built. There. Read!'

He stepped back and pushed her forward to the wall. Lucie opened her mouth obediently. The Mayor stood behind her; she felt the men's eyes on the curls at her neck.

'What does it say?'

'It says it was built in 1533, on the site of a former edifice.'

'A what?'

'On the site of a former edifice.'

'Who built it?'

'Two brothers. From Barcelona. They were extradited by the King and came here, and built this, and died here.'

'What did they do?'

'Who knows?' said the Mayor and then he made his excuses and put his bandaged hand back in his pocket. He walked away quickly, coughing. It was as if someone had called to him to come in and eat suddenly. He pushed his way through the gate and left them alone.

Arnaud was delighted with the wine on the table and he poured some for both of them, using the brandy glasses from the night before. He seemed relaxed now in the room, and warm. Lucie had kept a fire going for most of the afternoon and now she opened the lid of the pot hanging from a hook over the fire and stirred the stew thick with onions, tomatoes, peppers and potatoes. He watched her go about her womanly business and smiled comfortably. There was bread and a large slice of soft cheese, which Arnaud cut quickly and ate with his glass of wine.

He stood up to help her lift the pot from the fire. Lucie sat at the table with her hands demure in her lap. Arnaud leant forward, dragging his boots; already, she thought, his eyes had something of the countryside in them, something bright and hard like berries.

He ate hungrily, watching her. When he had finished his food, he pushed his bowl to one side and reached across the table for her hand.

'They are all so strange here, Arnaud.'

'You think?'

'The Mayor, with his cough and his bandaged hand, leaving like that, having pushed us over to see the plaque, which means what exactly? Built on the site of a former edifice?'

'It means built on something that was here before.'

'Before what? Before the fifteenth century?'

'Exactly.'

'But the villagers who say nothing, and do nothing? I feel as if something has happened here.'

He drained his glass. Then he pulled his chair away from the table and took it over towards the fireplace. He stood on the chair and reached his hand back through the bars and into the teeth of the wooden cage that was above the fireplace and was where he had put his gun.

'They would have kept the dogs up here, Lucie. Dogs to turn the spit.'

'Yes, Arnaud. Yes. I know.'

He slid the gun out of its cloth and turned it in his fingers. In the morning he would go out in the fields to check it was still in working order.

'This house was once magnificent,' he said to her, looking her straight in the eye. 'I think that if we work at it with all our hearts and minds we can make it so again.'

2

Through the winter, the crows kept watch; their watery eyes turned to her labours in the courtyard as she cleared the weeds and made space for herbs, for olive trees, a bed of lavender to plant in the spring.

When she had finished clearing the courtyard, it looked vast and ghostly; the ground was dirty white in places, rings of cracked earth around the giant fig tree in the centre.

Arnaud decided to remove the vines from the top vineyard entirely and leave the field fallow for a year. It took him days to haggle for the machines, and the men who came were not from the village but from another, up in the hills.

In the early-morning dark, he peeled back the blankets from his mattress in the kitchen and slipped out to warm his car for the drive. He was gone all day, coming back at the sinking of the sun in the afternoon, his face burnt in the wind, his hands torn, his breath bitter with alcohol.

Lucie watched the birds from behind the safety of the glass. She saw the way they strutted back and forth inspecting her wasteland and they reminded her of a teacher she had at school. Madame Tulson with her hair scraped back in a bun. It seemed that even the birds were ill-tempered, consumed with irritation for her lack of progress, mocking her inability to move on from the kitchen and into the other rooms. *You have made a prison cell for yourself, it's true.* 'Time to move on,' Arnaud said. 'We can't live for ever in the kitchen.'

But Lucie enjoyed her work in the kitchen. Going over and over the same things. Endlessly wiping the same surfaces, rearranging, moving things around. There was satisfaction to be drawn from this work and she lifted herself to the task. She put crates on the window ledges to store her fruit and vegetables, with tightly sealed jars of salt, flour, pickles and jam. In the centre of the kitchen the table was spotless and welcoming; on a strip of old lace she kept jars of mustard, thimbles of salt and pepper. Even their mattresses, as neatly made with blankets and cushions as beds in a doll's house, lay side by side on the floor, in front of the fire.

'We can't stay for ever in the kitchen, Lucie. Not for ever. We can't sleep in this room for ever.'

'No,' she said, but she didn't move.

'There is this whole house to live in.'

'Yes.'

A white winter morning. Arnaud and the men who worked with him came into the kitchen, unlaced their boots and sat around the table.

Lucie stood with her back to them; she thought again of Marie and the women in the room above the hairdresser's; how they would all laugh at this bunch of men behind her, their animal wrinkled skins, their inability to speak. Often she wondered what she was doing here among these people who never spoke, among the village folk who had not come round to pay a visit, not one of the women from the shuttered houses. In the square, their faces twitched with interest on seeing her, otherwise they slunk back inside, kept themselves to themselves. She wanted to follow them, knock on their doors and shout through their letterboxes: *I'm not a German, you know! I've got nothing contagious, no fear greater than your own.*

'Lucie,' said Arnaud when the coffee came and the men rounded like bears over their tiny cups. 'I'm going to go with one of these men to Toulouse to see about a new machine. I'll be away one night. Our neighbour said you can stay with his family if you would rather not be here alone.'

The men smiled knowingly and nodded their heads.

Lucie smiled. 'Of course I can sleep in my own house alone.'

'You'll need a gun,' said one of the men in an accent so thickly southern she struggled to hear what he said.

'Excuse me?'

He grinned. His teeth were brown and spaced apart. 'You'll need a gun. There are looters. Big places like this. Get looted.'

She laughed. 'Monsieur, there is nothing in this place for anyone to steal.'

'That's what you think, Madame,' he said and Arnaud's response was drowned out in the sound of their laughing.

—

They left in the early afternoon when the light was clean

94

and calm in the kitchen and the crows had gone. Lucie busied herself in the silence after their departure, emboldened suddenly by her independence. In the overgrown garden behind the house, she worked until her fingers were numb and then she bathed in the stone sink, sitting with her hair wet by the fire. She didn't let herself think about the rest of the house heaving and groaning around her like the great old ship she saw in her mind. In the kitchen she had found it easier to imagine that the rest of the building simply didn't exist.

She thought of the baby's blanket Arnaud's mother had given her before their departure from Paris and how she held it, spilling heavy and dusty white from its yellowed tissue. Conceiving a child, even figuratively, meant believing there was something to bring it to, something good and whole and not full of fragments; a world in which the act of remembering was sweet and nostalgic and not like walking into a room full of soft, open cuts, bits of vein everywhere, cuts and sinews of flesh on the floor, on the backs of the doors. What if she could not do it? She would let them all down. Mother, Father, Sister, Brother. Their expectations would fall like a pack of cards around her. And then they would claw at the absent baby like wolves gone mad for lack of food. Because her fear, even then, was that someone might see the doubts that sank to the silt in her mind, or that they might perceive from the look on her face the shadows of these hulks appearing, so sinister, at the edges of her thoughts. You had to believe you believed in belief, and Lucie had been given no reason, though she didn't really know it then, to believe in anything. There wasn't a role model of goodness and patience and faith and charity as far as the eye could see. And you had to see some goodness to believe in it, that was what she believed. Her mother-in-law was bent on glory and a screwy patriotism raged in her heart. There was wonder, the old woman shrieked, in the sloshing of buckets on hospital floors, in the plastering-up of old walls; there was hope in the cleansing rain of autumn, in the snow falling softly on northern graves. There was glory, she said, in the women returning to the hearth now, to fatten like hens and produce their eggs, to sit and fatten and squawk like hens, thought Lucie, in a great triumphant line of readiness to aim, fire and plug the country's gaping lines.

She didn't bother to mix the brandy with water but drank it neat, cradling the cup in her hand before climbing in beneath the blankets on the floor. The fire flickered in the grate. On the window ledge, the glass jars glittered, like a row of blinking eyes.

But the night brought strange dreams, dreams of the women from the village coming through the chateau gates carrying baskets. In her kitchen window Lucie stood, a much smaller woman than she knew herself, a girl in a nightdress, with hair curling thinly down her back. She stood in the kitchen window watching the women gather in the chateau courtyard, hundreds of them, squawking, with their little tiny aprons on.

She woke sweating, to knocking on the shutters, once, twice, a sharp rap, then silence and nothing. She put the dream to the back of her mind and stood slowly, comforted by the embers still glowing softly in the fire.

The shutters were rapped at again, and she walked towards them and opened them up to nothing but the white winter morning and the fog stretched three foot thick on the ground.

She could have sworn it was then that the bird flew into the kitchen because when Arnaud came back to Canas that evening he found his wife sitting under the kitchen table still wrapped in the thick cotton nightdress. All day she had been under there. She was hiding from the bird; you never saw anything so wild, she said.

3

The storm came at the end of February. The rain began and needled the ground; five days, pelting the courtyard, bringing up deep whorls like a thousand worms turning the earth.

From the kitchen window Lucie stared at the ground. It was 1950. The century on its fold. But the days were dark and seemed endless. She mopped the floor, washed the walls so that everything, inside and out, was washed in synchronicity. Life didn't begin again. It merely tried to release itself from the past.

The rain seeped into everything. Who knew what happened upstairs, in the rest of the house? She imagined pools of water, rain coming in through the roof. She imagined empty rooms with mottled and cracked walls. The temperature cooled. The streets ran red with sand.

'It's from Africa.'

Arnaud was leaning in the kitchen window, a cup of brandy in his hand. He wore a black oilskin with the hood slumped on his back. All the shutters on the ground floor he had repaired and painted a soft silvery green. But he didn't admire his work. Not for longer than a minute or two. He saw only what there was left to do. He saw only the vineyard, the endlessness of it, his need to clear it, to tug at the roots.

The light on his face was steely grey, the rain reflected in streaks. He was thin and hard, like an animal trapped.

'It's from the desert. A five-day storm. Tomorrow it will stop. Everything, the streets, the cars, will be red.'

'The vineyard?'

'What does it matter? We are pulling it up, vine by vine. It can just rain now and churn the earth and make it soft, make it new.'

'Yes,' she said, and she smiled prettily at his back. 'It might bring all kinds of goodness to the ground.'

She had dressed herself in brown; a thick wool dress bought several sizes too big at the market and tapered severely at the waist with a belt. Heaven knew what she looked like, but she was warm at least, and that was what mattered for now. Doctor Clareon had told her if she wanted to have a child she had to eat well – eggs, meat, cheese – and keep herself warm.

'You must think of yourself as an incubator. Fatten yourself.'

'Like a goose?'

'And try to be joyful, Madame. This white face, these dark circles about your eyes. No child could grow beneath this heart, which is heavy and takes up everything.'

She tried to laugh him off but the doctor bent his knees and placed his hands around her diaphragm, tried to lift her, his fingers between her ribs. He lifted her clean off the ground and the puff came out of him through grimaced lips. Then, just as suddenly, he let her down. She felt the colour rush to her cheeks. The doctor looked appalled. He turned round, looking for the other, more spirited version of himself.

Lucie hadn't forgotten Doctor Clareon's words, and she hadn't forgotten his hands either, the warmth and tenderness in them, the strength holding her up. There were other things he told her, about how to tell if a woman was ready to conceive by the heat in her hands, here, on her heart.

In the chateau kitchen she took the coffee cups down from the shelf above the cooker and polished them to make them shine. Round and round she went with the duster; not rushing but taking pride in the work, humming to herself as she went. She stretched up, her small feet on points, and lined the cups back on the shelf.

She would take them down in a day or so and polish them once again. She heard the rain clatter down. She teased the ceramic red hen to the side and stood back, her face intense with the business of seeing her kitchen look like this: clean and bright with a few modern touches, the spotlights from Arnaud's brother in Paris, the bin on wheels, the pressed stack of tea towels on the shelf straight from an American magazine. Soon the kitchen would be perfect and then the women would come from the village; she would get Arnaud to invite them all with their husbands and so they wouldn't be able to refuse. They would see her kitchen looking like a kitchen of Mrs America, and they would love her then – she felt sure of it – at last they would let her in.

In the grate, the fire burnt hungrily through dead vines, and a sweet-smelling smoke curled away from the rain and escaped from the top of the fireplace in waves.

She spoke loudly to make herself heard.

'They may not come today, Arnaud.'

'No.'

'Because of the rain.'

'I thought I would make a cake in any case. For when they come. I've got a basket of eggs from...'

'I haven't invited anyone yet.'

'But still they might come of their own accord.'

He drained his glass and belched. It was only recently that he had become like this. Sullen towards her, rude at times. He pressed her at night to lie with him but she found it so hard to relax here, she found it hurt so much she couldn't bear to let him near.

'Lucie, wake up. You are screaming. Your face. What is it? What's wrong?'

'You're hurting me,' she whispered as he leant towards her, clambering over the blankets on his own mattress to get to hers.

'God, have you gone out of your mind? We sleep every night in this kitchen. There is this whole enormous chateau to live in and we sleep, just in here, just in the kitchen, Lucie. Every night we sleep. Nothing else. How can you expect us to have a child like this?'

He placed his hands over her collarbones, moved his fingers under the cloth and ripped the material down over her shoulders, hooking her breasts out from underneath. She grunted. He held the breasts, like little fruits, in his hands.

'You're hurting me,' she whispered.

'But this is how – the only way to get what you want and make a child.'

'But I don't want to, Arnaud,' she said. 'I can't bear it.'

———

The Algerians came to help Arnaud in the vineyard. They arrived at dusk, pushing at the old gates, and stopping by the silvery brush of the olive tree, the men with dark coats over their dresses, a woman dressed from head to toe in grey, a black cloth covering her head. Three of them. Three bundles of cloth wrapped up at the entrance.

Lucie had been waiting for them, standing in the last of the light at the kitchen window and now she saw them and rushed out of the house without a cardigan on, her skirt swinging about her knees. She was thrilled to have some company at last.

'Come! You are welcome! Come inside!' she said, and she urged them into the house, not knowing at first what on earth to say. They had come from the desert, of course, and they would not know much, if anything, about the life of a modern woman. But Lucie knew that despite their differences they would be friends. She had made up a room for them on the second floor.

Inside, they sat in their coats and stared at the fire. The men looked up from time to time at the ceiling, as if to get a clearer sense of the size of the place.

Lucie fussed about, boiling water for coffee on the cooker, removing the cake she had made from its tin, sinking the knife into large slices.

The woman was looking down at her hands, the black veil making a baby of her head. In the village the dogs were barking. Their silence compelled Lucie to speak.

'My husband believes there is the best wine in the world to be made on these hills. But we are not there yet. When we came here just a few months ago, we had so little. We have acquired almost everything in this room since then. The rest of the house, we do not inhabit much.' She smiled. 'But we're getting there. You'll be sleeping upstairs. It looks big and draughty but there are only five or six rooms on each of the floors upstairs. It's not nearly as big as it looks. It's certainly formidable, though. And the weather. Come summer you will find it terribly hot. More what you are used to, I expect.'

The men laughed. They were dirty. They had heavy circles under their eyes. One of them, the one who didn't speak, was older. He had a scarf about his neck and a long, thick nose, like a beak. His eyes were hooded behind it.

Lucie felt for this woman being married to this man. It probably wasn't her choice. But the woman bore her cross gracefully. And this was to be admired.

'I've put a few things in a basket for you,' she said, 'washing powder, some Madeleine cakes, in the basket.'

The three of them were watching the fire, watching the shadows dancing on the wall. Lucie pushed the plates of cake and the cups of coffee towards them, placing things up, as neatly as she could. She was trying desperately hard.

'It's almond cake. We have almonds everywhere here. It's the most wonderful thing to have the blossom in the winter.'

Then she stood to the side of the table, biting the inside of her cheek, her little white face set with concentration. They fell on the food at once, poor lambs, and they didn't look up at her.

'My husband will be here in a minute.'

Lucie turned to the window. Arnaud wasn't out there. As always he was nowhere to be seen. Only the pine tree with its top-most branches swaying in the breeze and the pale pink sky. Only a bird banking ten feet above the ground, giant and inky black, its wings shining brilliantly as if it had bathed in preparation for their new guests.

The Algerians slept and they prayed, five times a day. Water ran through the pipes upstairs. By day they worked in the vineyard. At the end of the day the men came in and took off their boots and took the food Lucie made upstairs to share with the woman who was soon expecting a child. Nobody spoke about this when it became clear. Arnaud said the work they were doing in the vineyard was incredible. They were strong. Their backs and their arms were thick and strong. In the evenings, in the kitchen, Arnaud was pleased.

The weeks passed. Lucie spent time getting out and about in town. On a Monday, Arnaud took her down in the car. On other days she walked. She brought back cookery books, and a magazine with a picture of Mrs America. In the bookshop there was a pile of these: Mrs America bending down in a pretty dress with a wide mouth painted red and big eyes and rosy cheeks and a tiny waist, nipped.

Bosoms pointed. Mrs America. Her yellow kitchen. Appliances all over.

'The women all want one,' the shopkeeper said. 'The old women, they scoff and snort and walk past with their noses in the air. But the young women. Young women like you, my dear. You all want to be Mrs America.'

Lucie clutched hold of the woman's sleeve.

'Will you come? Will you come to my house for some tea, Madame? I'd so like to talk to a female. I'd so like to have someone like you to talk to.'

'Madame, you are shaking. What is it, please?'

'Oh God, I'm so tired, I can't sleep.'

'Then you must go to see Doctor Clareon. He has many things to help the women here sleep.'

Then Arnaud came into the shop. He tripped on the step and stood in the darkness, scowling.

'We have to go, Lucie. I need to get back, to work. I have work...'

'Yes, can I just pay for...?'

She hooked her purse out of her basket and clicked it open but Arnaud had already taken her arm. The shopkeeper said to pay for Mrs America next time. 'You keep it, dearie. You go now. Go to Dr Clareon now. We don't have to live in pain.'

Arnaud had been to the bank. On the way back from town, he drove the motorcar as if he was trying to run it into the ground. Across the heath the sky was brilliant blue. The sun shone down. Wild iris flower everywhere, deep purple skirts fluttering in the clear air. Spring was leaping. The Algerian woman was nearly due.

'I will go to Paris tomorrow, Lucie. I don't see that I have any choice.'

'To see your brother?'

'What can I do? I need money. He has money.'

'Will they know, the men, what to do in the vineyard without you?'

'Of course.'

Lucie came back to the fire. The nights were getting warmer now but there was still a week or so to go before they would sweep out the fireplace.

'I think she is about to give birth, Arnaud.'

'How can you tell?'

'By the way she walks. Her back is aching. In two weeks she hasn't left the chateau.'

Arnaud stood by the fire, teasing the burning vines with his foot.

'And you?'

Lucie closed her eyes.

The water was green.

'Not all true.'

'Um?'

'Not true that people can start again. Not really. I don't think I can.'

'What?'

'Start again. I don't know if I can.'

———

She lit the cigarette in its holder. Her hands were small. The woman upstairs, Fatima, her hands were also small. Lucie thought of the nice things, the bin on wheels, Mrs America, the hand cream in the basket, the spotlights from Paris. They were the things that kept her afloat. But she wasn't a fool. She knew what she did. She knew there was no escape from the past. There was never anything but the baggage, and each man and woman moving beneath it; sideways, lurching forward in a brief moment of light and forgetting, tottering backwards, collapsing under the weight. She tried to tell him. All he said was:

'We can't make a baby if you won't let me touch you, Lucie.'

'Arnaud,' she pleaded, but she knew of course that this was true.

———

Arnaud had gone to Paris. She woke in the night to the sound of someone screaming. She pulled on the brown wool dress.

Upstairs the moonlight fell on everything, seeking out corners, lifting everything in its ghostly tint. She didn't need the candle and she blew it out, placing it carefully down on the ground at the entrance to the room.

She had reached the door at the far end of the corridor, the fifth room. The Algerians told her this room had a fine view on the garden and the old stone storehouse nestled among its trees.

Lucie took a deep breath, holding the air in, using it to try to undo the knot of fear that sat high in her chest. Her heart thumped as she pushed at the door.

'Thank goodness,' said the doctor, standing as she walked inside, gesturing towards the figures huddled on the floor.

107

'How did you get here?' she whispered excitedly. 'How did you get in?'

'One of the men came to get me,' he said. 'Walked all the way into town. I brought him back in the car and we came straight up here.'

Lucie was pleased to see him.

'Two hours old,' whispered Doctor Clareon.

'Asleep?'

'Both of them. Exhausted. A long labour, made much worse by her fear.'

'Fear?'

'It seems she can't have a man about her now for at least seven days; she can't pray or fast now for forty days.'

'Were you here for the birth, Doctor?'

'Of course.'

'What name did they choose?'

'Baseema.'

'Baseema?'

'It's Arabic. It means "smiling". They will sacrifice a goat in time. Give her a proper naming ceremony.'

'A goat?'

'They will find a goat. They will kill the goat and eat it and give the child her name.'

'Baseema,' whispered Lucie, rolling the name around her tongue. 'I'll buy them this goat, Doctor. I'll sell something – anything – and buy them this goat.'

'That would be a noble thing to do, Madame.'

'Noble? God no, not noble.'

The doctor smiled; his eyes were kind but tired. Lucie placed her hand on the soft grey hairs at the back of the doctor's neck.

'Where is the husband now?'

'He's gone,' said the doctor quietly. 'He wanted air.'

Lucie felt her eyes moving all around his strong, confident face. Deliverer of children, kind, gentle deliverer of women.

'Is she happy, Doctor?'

'Yes.'

'And is it the happiest feeling of all, do you think? Does it wipe all else away?'

'No,' he replied, and he kissed her then, placing his hot lips very carefully, very neatly on hers.

'I think of you so often,' he said afterwards, and her eyes were filling up now, gazing up into his as if he might be seeing her soul at last, her sweet kindly gentle loving soul, as it should be seen here, like a nurse, in this room of birth and softness and life.

She kissed him briefly and pulled back and went over towards the sleeping mother and child. She put her fingers out to the mattress and knelt beside them with this feeling of strength and purpose inside, such as she had never before experienced in her short and disconnected life.

4

It was Lucie herself who bought the goat from the shepherd who walked his flock across the heath. She waited for him one bright morning and sprung out from behind the rocks. All she had was the ring she wore on her finger and the chain she wore around her neck. She gave the shepherd the chain and he used his rope to fashion for her a collar and lead so that she could walk the goat back to the village.

Lucie knew that the women of the village would be looking out, through the cracks in their shutters, as always, and so she approached the chateau through the vineyard, pulling the goat quite easily, while feeding it handfuls of grass from her hand. It was only her neat little round-toed shoes that suffered from the indignity of this journey, and these she was able to clean satisfactorily while the Algerians prepared for the ceremony.

Arnaud didn't come. 'Which suits me fine,' whispered Lucie to her new friend, and she and Fatima worked all day to clear out the old junk from the storeroom in the garden so that they could eat in there if it rained.

But it didn't rain that night of the naming ceremony and they made a wonderful fire and even the doctor came, parking his car outside the gates and walking discreetly across the courtyard and over to the garden room. He was a short man with a thick moustache but he was clever, gracious, and Lucie didn't mind him holding her and kissing the back of her neck while they stood behind the storeroom after the goat had been eaten and the Algerians had taken the baby back indoors.

'Just looking at you, standing there beside the fire, with the baby in your arms, Lucie.'

'Am I beautiful?' she asked him, and he kissed her hard then and it almost felt exciting to her, to know that her husband sat in his library deep inside the chateau and here she was outside with the doctor – kissing in the darkness – with the smell of a baby on her hands; new life and loveliness come to them all at last.

Within a week of the naming ceremony, Fatima was out to work in the vineyard with the men. There was a little money to be made on the land and Lucie agreed that Fatima should do it. On the Monday morning, Lucie stood in the doorway and waved her off and then she peeked into the blanket in her arms to see a little more of the honey-coloured cheek.

Dr Clareon said Lucie would never be able to have a child. But he so looked forward to her weekly consultations. He told her that she needn't be frightened or haunted any more; this memory of cuts he could wipe with pills that would keep her feeling upbeat and alive. He also gave her something to sleep. She would need to be strong, he said, because the Algerian family needed her now to care for their child.

So Lucie focused on the child in the house, she relished

the nesting; she fattened herself, and she took the pills. In the nursing chair she sung lullabies and when Baseema was sleeping she trotted up and down the stairs with washing, and clean towels, and cot sheets, and warm bottles of milk. She became an expert at making things last – using what was left of the meat to make soup and stew and thick casseroles and soon it would be harvest time and then they would be able to live more off the land. She was busy out in the courtyard too, planting fruit trees; pruning the fig.

'The yield on the fig tree will be tremendous,' she whispered to Fatima one evening. 'You just wait and see how much wonderful fresh food we will have here to feed us.'

Fatima was reticent. But she was flattered by all the attention and her heart softened to Lucie's advances. Soon it was easy for Lucie to spend almost all day walking around with Baseema in her arms.

'It's like I've got my own child,' she said to the doctor, when she went to visit him for her weekly check-up. He checked her pulse and kissed her wrist. He checked her breathing and his fingers teased the lobes of her ears. Doctor Clareon kept the shutters closed for her Friday appointment, and Lucie sat in the chair beside his desk while he kissed her and she ran through her mind the list of all the things she would need from the shops. Once or twice he got a little carried away; his hands became hot and he asked her to stay. But then, very quickly, he righted himself. The best thing about the doctor was that he did have this self-control and that was what Lucie loved about him – he was precise with his fingers, and neat and always controlled. And so she allowed herself to be petted in his chair. She gave him fifteen, twenty minutes; sometimes he wanted thirty. And then he slipped behind the curtain and pulled it across the bed while he took his trousers down and re-emerged a better man, he said; lighter in spirit, and mind.

In the village, of course, they all knew about the Algerian child and how Lucie was fast adopting it. In the café, the men who drank with Arnaud said his wife appeared to be thriving on it. Arnaud was getting bigger. His hair was long and straggly beneath his cap. He worked all day and he drank at night. 'When a woman is happy she cooks like a demon,' he said to the men in the bar. And so it became known in the village that Lucie Borja had a sense of purpose and cooked like a demon, and she tended a fruitful garden.

One by one, at the gate, the women started to appear. They came with ices. One or two of them even came to the chateau for lunch and they went to some trouble, she could see that, to choose an outfit and style their hair.

But something wasn't quite right. It was as if Lucie was trying too hard and the pressure she exerted made the women feel hot and thirsty. Always, she would be waiting for them, in a pristine pastel-coloured dress and cardigan, waiting for her guests on the top step, her eyes like beads. Down she would rush and come to meet them, chattering nineteen to the dozen, offering her cold little hands and compliments. Everything they said she agreed with emphatically, which was unsettling for these country women, and strange. Like children themselves they would be ushered through the hallway and out through the echoing kitchen to where the garden table was laid with a white cloth and covered in shiny fruit tartlets and sticky buns she had slaved over – and then the baby there, on display, but tucked up in a pram in the shade.

'Non-stop, she talks,' said the women when they got back, at last, to their houses at dusk and gathered for a quick discussion.

'She won't draw breath.'

'She dashes about, in and out of the kitchen, and she does all the work herself, slaving and slaving over the food. It's a wonder she doesn't run herself in.'

'Lord knows why she doesn't use the Algerian woman, Fatima.'

'It seems the charwoman has risen ranks in the chateau.'

They laughed. 'She bathes, don't you know; she was in the bath while we were having tea. It seems Lucie and she are friends!'

For the women, of course, in their grubby little kitchens, the talk lingered. Seditious and secretive as a second helping of chocolate sauce, it brought them together in an animated huddle, then drove them apart; each time the temptation strengthening their bond. And so it went on, month after month that first year and the next, shutters flipping open in the wall overlooking the chateau garden. Eyes that were trained to stay low in any case, looked once, twice, took it all in. Scarves were adjusted, shutters closed. They kept shoulder to shoulder on their way back from the post office, their baskets rubbing, their skirts swishing into each other as they whispered and veered off towards the fish van parked in the square.

For these women of the village, it was a way of speaking about themselves without saying 'I'. It was a way of laughing together, warming themselves on the inside while looking appalled on the out. It was affirmation, unification in spite.

⸻

The truth was that life in the chateau was simple and routine those first few years of Baseema's life. Fatima was a fine, hardworking woman with a sweet smile who was glad of Lucie's kindness and companionship – the more so when her husband and his brother returned to Algeria to fight for the liberation of the people. The two men went to speak to Arnaud about it in his library. They told him they had no choice but to return to their village.

Financially, Arnaud was in a slightly better position by then. He was making some money at last in the vineyard, and he had joined forces with other winemakers in the hills and was proving himself among them as a robust and astute businessman. He cared little for the domestic arrangements in the house – these days the women were all on one floor and Arnaud slept alone in his study at night.

Lucie knew that her husband was quite content that she was absorbed in something that didn't involve him. The day-to-day demands of a four-year-old kept her cocooned from the wider concerns of their world and for the moment at least, that suited him fine. Lucie knew too that he was relieved to have seen her finding a friend in Fatima. Four winters, four summers and the two women working together in the cold and the heat, taking care of the baby girl, telling stories to soothe her at night, whispering, singing, their hands moving together in the moon-light. One wouldn't have known that one was the server, the other being served.

Fatima liked to sing the songs she learnt as a child. Desert songs she called them. Crooning at the sink. They rolled up their sleeves together. Lucie showed Fatima how to curl her hair. Baseema skipped in between them. Lucie loved this little girl and her soft fat cheeks more than she had loved anyone and the thought that Fatima might take her daughter back to Algeria because of the deteriorating political situation was too much for her to bear. Time and again she mentioned the benefits of a French education, and extolled the virtues of the small local school. Fatima listened and nodded a lot but it was clear that things in Algeria were not improving and at some point, she said, she and Baseema would be returning to their home.

But then, soon after Baseema's fifth birthday, Fatima became unwell. Dr Clareon diagnosed tuberculosis, and suggested they move her out of the house and into the garden room.

It was Lucie herself who put the table and chair in there, a low bed, a vase of fresh flowers on the sill. Fatima was laid on the bed while Lucie sat at the table, arranging the flowers in the vase, her bottom pert on the chair.

From the fire the smell of sweet vine smoke filled the room. Lucie insisted on having the fire. Even in the heat of summer.

'Surely?' said Fatima, turning to the fire, looking aghast.

But Lucie said the doctor had told her to keep the fire burning for as long as the fever burnt. She didn't say why. The doctor had put medications on the bedside table. And a bottle of linctus she could take in a hot tea.

Lucie sat with the patient and she thought about how grasshoppers were larger than ever that summer. Huge and monstrous; they clung to the window ledges and reached into the rooms with their antennae. Fatima barely noticed. Poor Fatima. So ill she got, so fast.

As it turned out, the medication wasn't quite strong enough to destroy the bacteria that had formed in the woman's weak lungs.

The doctor consoled Lucie. When he came up to the chateau, he held her in the garden room and told her she mustn't blame herself. Fatima lay in the bed like a wraith now; all the fat from her limbs was gone and only her bones seemed to be there. The weight dropped off with such alarming speed; it was as if she were being rubbed out of the picture.

'Which she was,' said the women of the village, as they bustled into Mass on the day after the funeral. 'She absolutely was!'

Lucie feared the bad luck that spilled out of the chateau walls.

She took the child round and round the garden. They collected flowers; they ran together in the vineyard.

Lucie cried, quite quickly, in the doctor's chair and she told him that she would always be haunted by Fatima's sweet face in the garden room, the look in the poor woman's eyes, that brown hand trying to stifle a cough. It was so hot in the room, and the sweat had burst from them both. Lucie had herself closed Fatima's eyelids and held her hand to the open gasping mouth, she told the doctor, who kissed her and held her and wrote her another prescription so that she could sleep easier at night.

'You have a job to do now,' he said. She had to be strong and eat and get on. 'You're a mother,' he told her.

'Yes,' she whispered, with courage in her heart.

'That's the only thing that matters now.'

And Lucie agreed and was consoled by this and so she allowed him to lay her down on his bed behind the curtain and she found that the pills he gave her to keep her strong took the edge off the shock and the pain of penetration and the doctor was ever so grateful for her – the little neck, the sweet Parisian face – and the first time he lay on the bed above her and thrust and thrust with his trousers round his knees and he cried out in bliss.

Soon after, Baseema was moved into the master bedroom and she slept now on a little bed in the window with the porcelain doll Lucie ordered from Paris.

Out they bundled on a Friday morning and when the doctor called Lucie in for her consultation, Baseema remained in the waiting room for close to an hour playing with her doll under the sympathetic watch of the receptionist.

And if anyone had asked her, Lucie would say that the doctor had only ever been a trusted and loyal friend in a place where people were mostly cold and hostile to her. Mercifully, the doctor was able to advise her on so many things. He agreed, when she voiced her fears about it, that Baseema should probably wait another year before attending school and that, in the meantime, Lucie should continue just to enjoy all the time that they spent together in the chateau and out in the garden. Arnaud was never around.

If there was one thing that he asked, it was that Lucie found someone in the village to take her, just on a

Friday morning, so that they wouldn't have to rush behind the curtain, leaving the child sitting quite conspicuously with the receptionist in the waiting room outside.

5

Lucie wasn't able to find anyone in the village to look after her. It wasn't that she didn't trust them. It was more to do with the fact that the village women had other children – their homes were small and dirty and full of noise – and she worried that Baseema might prefer it there, might become used to the noise and the activity of other children and that this would bring about the first in a series of psychological separations that Lucie would be unable to bear. She was a woman in her own right now. She felt pretty in her Mrs America kitchen, reaching up on points in her full swinging skirts. In the evenings she made her clothes; by day she cleaned her house and played with her child. She made food that pleased her husband; she even had the women in the village to tea. So what need had she of the doctor and his Friday morning fumblings behind the white curtain? What need had she of all those mind-numbing pills?

So Lucie took the last of her pills and then Friday came and she would get through it alone.

The doctor didn't call. He was a gentleman through and through and he didn't come at the weekend.

On Saturday night she was bright as a button and she cooked a splendid feast for Arnaud. She sat with him in the library and chatted to him while she sewed. He sat and stared at the fire, listening to the radio and ploughing on through his bottle of wine, barely noticing a thing. No question his wife was more attentive, was chattier to him, and sweet. No question he was being fed like a king and waited on by a woman who seemed to enjoy making herself a slave.

They listened to the wind in the trees that night. They sipped the brandy by the fire. Then Arnaud said his intention was to bring her sister Marie down to the village for the summer.

———

A fortnight later, Arnaud carried Lucie into the surgery because by then she had got so weak and frail she could barely walk alone.

The doctor was appalled. He stood up very quickly from behind his desk and his face was white as the wall.

'She's done this to herself,' Arnaud whispered in the doctor's ear. 'She got some news she didn't like and this was how she responded. Her sister in Paris has a son. She didn't know.'

'When did she last eat?' asked the doctor, bending down beside his patient at once to check the pulse.

Lucie's mouth was dry and cracked at the corners. When she opened her mouth, the cuts opened and bled.

'My husband has a son,' she said. 'He's coming here in the summer to stay with us.'

'Of course it's not my son,' he hissed at his wife while the doctor stood as if to intervene. 'You're talking nonsense, Lucie. If you had something in your stomach…'

Arnaud picked up the pills from the chemist and he sat

with Lucie in the car while she swilled them back. Then he drove his family back to the chateau and for a few days things were back to normal. Every Friday the doctor came to the chateau to see Lucie and he would adjust the medication as was required.

Lucie took her pills and she got a lot of rest. She kept Baseema close to her, day and night. Soon things began to feel better. It was June. It was possible that it might even be fun to have a little boy about the chateau. Someone else for Lucie to mother as perfectly as she did Baseema, another reason to get the chateau shipshape as soon as she possibly could.

Lucie had Baseema. Marie had Paul. Fair's fair, said Lucie to herself as she hung up the bed sheets on the line in the garden. Fair's fair, she sang to herself as she went back into the cool of her house and busied herself, humming, and made the lunch.

It wasn't the nicest thing she had done, telling Arnaud about the doctor's Friday advances but she was so convinced of his affair with Marie and it guaranteed her the physical freedom she needed from him while ensuring he remained in the study.

She made a room for Marie beside the study; the children would sleep on the first floor with her. Lucie told Dr Clareon when he came the next Friday to check her medication that her husband now knew all about what he had done to his patient in his little chair and that all that would have to stop and would never happen again. Dr Clareon looked disappointed and he breathed heavily when he checked her pulse and her blood pressure, but otherwise she was left alone.

Which meant that Lucie had almost everything she

needed. She had her home and she had her child. She began to put on weight. From now on her husband and the amorous doctor would leave her alone. She would never be tampered with again.

—

July arrived with a heatwave. Marie and Paul were due to come on the day of the burning plane ceremony.

All was in perfect order. Lucie was looking forward to the village gathering up on the heath and she sang to herself in the kitchen as she bent over the sideboard pounding aubergines to a pulp. She spread these on the pastry bases. Then she sliced potatoes into flakes, which she lay in a dish she had rubbed with garlic. Then she poured milk and cream over them.

At eleven, Veronique from the house closest to the chateau came with a basket of seventeen eggs for the crème caramel. Veronique was shaped like a goose; long and stiffly necked, with a wide saggy behind. But Lucie had picked Veronique because she was more intelligent, it seemed, than most of the women in the village. She was a solid, loyal-looking person. And her husband was the most successful of the local winemakers, which gave her social standing and influence. With Marie and Paul on the way down from Paris with Arnaud, it was important for Lucie to put on a display to show her guests when they arrived how little she minded them being there, how happy she was in general, how well liked in the village. So Veronique was coming with the eggs for the crème caramel. They would make it together, the two of them. They would talk then and exchange all manner of intimacies, which Lucie knew would bring them closer.

Lucie went out and stood in the sunlight, one hand up to shield her eyes. The wind rustled in the branches of the olives trees.

'Will you not take my hand, Veronique?'

'*Mais non*,' whispered Veronique, husky with fat. '*Mais non*, Madame. Of course...' She smiled and moved forward and her whole body seemed to tremble with the effort.

Lucie tried to make a sweeping gesture around the courtyard and this gave Veronique the cue that she desperately needed.

'I am overwhelmed by the work you have done on the chateau. It looks so elegant, Madame. All these beds laid out for flowers, a herb garden here.'

Baseema circled Lucie's leg, one hand holding her hair back from her face.

'These olive trees are in exquisite shape. The shutters painted so neatly. You have done exceedingly well.'

Lucie bowed her head and felt the pleasure of her own humility. She said it wasn't the case inside the chateau but she thanked Veronique for her comments and held the woman's arm as they went inside for coffee. The doors to the salon and to the dining room, to the library and to Arnaud's study were all closed. But the interior was shabby by comparison with the courtyard and there weren't more than three pieces of furniture for poor Veronique to lay her eyes upon as she walked through the hall and into the kitchen. Lucie felt the embarrassment, the paucity of it, and she wrapped her cardigan about her chest, feeling the slightness of herself around the ribcage – so little flesh, so little womanly flesh – inside all this house.

It was said that Veronique's house was stuffed to the gunnels with objects. Of course, Lucie would have wanted to have some more furniture, some paintings on these walls, but all the money that Arnaud brought back from Paris or made in his vineyard went on the things they needed to live on and on the outside of the chateau, which seemed so much more important to him, she explained to Veronique.

'He also has a mistress in Paris,' said Lucie quietly. Behind her, Lucie felt the fat woman shuddering and she led her into the kitchen where a pristine table was laid with cakes in a small mountain of perfect pastel pink. Veronique gasped and sat quickly beside the cakes. Baseema came to the table with them and Lucie poured out the coffee. 'It's just that my husband is under pressure, you know? Sometimes he needs to let it go…'

The fat woman was nodding, her mouth open, and she tried to smile.

'We met in a restaurant in Paris. On Avenue Georges V. It was spring, and the air was cool and clean again. There was quiet on the streets. The women walked by in colourful dresses that were not made of curtains or cheap cloth. Oh Veronique, there was nothing like that spring. They leant on the arms of the ones who had returned, and smiled and laughed, as if there had never been a war at all. In the restaurant they drank Coca-Cola and ate. Arnaud kept saying how badly he wanted to leave Paris, you know, to give the city up and live in the country making wine. He believed it would be good for us… But I… when I arrived here I felt so strange about it all. It was so quiet. So lonely. I couldn't believe how bleak.'

'Yes, I find it bleak also at times. Too quiet. But we

take what we have, I suppose, and we try to make the best of it.'

'I agree,' said Lucie, sadly.

'I don't envy you, Madame Borja,' said Veronique, breathily. 'This place. There's so much of it to get through. Even with staff I imagine that...'

'Veronique, I never had staff to help me. I have done this alone.'

'But the charwoman, Madame. The North African woman. You must miss her around the house, yes?'

Lucie silenced Veronique with the cold press of her little hand.

'My husband believes me to be useless. It's because I can't have a child. His punishment is that I work in this place alone. Only Baseema helps me when we are not doing her tuition together.'

The Mayor's wife was looking at Lucie as if she pitied her.

'You also tutor the child?'

'Everything,' said Lucie. 'I do everything alone.'

'I can imagine that this has been terribly hard for you.'

'The tragedy is that Baseema doesn't need me any more. She is growing up. And away from me. Until now it has not been a thankless task. But the girl is making friends. She doesn't want to be with me. She wants to go to school.'

'Which is right,' said the Mayor's wife, patting Lucie's hand. 'You must try to be a strong mother. And let the child be.'

In her mind Lucie saw the women in the room above the hairdresser's. She was still young but her womb was rotten and grey. She closed her eyes till the feeling went away.

Veronique was looking around. 'And where is Monsieur Borja now?'

Lucie went quiet then, for effect. After a moment or two she got up from the table and she asked Veronique to come with her, she had something she would like her to see.

'Please bring the cakes, Vero,' she said sweetly. 'We can eat them as we go. It's not so big as you imagined, though, is it? It isn't as big, as formidable as you thought it would be. For a long time, you know, I was so overwhelmed, so scared to leave the kitchen. For months, we lived in the kitchen alone. I can tell you are surprised by it.'

Upstairs, they walked along the corridor that ran the length of the first floor. There was a door at the end there and the key was rusty, so small it was almost swallowed by the keyhole. Lucie pressed her fingertips on the wood and pushed at the door. There was a narrow hallway, which was empty. The walls were mottled, the ceiling damp.

'Where are we going?' Veronique whispered.

'The tower you see from the village, and from the road on the hillside. It's quite lovely, and very secret in feel. Every morning I come here, and open the shutters.'

They rounded the corner and entered a small, round space painted entirely in white. There was a cot in there, and a new pine nursing chair with a thick white cushion on it. Through the windows the sunlight poured into this perfect white space.

Veronique gasped.

Lucie had read in a magazine that if you wanted to have a baby you had to make the space for it in your house. She had painted it white, staying up most of the night, painting long after Arnaud had come up and stood there wrinkling his nose because of the smell. There was just something about the room: small and secure with the window in an alcove, old arched shutters, with one that had warped a bit; and the way the light moved through it at around four or five in the afternoon, a rich orange glow that stretched in a long, thinning triangle on the wall, then began to fade in a line and disappeared. Who knew what battles had raged around the chateau in the past? Who knew what beings had crouched in here, keeping watch on the hillside for signs of invasion? Now there was no sign of war; it was the quietest, safest room in the house and for hours, in the afternoon, Lucie sat here, rocking her thoughts in the chair.

'My husband is on his way down from Paris, Vero. With the son of his mistress. His mistress is my sister, Marie. For years they have been seeing each other while I have been left here alone, working on my knees to keep his home clean. You think I am overdoing it. I am. But the thing is, it's all true. I can't have a child, Veronique,' she said, again. 'I can't have a child. But when Paul comes later on today, he will have this room that was meant for mine.'

Veronique closed her eyes.

'I'm so sorry, Lucie.'

'I wanted it. So much.'

'Yes.'

'Are you? Did you know this? Did the women of the village know that I was barren?'

'Madame. I'm so sorry. I knew so little about you. We all, we know so little about you.'

And then, in the way that people turn when they get to see the vulnerable side of someone they thought was higher on the social scale than them, the Mayor's wife stepped forward and kissed Lucie Borja on both white cheeks. She hugged her then and her big fat heart opened right up to receive the little bird who was so much in need of love and support and friendship. She kissed little Lucie's head and she held her to her breast and let her cry.

—

They burnt the plane that night. The tail with its Nazi swastika showing had been found half buried in the woods. It was carried, in a ceremonial procession of trucks, up to the heath, where the village gathered to watch it burn in memory of those who had lost their lives fighting, or resisting the Vichy collaboration.

The largest paella anyone had ever seen was brought up from Canas and the couple who owned the *épicerie* in those days supplied the bread. The Café Union, as it was known back then, supplied the pastis and glasses.

When the villagers came traipsing up the hill at dusk, appearing first as miniatures beneath the pine trees, carrying their rugs and their babies and their bottles of wine, the air was already filling with the smell of saffron and the fish cooking in the rice. It was a party to top all others and there was music and dancing and children running around barefoot till the early hours of the morning. Meanwhile, in the centre of the turning field, on a tall bonfire, the black tail of that plane with its white insignia of fear lay fallen against the dark sky as if it had crashed into its own funeral pyre and buried its nose in the ground.

No one really knew why the tail of that plane had come to be there in the woods, nor where the rest of the plane had gone or been taken. They knew it wasn't a fighter plane but a carrier, most likely personnel, that had veered off course before being shot down on its way in from the sea.

———

When Arnaud's car pulled up at the heath that night, and the boy and the tall angular woman stepped out with him and came out to the place where all the villagers were standing in a circle round the fire, they saw Lucie chatting and laughing with everyone as if she were suddenly the most popular woman in the village.

In one of the pictures taken, Arnaud was standing in profile, the tip of a cigarette in his fingers in front of his mouth; a tall handsome man, exactly the kind of decent, honest fighting man the evening was put on to commemorate. And Madame Borja was standing to the left of the group, between the Mayor's wife and the doctor, just a young woman with a band of chestnut-brown hair, a light silk shirt tucked into high slacks, smiling round the shoulders beside her.

The picture didn't show the shame Arnaud was feeling nor the humiliation he experienced at finding his wife here, not lonesome and afraid and completely mad as he had suggested she was to Marie, when he had pleaded with her outside the apartment in Paris to come down – *please come to the country, see for yourself how mad she is, how crazy, please*! – but utterly at ease with these people, chatting, laughing with her friend Veronique on her elbow as she worked her way around.

—

Later Arnaud would say that Marie had simply wandered off somewhere, disgusted, he imagined, by the villagers' behaviour, which became more and more raucous as the evening wore on, as if the black tail rising up above them was winding them up somehow, giving them an outlet for something that wasn't quite patriotic but felt violent nonetheless.

A few of the men whipped round the edge to wake the women and children who had fallen asleep on their blankets.

The crowd moved towards the turning field and some of the men broke into drunken song, wartime songs, and the children rubbed the sleep from their eyes and rushed forward towards the plane, their faces lit up with excitement.

The young village boy they called Lollo walked on his own at the back, his hands in the pockets of his shorts, his shoulders hunched against the crowd.

It was Lollo's thirteenth birthday, and he was used to celebrating his father's memory, the village hero who had died as a hostage strapped to the roof of a retreating German truck.

People said it was because the boy was angry. The villagers were getting carried away with the plane, forgetting the heroes who had died for them to be free. Others said it was because he had this need to prove his bravery – he wanted to be a war hero. He waited till the fire was lit and the first of the flames began to take hold of the logs and the children were standing rapt at the front, holding their hands out to test the warmth. Lollo hurled himself onto the bonfire and scrambled up to the top in his bare feet and sat himself on the tail of the plane, straddled it and rocked himself backwards and forwards till the thing began to shake. He was holding his hand in the air like he was riding a bucking horse and people were screaming by now, some with enjoyment, others with fear. But after a few minutes, the boy hadn't stopped and none of the people crowding round could comprehend what he was doing. The flames were leaping higher. A few of the bigger men came forward, shouting, trying to bat him down with their hands. But the boy didn't come down. And the fire burnt and got more and more furious and began to lap round his legs and now everyone was screaming. It was then that two or three of the men went in to rescue him, leaping up into the flames and grabbing a piece of him, a foot, a hand, and pulling him down, him and the tail, sliding him down onto the ground and away from the fire.

—

Arnaud drove Lucie and Baseema and Paul back down the hill in his car. It was morning when they arrived at the chateau and the sun was coming up. Baseema was asleep before they even carried her out of the car. Arnaud laid her down in the cot bed in Lucie's bedroom while Lucie put Paul to bed in the nursery and then went upstairs to check on Marie. She found her sister asleep in bed, sleeping off the journey. For a moment or two she stood and stared at her sister, who looked lovely asleep in the bed, with her hair all choppy and pixie-like on the pillow. She was glad her sister had got prettier. She was glad there was something pretty for Arnaud to put his thing into at last.

No, that didn't worry her at all. What worried her was the effect that her sister's boy would have on Baseema this summer. She could feel the change coming already, and she knew that soon, the child would let her down.

BASEEMA

1

Hotel Soleil, the Pyrenees, March 2006
Paris was the mountain. The well-spring of immigrant
violence came from that mountain and trickled down
through the rest of the country, reaching various troubled
industrial cities where it swirled under the bridges and went
again, thinning out through the rest of France, where most
people tended to live quietly with log-burning fires and
family meals and some people, right out in the middle,
couldn't yet read. By the time it got to the Pyrenees, you
wouldn't know much about it; only a trickle of something cold and wet that leaked into conversation in the
dining room but was nothing that couldn't be muffled
in a glass of something at the bar or mopped up with a
beautiful new towel. If you kept yourself clear of the daily
news, and you didn't go into the *banlieue*, you probably
wouldn't know much about it. When it all came down to
it, most people wanted peace and tranquility; they wanted
to work an honest day and sleep, to eat with their children
and come to these mountains to ski. They wanted as much
of the bounty of niceties as their circumstances would allow. Baseema had put the bath towels she had ordered in
all of the bathrooms now. They were white and fluffy and
folded on a heated shelf. She had taken the delivery herself, out in the cold driveway this morning, from the man

who complained about the roads. It was March. There was unemployment. In Paris there were labour protest riots. In the *banlieue* the immigrants were still torching cars. But that was Paris. And Baseema felt no connection to the city or to her roots. It was only Lollo who knew and liked to remind her. *Maghreb*, he would murmur when she made a sauce that was too piquant. Baseema ignored her husband when he said such things. She ignored him quite a lot these days and left him on his hateful sofa while she busied herself with the tasks that were required of her as hotel manager. Each morning she pulled on a clean turtleneck and coiled the thick length of her silvery hair into a neat bun at her neck. One of the chefs said that Baseema was like a swan.

Lollo felt she was up herself and by this he meant aloof. He said his wife had taught herself the pragmatism that comes with a certain inner desolation. She was cool on the inside. Which kept her calm. But Baseema was an intelligent woman who'd found it was easier, as she got older, to find the end of a thought, and leave it there. She had begun to feel that there were sinkholes in her memory. She saw what it was like in the blind man's paintings – the man who came to eat from time to time in the restaurant at the hotel, who painted people without faces. He did little sculptures too and she kept a few of them beside the till. Even the sculptures didn't have faces, they had been smudged out – a thumb pressed into the clay – making a splodge of what used to be a nose, the pinprick of an eye. Baseema loved these smudged-out empty faces, for all that they kept private and unexplained. Memory was a fickle thing. Who could tell for certain what had happened and what was real when so much depended on perception and the storing of data in the fly-by-night filing system of the mind?

In many ways it was remarkable what she had done; how she had managed to draw a line between the life she had led there in the village and the years she had been here, high up in the mountains, working in a place that clung to the edge of a flinty outcrop – only snow in the winter, and trees. It suited her. It went with the detachment. She was good (she had always been good) at rolling up her sleeves, pressing on, not stopping to wonder much, to analyse or peer. Feeling led, more often than not, to nothing but pain, which was a hindrance and to be avoided as much as possible at all times.

Which was why, when she received emails like these at her desk from Sylvie, she didn't trouble herself with images of her daughter sitting, shoulders hunched, her freckly face pockmarked and glistening in the light of the screen. Sylvie had gone back to the village because she wanted to. For a long time now she had been there living her life with a face that was quite unspeakable. What else could she do? From his sofa, Lollo had looked at the photograph of his children when Frederic was seven and Sylvie almost six and cried. But what could they really know about how Sylvie was managing these days? Humans had their own ways of coping and Baseema felt it was wrong to pry into someone else's way of doing things and patronise their attempts to get on. It would be the worst possible indiscretion to impose her own feelings on the beret that Sylvie wore to hide the scars on the right side of her face and the drooping eye – the only structural reminder of the steel girder she had worn to hold the pieces of her face together in that hospital in Toulouse.

Instead Baseema thought, without sentimentality, of the length and thickness of Sylvie's hair. She thought of the window boxes of bright geranium, and the house on the square. She was well liked in the village, and the dog – whose name was Coco – brought her companionship and warmth without the stress of a human relationship that Baseema supposed her daughter was too vulnerable to bear.

———

3rd March 2006
From: sylviepépin@aol.fr
To: Baseemapépin@aol.fr
Subject: For Sale?

There's so much excitement in the village now,
Ma, since the news came from Paris that
Madame Borja died and the chateau is going
up for sale. Suddenly everyone has something to
talk about. People make sick jokes. Underneath it,
everyone is intrigued. We all want to know what
will become of the place and, indeed, what became in the end of her! We know she went to Paris
after the fire. We don't know anything else. Did
she ever see Daniel for instance? Did he go to her
in Paris to make peace with her before she died?
Do you or Papa ever speak about it? Do you ever
think about it all?
    I know you are well shot of the place, Ma, but
well you will remember how gossip thrives and
multiplies here. There is talk of Americans coming

to buy the chateau and turn it into a hotel!
Also, there is talk of the Glovers, who are staying
here for the winter, expressing an interest.
The Glovers are staying in no 17. They are an
exceptional couple and though it's all speculation,
I would love it if they did decide to buy. They are
glamorous, and full of energy. She is very pretty
with nice skin and bright white teeth. She tends
to walk around a lot with her arms out to her
sides. I have become quite friendly with Kate. And
we have talked about the prospects that would
be available to some of the locals if she and her
husband were the ones who decided to buy, She
laughs it off, but you should see how much time
she spends at the place. There would be renovation
work for some of us. A lot of work, in fact.
But there would be questions to answer too, I
expect.

Baseema smiled to the young man in the burgundy scarf making his enquiries at the desk. Her hand moved the mouse onto print while she kept her eyes on her guest. Inside the mechanism something clicked, the light flashed blue.

It was white out; snow had been falling on these mountains for three days. Tiny flakes of snow dancing, as if someone grand had opened a compact of loose silvery powder and shaken it over the hotel. It was a good thing to have it, though, because the season hadn't been a good one and the slopes were much in need of a little fluffing here and there.

Baseema's gaudy bracelets chattered about her wrist as she slid the local magazine across the desk.

'There's a lovely concert in town, Monsieur. For Easter. This will tell you everything. It's candlelit. They begin at five. They sing to start with in the dark. Then all the candles come on. It is quite enchanting.'

'But is there somewhere in town I can buy a newspaper?'

'We've got an art exhibition too, Monsieur. A local artist, he paints these mountains, both in summer and winter. Lovely abstract paintings. I could draw you a map.'

'That's ok,' he said. 'Maybe later. But I'm a journalist and it would be good to have the papers delivered while I'm here. I'm covering the riots in Paris. I guess there's an internet connection in the room but still it would be great, you know, to have the actual papers.'

Baseema folded her hands in front of her stomach. She smiled.

'Many of our guests ask not to be given a newspaper, Monsieur. Not be shown anything that resembles anything close to a newspaper. We provide refuge, you see, from the noise of the world. It's a peaceful place. Space and comfort. Far from the chatter and madness.' She smiled. Her voice was soft and clear. 'People come with their loved ones. To get close, you see? To walk and ski, to eat well. We have a pool. It lights up in the evening.'

'Right,' he said, and he flicked his hair away from his face. He was a lovely-looking young man, and patient with his success, which was rare in such types, she felt. No, he wasn't finding this a problem. He held out his hand. It was springtime in the Pyrenees. He was here for a long weekend with his sweet beloved girl. Perhaps they would wander down to the concert together. Hold hands at the back, in the shadows. After that they could go to a wine bar, have some sweet, hot wine.

'I must tell you about the *patisserie*, Monsieur. They sell the bread for which we are famous here. And "Le Petit Blanc", the *chocolatier*.'

The journalist was smiling as he backed away, shaking his head. He knew he had the upper hand. He was the guest, she the server. He didn't bother to look her in the eye before he turned and picked up his case. He didn't need anything from her. He had his views on Paris, and his face in the national newspapers. It was a question of power, of identity. France was struggling with hers. Clearly, this confident, well-mannered boy was sure of his.

—

There's a real estate person coming here from Béziers tomorrow to take a look at the chateau. It's hard to estimate how much it would cost. Just all the renovation it would need. I guess it would have to be like a millionaire or something. But in the shop all they say is American this and American that. It's Americans, they say, like everyone knows what had been decided already when the agent hasn't even been to value the place. But what if someone did come and turn the old place into a hotel? Can you imagine?

I'll keep you posted

143

Big kisses
XXX Sylvie

P.S. In the café, I had such a strange conversation
with old Monsieur Surte. He said he felt, deep
down in his gut, very sure of one thing. Lucie
Borja never left this village, he said. Not after the
death of Frederic and the fire and never after. He
looked at me with his crazy eyes and looked very
still for a moment. Then he smiled at me and I saw
his black teeth. He said: 'As God is my witness,
that woman is still there rotting away in the dark.'
Rotting, he said, in the dark! Poor Madame Borja.
Straightaway I said a quick mental prayer for her,
for all the things people have said about her and
for the fact she never fit in and should never have
come here in the first place. Somehow now she's
dead I feel guilty that everyone hated her so much.
It was Daniel that caused the trouble here, Ma,
and broke all our hearts. It was Daniel who was
setting fires and running away and dancing along
the chateau wall with all the alcohol in his veins.
Remember that long coat he used to wear?
Remember his eyes, Ma, his deep blue eyes?

Monsieur Surte said he reckoned Daniel had
gone off to join the foreign legion or something or
that he might have even ended up dead, shooting
his brains out in some shitty hostel in Morocco
or somewhere. I didn't even know that Mr Surte
knew expressions like that. It was weird though,
you know. He said all this and his eyes were blazing red as the sun, like a man on fire. He spoke

with anger, such fury. It was blinding to see and
I couldn't help wondering, why on earth? What,
really, did the Borjas ever do but not quite fit in? It
makes me think how stupid it is to stay in a village
your whole life and never go anywhere else. How
the brain shrinks and shrivels like a pip before you
get laid out in the ground. That's what I was beginning to think anyway before the Glovers came.
I think I will talk to Kate about this. I will invite
her for coffee. I like her so much.

Please give my love to Papa. I hope he likes the
scarf. I hope he is ok. People in Canas still talk of
you both sometimes.

x

4th March 2006
From: Baseemapépin@aol.fr
To: sylviepépin@aol.fr
Subject: For Sale?

Dear Sylvie
It's good to hear from you. And thank you for the
scarf, which arrived by post on Tuesday. I'm glad
it got here. I was waiting for it out in the drive and
the buttons are delightful. Where on earth did
you find them? I hope that all is well and that you
managed to sort out the skin trouble of Coco's.
Did the vet prescribe the cream I suggested?

We are fine here. The hotel is full, of course,
and I am exceptionally busy. Thank you. Heavy

snow is predicted for next week and I expect we
will have many guests who will find themselves
unable to ski.

Your dad says Hi... He isn't up to much but the
scarf will make him smile.

I was wondering (it does all feel so long ago)
who did you hear this news from about Madame
Borja? Where did she die?

Thanks and kisses

Maman

———

At the desk, Baseema sat for a moment, waiting on a
response, waiting for the email to arrive in her inbox, its
presence made known to her by a message box that flashed
into view in the bottom right corner of the screen with
the first few words of the email. It was a message that
popped out of nowhere, stayed for a moment, and was
gone. Like a hint of someone's true nature that appeared
on the surface of things, and then disappeared, sunk back
into the system. She polished the desk with her fingertips
and waited for a few minutes but the email didn't come.
She pulled the collar of her roll-neck sweater up and held
it there for comfort beneath her chin. Still the email didn't
come. So she pushed the keyboard back beneath the mon-
itor and roused herself to get on.

———

In the lobby at midnight, she buttoned her cape and used
the lights left on in the entrance to find her way on a path

through the snow to the small log cabin built in to the side of an escarpment behind the guest rooms. The sky was clear now – clear and cold. On the wooden steps outside the cabin, she kicked the snow off her boots.

Downstairs, in the living room, which sloped off the kitchen down a couple of wooden steps, Lollo watched television through an ancient set, and drank beer from a series of cans she got cheap for him from the wholesaler. He sat with one leg crossed over the other, a cloud of blue cigarette smoke floating above his head.

From behind the sofa, she could see the wiry curls and that little foot in its old bald sheepskin slipper pumping the stale air. They didn't look at each other when they spoke. They hardly spoke. It was too hard.

'Baseema?'

'I had some news from Sylvie. Lucie Borja died. The chateau is going up for sale.'

The leg stopped.

Baseema's eyes roamed anxiously around the dark room with the toilet in one corner, a gingham curtain across the single dusty window through which one could see far across the valley. But Lollo didn't open the curtains during the day, except once last year, when in a fit of activity he had taken them down and washed them on a hot cycle so that the red squares leaked into the white and now the curtains were pinkish, like in a child's bedroom. The room was small and cramped. The air was stale with the smell of old smoke.

Lollo flattened his cigarette into the ashtray on his stomach and stood up. His face was grey and small like a rodent's face and his chin had collapsed leaving only a sad little swallow of fat on his neck. He had one very mottled tooth at the front and when he spoke he tilted his chin up in some small effort of defiance at the world.

'So?'

'I'm thinking, Lollo... It's been twenty years. More than that.'

'Daniel will get everything. You do know that. He's a good-for-nothing. And what about us, huh?'

'You don't know anything,' she said, quietly. 'It's all rumours at this stage.'

'It's time he learnt the truth.'

'What good would it do?'

'It would humble him, Baseema. Bring him to account for himself.'

'But what's to be gained from that?'

'It might give us a slice! Something at last for our pains.'

'Our pains?'

'Only you can confront Daniel, Baseema. Only you can tell him the truth.'

'But who knows where he is? It's been twenty years. He could be abroad. He could be in the army. Anywhere!'

'Don't you think you owe your family, our family, at least the effort of trying to find him?'

'Ah, for what, Lollo? To rake it all over again? Sylvie's doing ok. She has the house, her friends in the village. And me, too. We've done well coming to these mountains.'

'And Frederic?'

Baseema said nothing.

'And me, Baseema?'

'People have offered you work.'

'Shit work, though. Painting. Toilet cleaning.'

'Does it matter?'

148

'What?'

'Isn't it just work?'

'Ah yes.' He was silent for a moment. 'It's just work. Not to mention I had my own café, my house, my friends in the square!'

She turned to go. Lollo slid back into his seat. He lit up a cigarette and threw his voice over the back of the sofa towards her.

'We had a life there, Baseema. Now we have nothing. We live in exile.'

'We do not,' she hissed and still she held herself tall and graceful – still her shoulders were broad and straight and strong. Calmly, she looked at the large square nails on one of her hands.

'It's his fucking arrogance, Baseema. His lifelong fucking arrogance. And your denial.'

'You can't speak to me like this.'

'Daniel stands to get everything unless the truth comes out. It's about time that he and you faced up to the truth. To everything.'

She turned on the stairs. Her voice was weary.

'We're not in exile, Lollo. Here we have control. We don't owe anyone.'

'*Pah!*' he said. 'That's bullshit and you know it!'

There was nothing she could say. In all these years she had never got further than this in conversation with her husband about her family. She had failed, repeatedly, to cross this line. Now she was tired.

In the cabin kitchen, she hung her coat and hat on a peg. She slid her feet into the warmth of her sheepskin slippers and lit the stove with a match. She cut a slice from a lemon and waited for the water to boil in a pan. Up a flight of stairs, she shut the bedroom door quietly. Then she washed herself at the sink, using a hot scented flannel to remove the day from her face and neck. In the tartan pyjamas which she wore buttoned up to the neck she sat on the bed and drew up her spine and tried to breathe.

On the wall above the bed was a painting of three children playing on a barrier of sand. Around them, the sea was still and grey in the low light of afternoon. But the children weren't seeing how the day was ending, so intent were they on the sand and the channels of water they were making, the miraculous disappearance of water so soon after they filled the channels up. All three of the children had tousled locks of bright blond hair. It was hard to tell if they were boys or girls. And one of them was crouching, a blue bucket dangling from a hand. The other two were standing, clutching spades, their legs bent, eyes downcast, preparing to dig the sand.

2

She had married Lollo quickly, she was sixteen – quickly and simply – it had to be quick – and though she doesn't remember much, she does remember how cold it was in the church, and the giant vat of chicken cooking on a fire in the square, and the relief, she was almost doubled over with it, of being outside the chateau gates at last. Daniel was two. Lucie had dressed him in matching knickerbockers and let his curls loose down his back. She used to sit and watch Baseema feeding him. She would stand over at first, pushing the breast into his mouth, pinching it to make sure he got enough. Then she took him away. The cot was in her room. Baseema lived upstairs. She got paid for it, though. That was the thing. She got paid more money than she needed. One day she would have her own restaurant. She would make the nicest food in the world. She told Lucie about it while they were nursing and Lucie sat there sewing things, driving her needles in and out. They sat together in two wicker chairs and they talked. They got on well. Baseema was excellent – the best in the world – at trying to please.

In terms of a husband, Lollo was the first and easiest choice of the boys in the village. He loved her instantly. His mouth fell open when she spoke to him. Her thick hair spilled around her shoulders and she told him about her money. They bought a house in the village. It was right on the square. Right in the centre of everything.

'Arnaud Borja is very, very rich,' she told everyone at the wedding reception. She was drinking, getting carried away. 'He's so rich he can have whatever he wants in the whole world.'

She told them how impressive the Borjas were, how kind they had been to her. She drank back the wine. She was free now. She could make up everything.

To all intents and purposes, Baseema had merely been the carrier, never the mother, and no one knew even that. Everyone believed what they'd been told. Even she almost believed it. The alternative was so unreal.

The story went that at the age of fourteen, Baseema had gone to Paris to live with the brother of Arnaud Borja and she had studied there and gone to a local school in return for helping at the weekends with his children. During this time, Lucie Borja had finally given birth to a child which was a surprise to everyone, because no one at all had seen her in the village and assumed that she had also gone to Paris. When the child was one, Baseema had 'come back' to help them. Of course, by then the Borjas were rich and successful; the chateau was gorgeous; they could have had anyone to care for their child. It was Baseema they wanted, though. She was kind and willing and had lost none of her lovely charm. And so the girl was brought down from the tower room where she'd really been all year, with Lucie in the room next door, and she became the nanny who also happened to be nursing the child. Then things got complicated. Of course they did. Lucie wanted Daniel all to herself. It was time for Baseema to pack her bags and leave.

She was tall and graceful on her wedding day, narrow-waisted, her hair in a thick glossy plait down her back. She was paler than she had been as a child. Still a deep olive colour but paler somehow, almost white from the neck up.

'*Such a beautiful child, wasn't she?*'

'*But no, she still is.*'

'*She was more beautiful as a child.*'

'*She was wrapped in cotton wool.*'

The women were talking across her. Everywhere they talked. It was the big village subject. One was rubbing the top of her breast, her glistening breasts nearly out of her dress. It was a hot, black night. The children were running around the fountain. The fire leaping beneath a vat of food. Monsieur and Madame Borja were helping Daniel lift the bolt to shut the gates behind them. They had been for a drink and now they were leaving.

Baseema closed her eyes when they shut the gates. She was out. Daniel was in. He was theirs. She had got her freedom. She turned to look at the house the money had bought her. It was a fine and handsome house. She had a fine handsome man. She was still a child herself. What good would she have been to Daniel then? They had told her that: all over France people do this. There are some people who are lucky enough to have a child. There are others who can't. We share the seeds. This was what they had told her. *We share the seeds*.

But Lucie Borja had become very pale, very thin by then. She scuttled about in the village, her black eyes wide and haunted, her shoulders hunched and her hair oddly sprung on top of her head, as if even the curls on her head had tightened in the static tension of her atmosphere.

In the *épicerie* the women said that Lucie Borja was paranoid, a fantasist; she believed some people were coming to try to take her little boy away. That was why she never let him out, nor let anyone in. She talked to the birds in the courtyard. She thought the birds were women. Dressed in black. Chattering about her. She dressed Daniel up like a prince. He had black beautiful curls and pale blue eyes. He took people's breath away. But Lucie wouldn't let them linger. She was furtive and always suspicious. Scuttling away from everything before anyone had a chance to talk to her, to ask her what on earth was wrong.

———

Only once she was married and out of the chateau did Baseema begin to understand just how much the Borjas were disliked in the village. She drank this knowledge in and she settled into the village house and within a month of the wedding she was pregnant. This time it was easier. She knew what was happening and she threw herself into life as a housewife, keeping everything neat and organised, and she threw herself into life as a wife and she tried not to think about Daniel.

Within a year, Frederic was born and Sylvie followed soon after. Lollo's parents had moved into the village house with them and the life of cooking and washing and cleaning and managing a household of six was easy enough.

There was warmth and comfort to be found in her family. Lollo's parents were old and frail but they were kind people, and she found that she enjoyed looking after them. They delighted in the children growing rapidly at their feet. And Lollo was kind too: hardworking and quiet and kind. Uncomplicated was the word she used to describe him to herself. Unfussy. Mostly, she was grateful. He worked well in the café and was regularly seen out in the square with his children, playing with them when he had the time, letting them sit up at the bar and drink ice-cold drinks on summer afternoons. Frederic grew rapidly one summer and this became a source of pride to them all. He could help his father with the crates in the café, and Sylvie entertained them all with her sweet little songs and her skipping about at sundown in the square. Baseema tried not to think about Lucie and Arnaud and Daniel behind the chateau wall. She found you could make yourself good at being practical and then push yourself to work until you were tired. It was all a question of discipline; learning how to control the mind. Sometimes it slipped, on the long-hot afternoons. And sometimes, when Lollo had closed the café and driven his wife and children out to the vineyard to sit and eat with the boot open and the radio playing, he would see his wife wander off and crouch down in the dirt and beat her fists on the ground there, which was her way of stifling the urge she had to cry.

It was a simple life but it was a good life. It was fine.

People said what a good father Lollo was. And what a brilliant housewife Baseema was. Her hair pinned up on her long neck, a crisp white apron on over her pretty summer dresses. They all admired her in the village; the way she would carry two children on her hips and never even sweat. She would carry a basket of logs, drive the truck to market in her pretty dresses. She was strong, people said, as a horse.

When she was fourteen she had learnt from the Borjas that women had to be strong. Strong and fit as horses. And that is precisely what she became.

3

13th March 2006
From: sylviepépin@aol.fr
To: Baseemapépin@aol.fr
Subject: For Sale?

Thanks for your message. Yes, I did get the cream.
Coco is better now and I've started her on those
biscuits you can get at the supermarket which are
meant to be a bit better than the tins. She quite
likes tuna now which is a relief because a massive
delivery of stuff came into the shop which was
almost out of date and so they put them all on
special and me and Coco brought a stack load. It's
all we've eaten for a month now, tins of tuna and
salmon mashed up with mayonnaise!

But... I was cleaning in the Mayor's
office this morning and no one was in and so
I answered the phone, which they like me to do
from time to time when I can. It's nice to sit at
the desk and think for a moment that I might be
working in an office. I picked up the phone and
said, Mayor's office, hello, and a man was on the
end of the phone. He sounded a bit foreign but he
asked in French if it was true that Lucie Borja had

died and that the chateau was going up for sale. I asked him who was calling but he didn't want to leave a name. He just made a coughing noise like people do when they don't know what else to say and then he put the phone down. Of course I knew who it was. You don't need a face to remember a voice. And I checked out the number – Paris, for sure. I know it was Daniel, Ma. But I will try to do some investigations when I get a minute. Kate is lovely, so chic and funny. She is free in spirit and mind, Ma. She even lies down by the road sometimes. When she laughs I feel myself come alive.

As for your question about Lucie Borja. Well, yes, she died in Paris. She lived with her nephew, Paul, in an attic room above his flat. I don't know where it was but I'm sure I can find an address. Apparently she fled there on the night of the fire and stayed there all these years. We don't know how she died. Old age probably. Grief?

I'll keep you posted.

xSylvie

p.s I was cleaning out my wardrobe the other day because of a funny smell in there and I came across that bin liner of material that Lucie left out in the entrance to the church all those years ago. It made me stop for a moment or two. I sank down on my knees and pushed my hands into the bag, pulling all this old cloth out that was all full of holes. Poor Madame Borja. Do you remember that summer of the village sewing competition that we

ran through the shop? Everyone knew that despite
her initial enthusiasm, she couldn't face it after
all and everyone knew how she'd crept out
in the middle of the night leaving all that cloth in
the plastic bags outside the church. How people
sniggered, I remember. Do you remember how
everyone came to the café and talked about it?
How they all laughed. And we divided the cloth
among us. Some got on with the business of
making things. Others just stuffed the bags
to the backs of their wardrobes and forgot all
about it.

It's like that in every village I suppose.
Sniggerers, makers, stufferers to the back of things
– faithfuls, atheists, hypocrites maybe. Or maybe
it's the other way round. Maybe we're all a
combination of all of these things. But the makers
are the best, Ma. The makers who get on with the
business of doing things. Maybe if I'd bothered
to make myself a beautiful dress that day then
Daniel might have loved me back; he might have
loved me when I was lovable and then I might have
been saved. Which makes me sound like an idiot. I
know! Maybe I'll take the cloth round to Kate and
ask if she can sew. I think she's quite good with
her hands. She looks like she can turn her hand
to anything at all. She's a maker, Ma. I think she
might have been a stufferer to the back of things.
But down here I think she's becoming a maker.
She has one of those faces that tells you everything
that's going on inside. It's fascinating to me.

At lunchtime, the guests came in from the mountains and tramped into the steaming dining room for bowls of hot soup, for cassoulet, and wine. Baseema moved about the dining room, answering questions, chatting about the walking conditions outside. At one of the tables, a woman leant over and said how last time she had been here it was December and the light had been disappointing and their guide had taken them off the trail and into the middle of nowhere. How frightening it was, she said, being lost like that, and the light fading, their bright suits disappearing in the snow.

'Here's to being safe and warm,' said Baseema and the woman with the small diamonds in her ears took Baseema's hands and held them in her own. It was remarkable really, to think how far she had come.

At half one, the new cleaner rang to say she had gone down with the flu and so Baseema rolled up her sleeves, working through the bedrooms and the bathrooms at speed.

Room number 6 was the one she lingered in. It was the room belonging to the journalist and his girlfriend from Paris. Everywhere their lives were strewn and Baseema worked quickly, carefully folding the cashmere sweaters and putting things away with her mind, as she always did when she was working, completely in neutral, and without the destructive need some parents had to make comparisons between other people's offsprings' lives and their own.

In the bathroom, she replaced the lid on a shiny pink lipstick. She rinsed the paste off two electric brushes, and stood them up in the rack. She rinsed the water glasses and stripped the sheets right back, letting the satin bedspread slide down to the floor. Baseema wiped the surface of the plasma screen television, used the remote to direct it back into the wall. She moved about silently, picked up a novel on one side of the bed, a small white clock, a tin of sea-kelp lip balm, a pair of pink silk knickers twisted up in a corner of the room. There were bottles of water everywhere, on the bedside table, on the desk with the writing paper and the pen laid out. A hairdryer discarded. Bottles of perfume, massage oil from Provence. Two passports in the drawer.

But how careless people were with their precious things, Baseema thought, opening the passports, running her fingers over the pictures of the blonde thing grinning and the doe-eyed man frowning at the camera as if he had seen too much of the truth and now carried on his shoulders all the weight in the world.

Lollo said he was going to leave her. He had a friend, he said, who ran a bingo club in northern Spain. Tossa del Mar. This was on Tuesday. He was lying with his arms up above his head on the sofa. He heaved himself upwards and switched the volume down suddenly. On the television there were elephants walking around an enclosure.

'I'm going.'

He said it louder.

'I'm going, Baseema...'

Then she laughed. Which was almost fatal. She was rearranging the flowers on the table behind him. He stood up from the sofa and let the blanket slide to the floor. He walked slowly around behind the sofa; the elephants were being hosed behind him. She thought he was going to lunge at her and she backed away. But he didn't do anything. He simply stood where he was and let the tears soak his face.

'I shall make you some coffee,' she said, and she was in a panic – she might have slipped; she was wearing stockings without shoes and the carpet on the stairs was worn thin and smooth. Instead she went into the kitchen rolling the cream wool of her sweater up over her mouth.

Behind her she could hear him kicking something, the wall perhaps, and she felt suddenly ashamed. It was the Borjas he hated, her he was merely frustrated with. But Baseema felt responsible. There had to be another way.

She would say something about it, acknowledge the pain at least. She waited until the morning. He was hungover then, more slunk in the sofa. She took him some breakfast on a tray; fresh croissants she had been over to the kitchen for, and a bowl of steaming chocolate.

Lollo sat up but he wouldn't eat. His face was grimy and white, his eyes like pieces of grit.

'We had a life there, Baseema!'

Suddenly she felt too heavy to continue. She put the tray down and went off to work.

19th March 2006
From: sylviepépin@aol.fr
To: Baseemapépin@aol.fr
Subject: For Sale?

So the Mayor went in with a tall man to have
a look around. I think he might have been
American. It was so strange to walk past the open
gate on the way back from the épicerie and to see
the front of the house like that with the olive
trees still standing in the courtyard, still growing
fruit and leaves. I said to Kate, who came in
with me this afternoon, that she should be the
one to buy it. Heaven knows if she has that
kind of capital, Ma, but she is so creative. She
would do something with it.

I brought her back to my house then and we
had coffee together and chatted casually about all
sorts of things. She likes to smoke my roll-ups. She
liked the way I do them for her. I'll pay you back,
she says. She wants to talk about the chateau too
but I don't say much.

All day I've had this feeling, Maman, that
something will come of this and the sale will
bring them all back – Lucie, Arnaud, Daniel and
Frederic – I mean, I know, it won't bring Frederic
back but maybe, at least, some dignity for us, for
his memory.

———

Baseema didn't believe in ghosts. She knew that the
sale, when it happened, would bring no one back to the
village nor anything new to light. Frederic had died in
the bathroom that night. The Borjas had asked her and
Lollo to leave because they hadn't wanted a fuss; they
hadn't wanted an inquiry. Lollo was right. It had been

weak, more than weak, of them to have left when asked to. They should have been ashamed of themselves for having been the kind of people who just rolled over and did what people asked them. But in her heart, Baseema understood the indifference of the well-to-do and that this was why Lollo's begging for a portion of the money to heal an ancient wound was futile. Her meek little question about the will and Daniel's whereabouts delivered on a doorstep in Paris would be something Madame Borja's nephew, Paul, living quietly in scented drapery in some genteel apartment, would hear faintly, like a sound heard from the street outside through the window – a call to prayer from the mosque perhaps – that he would barely understand.

In the cabin that night, she fried a handful of lardons and sprinkled them over the chicory and the spinach leaves, which were dressed already in olive oil. She took his plate downstairs on a tray and sat with him. On the news, they saw a boy being carried between two policemen away from a burning car. Lollo's face was lifeless beside her. He watched the newsreels and said nothing.

'If working-class people are the onions,' said Baseema, after a while, 'then who are these people?'

He shrugged. He held the sides of his plate in his weak little hands.

'I was thinking you might have a vegetable for them...?'

'Couscous,' he said gently.

It made Baseema smile. She was patient with him; she

watched through the reels. 'And the well-to-do?'

'I never met any well-to-do,' he replied. 'You think the Borjas were that but they weren't. They came to the village after the war with nothing.'

'I don't think there's a vegetable for them, Lollo. They're more like fruit which goes rotten quicker. Figs, for example.'

'Figs are too common.'

'Ugli fruit then,' said Baseema, turning her eyes to the side to see if he would smile at all. He didn't.

'My bosses here are well-to-do.'

'New money.'

'What difference does it make?'

'It makes all the difference. No one is who you think they are, Baseema. Your bosses are Euro-trash. We never knew any well-to-do.'

'If Daniel is innocent, Lollo? What if he didn't do it?'

'He did do it.'

'But in my heart I don't believe that he did.'

'He was starting fires since the age of seven, Baseema. That boy was on a mission to destroy. He killed Frederic. He hung him up and then he started the fire to destroy the evidence and make it look like it was a suicide. He was fucked in the head because Frederic was leaving and off to be a man. Off to take responsibility. Stand on his own two feet in the world. It was more than Daniel Borja was capable of. And he knew it. Daniel was jealous. And Lucie knew that. It was her fault, of course. For raising him like a pet. Making him think he was too good for anything. Making him think his health was poor so he wouldn't find the strength to leave her. She knew it, all right. Her poor little adopted child.'

'I think that Frederic killed himself. I think that he was afraid of being gay.'

'*Ridiculous!*'

'There was no inquiry.'

'Because we did what we were *told* to do. Like a pair of mugs. You should have seen yourself, Baseema. All tickled red with shame. What a sight we must have been. And who knows what happened to the café, to the people who went there next morning waiting to be served. Gone, poof. We were gone, just like that. And all because...? Ah yes. Because we were *asked* to!'

Lollo lit a cigarette. For a long time they said nothing to each other. Baseema turned the sound right down. Then she changed the channel to a comedy show and he took the remote control and sat there clutching it while he laughed, high-pitched, like a maniac. It was how he had behaved on the night after the fire. Like a man with a sudden case of dementia. Wandering round and around the car in nothing but a T-shirt and sandals, no underpants, and talking to himself about all the things they would need to remember to do on the way. He had crammed what he could into the back of their car and held it down with rope. He had driven in his vest and sandals, his manhood curled like a grey mouse in his groin. It was dark. September hot, but dark. And quiet. Even the cicada were silent.

Sylvie had been taken in an ambulance to the burns hospital in Toulouse. For months, she lay there with her face wrapped under bandages; a steel girder keeping her ear from sliding down to her neck. Maybe she cried under all those bandages. Cried for Daniel. Cried for her brother. Maybe she didn't. Nobody could tell. Daniel had run away to a place even God didn't know about, and Lucie Borja had gone into her chateau through the great big entrance and then she had packed a suitcase and disappeared.

Baseema had looked away from the chateau as Lollo drove them away. Smoking as he drove. One cigarette after another. All the way to Toulouse. She could barely see through the smoke. But she didn't care. There was only the pain to manage, to be borne through the night. Then the sun came up and turned the land orange. And Baseema watched it with a tissue pressed to her mouth, which was parted slightly, in a stiff, silent scream.

After that, it was focus on something or die. Work to make things better. Try to get on. Small things to start with. A pair of shoes for Sylvie for when she came out of the hospital. Something shiny to make her smile. Small things. A book, a magazine, some flowers. Day by day. What else could she do?

She worked hard, taking on as many hours in the restaurant as she could. Lucie and Arnaud Borja; the vineyards, the village, the chateau itself: these were easy to force out of her mind. And when the children came back to her – afternoons in the square with Frederic and Sylvie, and the red sun rising over the vineyards in winter from where she had looked out with Daniel as a baby from the tower room, Sylvie growing up, Frederic – she let things come, for a moment, just to make themselves known, a vision, but a vision without feeling, without substance, just a memory, like a room full of air kisses.

Baseema climbed the stairs and washed the dishes and laced up her boots. It was cold and dim outside. There wasn't any moon. She walked down the drive and stood for a moment watching the wind moving in the pines. Her mind was empty now; she was tired; her thoughts were still. There was nothing more she could do for her husband or anyone tonight, so she put her hands in her pockets and walked with her clear still mind.

She found that the fire door to the swimming pool was open, the hot air escaping. There was a tinkle of a piano coming from a shiny white box off to one side of the pool. Baseema didn't know this kind of music. It was what the young people would be dancing to in the cities. Instinctively, she knew that the swimmers were the couple from room number 6 and she hid behind the pillar and listened.

After a while, there came a lull in the music. Something clicked off. She was summoned from the shadows.

'Have you come to tell us off?'

The young man's chest was smooth and bare as a boy's. His face was perfectly round; his eyes were mischievous and alive. 'I spied you creeping in, Madame! Sorry, we know it's late.'

Baseema looked at her watch. It was late. But what could she say? She smiled to see them swimming like this. How reckless they were. How impulsive. But they were happy, these fish. Uncontaminated, free. The past no more clung to them than they to a rock. They were swimming forward, in good clear water, their channels flooded with light.

'I just wanted to tell you about the newspapers. I managed to get hold of them for you. All the ones that you wanted. They will be delivered to your door in the morning.'

He held a thumb up out of the pool.

The water was streaming off his arm. Baseema watched the girl giggle and dive back beneath the water. They would get cold soon, these fish. They would wrap themselves. Go back and get cosy in their deluxe shiny room, slide a DVD into the machine. It would be nice for them. It was what young people should be doing. Baseema knew this. And the sheets would wrinkle beneath them, the towels dropped, like peasants, on the floor. But that wasn't something to worry about. Not enough to worry about. Life was short. Baseema knew this. The sheets, the towels. Everything could be changed these days; everything replaced so that the lucky ones could move on. And someone would change the towels and the sheets in the morning. She, personally, would change them in the morning. Like the snow, she would fall in silently and cover over everything, wipe the past away so that the luckier ones could find a way to move on.

4

In Paris, six weeks later, it was a quarter past three in the afternoon. Baseema was much too early. She walked quickly to the café on the corner and sat for a while playing with a teaspoon, running her fingers over and around the edge.

Lollo had got up early and emerged to see her off. On the step, he'd stood with a purple dressing gown pulled tight around his waist, his hands deep in the pockets. The early light made his skin look bluish; his eyes were mean.

'Remember,' he had whispered into her ear as she carried her suitcase down the steps to the taxi that was waiting. 'We are the losers, the lost ones, Baseema.'

But were they?

The sun was appearing through the clouds now, casting one side of the street in a cool, white frame. She paid the bill and left, walking quickly towards a hairdresser's across the street. In the gutter, there was rubbish, chippings of paint.

In the green cross outside the pharmacy with the posters advertising glasses for old people who had white teeth and skin like butterscotch, the halogen light was broken and flashed intermittently, in a weak rhythm of its own. Baseema stood and watched it flash. She counted to ten and then moved up to the door.

The door was grey, thick and scratched. There were doorbells for the apartments above. She pressed the lowest of the three bells and waited. There was no response. She rang the next one up, pressing her finger carefully on the button and holding it there long enough to hear a bell ringing somewhere inside.

There was the crackling sound of the intercom and then a voice, small and distant.

'My name is Baseema Pépin.'

The crackle of the intercom faded on the street.

'Please,' said the voice from inside, 'push at the door. I will come down.'

Paul was a middle-aged man in a faded blue sweatshirt and jeans. What hair he had was reddish brown and drying from a wash behind his ears.

He kept a hand on the banister as he came down the stairs, one foot placed carefully in front of the other.

'Are you the nephew of Lucie Borja, Monsieur? Have I come to the right place?'

'Oh,' he said quietly. 'He's dead!' and he pulled the corners of his mouth down.

Baseema looked into his face, confused.

'No. I'm sorry. That was just a joke. A weak one. You will find I haven't changed much in fifty-odd years, Baseema. Please, do come in.'

'I'm sorry to disturb you. It must seem most strange.'

He gasped and put a hand to his mouth, the sarcasm widening his eyes. But the eyes were kind. And playful. She wasn't expecting this.

He put a hand lightly on her shoulder. 'Hello, Baseema. I'm being a fool. Do you not remember your sickly old friend Paul?'

'Of course,' she said slightly stiffly, and she fiddled with the silk knot at her neck and tried to loosen it a little; she shouldn't have come.

'Please come in.'

The hallway was thin and dark. When Paul put the light on, she saw the piles of white, hand-addressed envelopes lined up on the ledge. She read his name and address on the label.

'Did you have a pleasant journey?'

'It was fine,' she said politely. 'I took the high-speed train from Perpignan.'

'Sometimes, it's just perfect the train, isn't it? Time to think and time to... rest.' He shrugged, his eyes twinkling a little. 'Who knows?' he added, and then he laughed with forced abandon. 'Did you get refreshments?'

'Yes.'

'Good.'

She followed him up the stairs. 'You seem as if you were expecting me.'

'I was,' he said, and laughed. 'You called to say you were coming.'

At the top, he opened a door onto an old kitchen with dull terracotta tiles on the floor. The air was thick with dust and the windows smeary, the surfaces cluttered with books and newspaper. There was a line of clear plastic bottles on a shelf above the sink.

'The hairdresser's is downstairs; it closed down last year,' he explained. 'No one has been round, though, to take away the chairs, the mirrors. Some of the hairdryers are still there. Please, if you would like me to cut your hair I...,' he was smiling, kindly, embarrassed at his own attempt to make a joke. He looked like the kind of person who didn't see many people. Baseema liked him. He was gentle, soft as the woolly hair on the back of his neck.

'Really... why were you expecting me?'

'Please, take a seat. Can I take your coat?'

He cleared a newspaper from the chair, tried to find somewhere to move it to. There was none. He folded the crust of bread he had been eating away in a paper bag and stood holding it. He was a nice-looking man. On the table, there was an open pack of butter.

'Can I offer you something, coffee?'

'I'm fine, thank you. I had a coffee on the train.'

'I have fruit juice. It's freshly squeezed. I could pour you a glass.'

Baseema nodded and the smell of the inside of the old refrigerator filled the room. 'Why were you expecting me?'

'Because from time to time she talked about you.'

'Oh.'

Paul smiled and put a breadcrumb in his mouth. He sat down opposite her at the table, and crossed his legs to the side, folding his shoulders forward.

'She fell down the stairs and cracked her skull,' he said. 'Her heart stopped just like that. No surprise, of course. But she'd been with us so long. My mother's friends used to joke that we kept a lizard upstairs. She made so little noise. When my mother died, Lucie came down for the funeral and for lunch at the restaurant on the corner. She bought a magazine in the newsagent's and then went back on up the stairs. There was a kitchenette up there, which she didn't use – I tended to take her meals up on a tray – and a shower which she did use. At least before the sealant went. And then she began to lose her sight. I think it was about nine months or so later, and six months before she died that we got the diagnosis. Forgive me, Baseema. I'm mumbling.'

'It's fine,' she said.

'She went blind as a bat overnight then.'

'I've heard it can happen like that.'

'Poof!' he said and he lifted his hands together and clapped quite triumphantly. It made him feel awkward. He got up and placed a pan under the tap to rinse it. Water screeched through the pipes. Baseema's eyes travelled around the room, taking in the disordered piles of things, the linoleum floor, the smears and stains, a bowl of cat food spilt in the corner.

'How long did she live here, Paul?'

'Twenty years.'

'Here?'

'You are surprised.'

'Yes, of course.'

'We got by.'

'Did anyone go to the funeral?'

'I cremated her. No one came.'

'No one?'

'Who would have come? My aunt did nothing here. She sat in the room upstairs for twenty years. She went nowhere. She wrote the addresses on envelopes for a few years to make a little money to help us with the rent.'

'I see.'

'I'm a printer. I have a workshop down in the basement.'

Baseema stood, finally, and took her coat off, which she hung neatly on the back of the chair. She sat back down and lifted her head up then. She took a deep breath.

'Do you know why I'm here, Paul?'

'It's not a courtesy call.'

Baseema smiled. 'Lucie's will,' she said, feeling the discomfort as a pain she tried to rub out of her chest. 'Is there...?'

He looked away from her, tried to redirect the focus. Baseema was used to this behaviour in men. Their awkwardness around money and women, the combination. It amused her when the female clients came to pay the bill and the men had to leave or stand off to one side. Their weirdness about it empowered her. She spoke clearly.

'Is there anything in the will about me, Paul?'

'No,' he said.

'Nothing?'

'Nothing.' He sat back down at the table then and folded his hands in a business-like manner. 'She left everything to Daniel. There was never any discussing it.'

'Did she see him?'

'Never.'

'Never?'

'We heard nothing from him. In all those years. Nothing at all. He made no effort to contact her.'

'Why would he? Of course...'

'I'm sorry?'

'He hated her,' she whispered, almost to herself.

'Yes,' he said, softly, and he coloured a little.

Baseema took a breath, tried to sit higher up. Finally, she pushed herself up out of the flimsy little chair.

After the juice, Paul led her down the narrow flight of

stairs behind the hairdresser's, then down again into the basement and switched on the light in the printing room. Here there was paper everywhere, delicate pencil drawings, thick sheets of paper hand-made and tied with ribbons, parchment in tubes. There were shelves on which books were lined up in alphabetical order, cards with drawings of lovers, poetry inside. Baseema was silent as she followed him around.

From the windows on the pavement the light came in and sifted the dust. Paul bent his head as he dipped beneath a poster hanging off a strip of wire.

'What an urge I have to clean,' she said.

'Perhaps we are best not to bother, though. There will always be more.... sooner or later...' But he didn't finish. Instead, he bent to the floor and took a box, which he lay on a photocopier and opened. He peeled back a layer of tissue paper and took out a leather-bound book.

'This man used to eat sometimes in the café on the corner. Meat and potatoes in sauce. That's what he ate.'

'He was a poet, then,' she said, a bit flatly.

'No. Not really. He wrote, in his lifetime, maybe nine or ten poems. Take a look.'

Baseema turned a page.

'It's beautiful, no?'

She ran her fingers over the deep gold lettering.

'I guess it is. Yes.'

'He came to see me some time before he died. He was holding these loose pages in his hand, all covered in his handwriting. He said he would like his wife, Marianne, to have a book with these poems of his printed in them. He gave me what money he had.'

'And you believed that was all the money he had?'

'I didn't believe anything. He didn't have a wife. That's the funny thing. It was a complete stranger he was in love with. She used to walk by the café sometimes with a dog. At least, we think it was her. When I finished the book, I took it to the address he gave me, which turned out to be a poodle parlour. There was no one in there by the name of Marianne. They all turned to me and laughed. The man was dead by then, which is why I have his book down here gathering dust.'

'Well, isn't it funny the way life goes,' said Baseema and she sniffed and flicked the angry little tear that had popped out of her eye.

He took the book from her and placed it carefully back in its tissue paper and box.

'Do you know that Daniel Borja was my biological son?' she said finally.

Paul nodded.

'You knew?'

'Yes. I knew.'

She inhaled slowly through her nose. She wanted to ask him how he knew but it didn't seem to matter much. Nothing did, in the end. Except money.

'I did see him. When he was a child. I did try to see my son. But Lucie was paranoid that I would try to take him away.'

Paul nodded. 'It must have been hard. To be living in the village. And Daniel there, but divided from you by a wall.'

'I was tough, though. A survivor. I have that. I don't know where it comes from. The desert, perhaps.'

'She said that to me once.'

'About the desert?'

'No. That you had strength.'

'"You've a quiet strength, Baseema," she used to say. With the emphasis on quiet. Believe me, I would have shouted my head off in those walls if I could.'

'She envied it,' Paul said.

'What?'

'The strength. The energy.'

'Perhaps...'

'And that was why she kicked you out?'

'She had got what she wanted. She wanted a child of her own.'

'And you?'

Baseema was quiet. She looked up towards the windows.

'I had a house in the village. I got married. I had my children. Frederic and Sylvie.'

Paul said nothing.

'It doesn't matter what others think of us,' she whispered. 'Most people are too busy. But your curiosity for others is unusual and, I think, benign.'

He shrugged modestly.

'The truth is I did try to see him. When he was small. Daniel was five. I saw him playing, climbing the wall. It was summer and I managed to persuade him to climb over. I gave him my hand. I was so desperate. I would have done anything. From then on, it was ice creams. One every day. And for almost a week we got away with it. We walked together. In the avenue. There were these trees.' She smiled stiffly.

Paul nodded.

'It was cool under there. In the height of summer. It was cool in the shade of the trees. Holding his hand as we walked along. I can feel it now. The warm clutch of his hand as we walked along. That hot, solid stickiness. How intelligent he was. His eyes were so blue they startled me. You know? As if he'd been swimming underwater. As if he knew, when he looked at me. As if he knew, and also understood somehow that he couldn't ever tell.'

'Did he find out who you were?'

'Of course not. In a few days he stopped coming to the wall.'

'Lucie must have seen you.'

'It was Arnaud. He was driving back from town one afternoon. He simply stopped and opened the passenger door. Daniel knocked his ice cream as he climbed into the car. For three weeks I didn't see him.'

'Almost a summer.'

'For a child, certainly.'

'No one in there but him, Lucie, Arnaud. No one to play with.'

Paul kept the box in his hand as he switched the light out above their heads. The back of the basement was in darkness now. She followed him back up the stairs. She wanted to tell him then that the reason she had come was nothing to do with the sale of the chateau and the money but about Daniel, to think for once about what had happened that night in the fire, to begin the process of finding a way back to her son. She wanted to tell him she had learnt, her whole life, about getting on; she had managed fine. It was just that...

—

He opened what she had thought was a cupboard door at

the back of the kitchen. He reached his arm around inside and pulled the step down with his hand.

'Usually we kept the door open, the stairs unfolded. It became quite dangerous for her. Please. It's ok for you to go up.'

He followed her up the steps into a narrow room that had been walled off from the flat upstairs and into which the light poured through a tiny skylight above. There was a narrow bed and a chair against the outer wall, a wooden crucifix above the pillow. On the opposite wall was a low shelf with a microwave, a small television, a pile of magazines. There was a pair of black shoes tucked under the shelf. A brown cardigan was folded on the armchair in the centre. A pair of gloves, woollen socks. Baseema stepped over to the armchair and sat down.

'This annexe was used to hide people in the war,' said Paul.

Baseema thought for the first time, with a stab of unhappiness, about what Lucie's life would have been like in the war – the two sisters, working as nurses, using whatever they had to patch and stem and perpetuate life. Now Baseema could perceive how the journey south and her life in Canas with Arnaud had failed her.

'Lucie arrived at the station very broken. My mother was waiting for her. She'd got it into her head that her sister had been abused all those years, living with a man who spent his time outdoors, she always in. Marie and Arnaud had fallen out long before. There was no correspondence for years and years. Then suddenly we had this call. There had been a fire. Daniel had gone. Lucie was leaving the village and taking the train to Paris. She was leaving for good, she said. The journey took her three whole days.

She was in such a terrible state. She had this bald patch at the back of her head as if she'd plucked her own hair out. We thought she would simply disintegrate. We brought her back here and Lucie quite fell into my mother's arms, I remember.'

Baseema was listening to the silence in the room. She could hear water gurgling in the pipes; outside the muffled roar of cars. In winter it would be cold up here.

She put a hand on her heart and rubbed at the skin, but the look of pain on her face was hard to disguise.

'Are you all right?' he asked. 'You have gone quite pale.'

'It's just strange,' said Baseema, 'for me to be here.' She stood for a moment looking into his eyes with her fingers pressed to her mouth. In her mind she saw the lizard up here – white and small – drying out.

In the kitchen, she picked up her coat. Paul stood to one side, smiling shamefully at the floor. Something had been said between them that should have remained buried.

'I wonder,' he said, blinking at the back of her. 'I wonder what you would have said to her had she been here.'

'Quite simple,' said Baseema, knotting the silk scarf at her neck again. But she didn't continue. The sun had gone in now and the kitchen was grim and brown. She felt cold suddenly.

'I've seen Daniel. He's here, Baseema. In Paris.'

Baseema cleared her throat. 'I would like very much to see him.'

––

Baseema rang Lollo to let him know where she was and that she was safe. The phone was in a vandal-resistant aluminium booth.

'Where are you?'

There was silence on the end of the phone.

'Lollo?'

'Yes.'

'Did you find the soup?'

'Yes, I found the soup.'

She put the phone back on its hook then, quietly, without saying a word. She stood for a moment with her hands on her handbag, her chin tilted up to the ceiling.

Arab cunts. Fuck the cunts. She dialled the number again. He picked up. His voice was weak and slow.

'Lollo?'

'Yes.'

'It's me.'

'Yes.'

'Lucie died here in Paris. She fell down the stairs. She left the chateau to Daniel. Nobody else was mentioned in the will. Not even Paul Prevost, her nephew.'

'Does he know where Daniel is?'

'Yes,' said Baseema. She felt her heart beat a little faster. 'Daniel is here. He lives and works in Paris.'

'Where?'

'In a restaurant on Boulevard St Michel.'

Lollo's voice wasn't menacing, only flat, without life.

'You will see him.'

'Yes. Tomorrow. I want to.'

'He'll manipulate you.'

'We'll see.'

'No one is innocent. You romanticise him.'

182

'Everyone does.'

'It stinks.'

'He knows that Lucie died. He knows the chateau has passed to him.'

'And?'

'He has not been in touch since.'

'But?'

'Paul says he is a kind person. Calm. He suggests I try to write to him.'

'Write to him?'

'To get my thoughts down. In order. It's easier to say what one feels.' But she felt no need to go on. 'Bye,' she said. 'Night.' And then she put the phone down.

Right up until the time they had moved away from Canas, life with Lollo had been fine. He was a quiet, hardworking man – soft as skin; sallow, harmless, with little black eyes and features that were small and close together. He had occasional but very occasional bouts of nastiness that had him rearing up to snap and writhe – like a small snake – before falling back and sinking, deep into the listless quiet of himself. The emotional bruises she got from these outbursts weren't bad, and they were few and far between. After these episodes he barely said a word. Simply went to work at dawn and came home again for lunch with her and Frederic and Sylvie, then went back out again to work. Life was quite normal. The children were mostly happy; they did what all children did, which was play and wander and try to explore. They chattered a lot and watched TV when it got too hot to go out and they hung out in

183

the square with the other children who played around the fountain. Frederic liked to go out to the vineyard and ride the machines. He was a tall and silent boy who loved his family and his collection of bugs in the yard. Weeks went by. Autumn gave into winter. Winter folded away. The village was quiet; time there moved in its own gentle rhythm; it held her in.

Sometimes, she wondered if Lollo's outbursts had something to do with the weather. High winds on the hillside got to him, and he'd stop at the bar with the wind still howling in his ears.

So there was the work, and then the bar. Then there was coming home. That was what Baseema thought the problem was: the stimulation, the testosterone of men pent up their whole lives inside themselves with nothing and no way out and then them coming into the kitchen with it all hanging out and electric, looking for a fight. She could tell what was coming from the way he tried to cover up what he was feeling by whistling. He looked smaller than ever on these nights. When he was trying to look big. She'd never realised how small his features were, how feminine his nose. Right away she would make him coffee and then lock the door to the bedroom and turn the television up. Once or twice, he kicked at the door.

But life was difficult at times for everyone. The point was to look at it positively. And, generally speaking, life in the village was comfortable, and familiar and fine. Then Frederic's behaviour and his way of walking became the topic of conversation in every little kitchen, whispering and sniping behind the yellow mosquito screens, windows open to let the cooler air in; no one knew how their voices carried – no one in the village had any idea of the damage they were doing – silly women always doing their whispering...

And because Baseema was a perkier, more sensitive person than people gave her credit for, she started hearing a few too many stories about her son, about his friend at the chateau, about her husband the café owner and the looks of disdain he gave his own boy, and it was round about then – Frederic in puberty – that she discovered the needles of shame underneath his bed and how bad it could be when they dug right in and needled away, needling a person back through all kinds of other shameful moments.

Everyone knew that if you told someone they were this or that often enough, they would become this or that. And when she heard the villagers saying how she was either crazy or ought to be ashamed, turning her eye from the two teenage boys who were spending so much time together, she found the shame guiding her into town to spend half of the money her husband brought home on food for the family, on nicer clothes and shoes, on skincare, and six francs in the *salon de coiffure* having the shame styled out of her or herself styled out of the shame, so she could drive home and walk into that house and see her husband sitting there – he was a stupid man, even stupider than her.

For a long time that night, Baseema sat with her ankles crossed on the crisp cotton sheets on the bed. In her hand she held the address that Paul had given her for the restaurant on the Left Bank where Daniel worked. Boulevard St. Michel. 'He's a nice guy,' Paul had said. She had already asked the concierge how long it would take her to get there, how much time she would have before her train back to the south. Paul said he was a nice-looking man – 'easy-going'. He had tried to describe the face but it could been have been anyone. Baseema felt that perhaps it would have been best to write to him first. Not turn up unannounced. Not squeeze him in between taxi and train. He's very calm, Paul had said. 'I imagine that he would take it in his stride.'

But would she? That was the thing that worried her. Baseema stared through the ring of soft light from the lamp on the ceiling. From time to time, cars roared past outside with music pumping from their stereos. In the closet her suit was hanging, soft and old, and her green shoes would never do. She tried to think of what she would write to Daniel. For hours she ran it through her mind.

If she didn't go in the morning then she would have to face Lollo with her failure as soon as she returned. She hated him. But hate was easy. It was love that was hard. She should write that to Daniel, she thought. But how could she write that? What a thing to say. No, her green shoes would never do. And besides, she knew from her own experience how busy things got in a restaurant. Daniel was busy, and she needed some time.

5

From the Pyrenees it took Baseema only three hours. She had got back without seeing Lollo and taken the car. She would ring him from Canas. Then she was purring along the avenue of trees, headlights on, seeking out, between the trunks of plane trees, glimpses of the old chateau wall. There were holes and lichen growing; all was dark.

She parked in the square. There was no one around. The café was closed, a single streetlight shining on the zinc tables piled high beside the doorway. The air was warm. Baseema switched the lights off and sat for a moment, listening to the tick and whirr of the engine as it cooled.

The car door shut behind her and she locked it up. She was wearing the trouser suit with the green shoes but she had managed to bring some clean shirts, another pair of trousers. She stood still and heard the water trickle in the fountain.

A new streetlight had been put up outside the church of Saint Perpetua and just a few of the houses had been repainted, some with lights in the eaves above the doors. Things had been patched up. There was a new awning over the café, a new bench outside the Mayor's office, other benches dotted about. There was less memory, less of her life here.

At the Pépin house she knocked, once and then again.

Sylvie was there in a black tracksuit with the hood up around her head. She sniffed and dragged a finger under her nose. It was red and puffy. It looked as if she had been crying. She burst, with her sleeves over her hands, onto Baseema's shoulders. Baseema inhaled the warmth of Sylvie's small body and buried her head.

'They're gone, Ma,' said Sylvie feebly.

Baseema pulled back and focused her eyes on Sylvie's.

'The English couple, Ma. Kate and Stephen. Her mother died and they went back to London. She hasn't come back. I liked her being here.'

In the kitchen, Baseema stood at the sideboard and sipped the thimble of wine Sylvie had poured. She looked at the bin in the corner, the soda cans spilling onto the floor. Sylvie kept the hood up around her head and she pushed the glasses up on her nose as she bent down to the oven. In the sweatshirt she was wearing there were rings of sweat under her arms. She put some rock music on quietly and clomped about the kitchen in her boots. From the fridge she peeled back the clingfilm from a tin of anchovies and stuck her nose in.

'What makes you think they won't come back?' said Baseema, after a while.

'Mr Glover hated it here. He's the husband. He was jealous.'

'Of what, Sylvie?'

'Us, Ma. The quiet peaceful life she found here!'

'And the chateau?'

'An agent came. They locked it back up with a new chain around the gates.'

Sylvie shook salt onto her chips and put one in her mouth. She didn't look at her mother when she ate and the chips were hot so she chewed them fast with her mouth open. There was a jar of mayonnaise on the table, which Baseema tried and failed to open. She put the jar back on the table and told Sylvie about Paul.

'Under French law if the owner dies then the property is passed to the children.'

'Yes,' said Sylvie, blinking rapidly as her father did as she looked up into her room. 'I know all about French law, Ma, you don't need to tell me. And so Daniel will come back because he will have to, won't he? Whoever buys the chateau, Daniel will have to come back to sign a paper or something. I did want the Glovers to like it.'

'Someone will buy it,' said Baseema soothingly. 'Someone will buy it but, in the meantime, there's something I need to talk to you about.'

Sylvie was staring, her mouth hanging open. After a while, she got up from the table and went and sat down with the dog.

'You want ice cream?'

'No, love, I'm fine.'

'If you're here to tell me you left him, Ma, then spare me the details, ok?'

'That's not why I'm here.'

Sylvie sighed. 'In which case we can talk tomorrow. I'm tired. And Coco needs to pee.'

⸺

Baseema gathered up the dishes. She put them in the sink, running water from the tap until she got something that felt hot. She rinsed and filled the cloth with hot water and then rubbed at the plates and the pile of chipped ceramic

189

bowls until they were clean. Then she stacked them on the draining board and wiped behind the sink, over the rusty tap; she cleaned the shelf behind the sink, removed a spoon from where it had stuck to the shelf, and wiped it clean.

She took the Spanish plates off the wall and refilled the sink, plunging the plates into water that was hot and soapy, and which covered her hands and wrists; she held the plates down there for a minute or two (they had been a wedding present to her and Lollo) and she tried to remember who had given them but the name was gone; there was only the object left – old and sticky, meaning nothing to Sylvie and nothing to her mother. She turned back to the table, having dried everything on the sideboard, and saw Sylvie had come back in and slumped there, the mass of her hair spread over her arms to sleep.

It was quite late already but Baseema wasn't tired. She wiped the crusted legs of the kitchen table, the backs of the chairs. Quietly she stacked the chairs in the corner of the room and moved the dog to its bed by the door. She lit a candle in the window, swept up the dust and the dog hair and then she mopped the floor.

She cleaned the oven and made a tea; then she sat at the kitchen table to drink it, listening to the rise and fall of Sylvie's breathing, to the quiet tick of the oven clock. The room was clean. It made her feel better but it was still unsettling to be here.

She thought of Lollo, she wondered whether he had eaten the food she had left on the stove. She thought of Paul, alone in his cluttered kitchen, some small part of him still listening out perhaps for the cries that no longer came from upstairs. Guilt was something we should all try to live without, she thought, staring hard at the candle that was guttering in the window. She looked at her shoes then, and got up to polish them.

It was almost midnight but she wasn't tired and her steps were soundless as she hurried across the square. Sylvie's dog lumbered behind her, his long nails clicking quietly on the asphalt.

The air smelt of dust. Baseema turned down the passageway off the square. There was no one around. She drew up silently and she pushed at the iron gates.

The dog turned itself round and round in a circle. Baseema pushed harder; tried to jump up. She knocked at the chain with her hand. In all her thoughts of returning here there was never this thought of trying to get in, being locked out, unable to break back in. It was simply, in her waking and night dreams, a question of being there, back in the room at the very top or running in the halls. Never had she thought it would take any effort to get in there, nor that she might need a key.

The gate creaked and the chain rattled but she couldn't push it open. Baseema straightened her collar and stared down at her shoes. She pictured a little girl running, her velvet hair. Running along the corridors. It was almost as if it wasn't her, and the memory not something she owned any more.

She dialled Lollo as soon as she got back to Sylvie's house.

'Baseema?

'Yes, it's me.'

'Where are you?'

'I'm in Canas. What's the matter?'

There was silence on the end of the phone.

'Lollo?'

'Yes.'

'Did you find the casserole in the freezer?'

'Did you find Daniel in Paris?'

'No.'

There was silence.

'Sylvie needs to know first, Lollo. I need to spend some time with her. Talk to her a little about it all.'

'Why does she need to know first?'

'Because of what happened that night. And because she's one of us. She has a right to know first.'

She took a deep breath.

'So I don't know when I'll be back. They all know at the hotel.'

'At?'

'At the hotel.'

'They all know what?'

'That I'm here. That I've come to Canas.'

'That's fine then,' he said and put the phone down.

6

Three days later, Baseema was on her knees polishing the wooden stairs outside the door to Sylvie's room.

'It's too much, Maman. What you're doing here. It's breaking your back!'

Sylvie was standing, halfway down the stairs. Her hair was wet and combed down her face in a thin black curtain.

'I haven't seen you all day. Where have you been?'

'I don't know why you're doing it. Every room in this house is being changed... I don't understand. This was meant to be a holiday for you.'

Sylvie pushed her glasses up with a finger and went into her room.

'I thought it could do with a freshening-up. Thought I'd do it all in one hit to surprise you. You're not pleased?

'Well, I've never seen it look quite like this, I guess.'

Baseema looked around at her efforts, tried to see how clean the windows were, how shiny the tiled floor of the bedroom and the look of the white tablecloth on the round table in the window, the crystal vase of fresh-cut roses, the light clear in the water, pale green stems.

'Oh God,' said Sylvie, laughing. She pointed to the turquoise and blue silk cushions piled up where there used to be a falling down armchair with a broken seat in the corner. Baseema had chosen a mix of round and square cushions and she had heaped them in a pile for when the sofa came back.

'I'm getting the seat fixed, getting it re-covered in cream.'

Sylvie looked down at her feet. She spoke quietly: 'Thank you, Maman. It's like being on "fix your space up".'

'Tssh!' said Baseema. 'I wanted to help.'

'But I didn't ask for it, did I?' said Sylvie, suddenly sounding nasty.

'What's the matter with you, Sylvie? Where have you been?'

'To the Mayor's office. Where else would I have been on a Tuesday morning, Ma?'

'I don't know why you're so depressed. Is it because the English couple have gone? Is that all this is?'

Sylvie turned her head defiantly towards the window, the soft puffy jaw striving for an edge. The scars on her face were glistening, almost weeping.

'You don't live here any more.'

Baseema played with the gold bangle on her wrist.

'I thought that you were depressed. I wanted to help.'

'But why? What with?'

'With your happiness, Sylvie.'

'I'm fine!'

'You're not fine.'

Sylvie was scowling, there was spittle at the corners of her mouth.

'No,' she said. 'You're right. As usual. I'm not fine.'

'You're on your own.'

'And you?'

194

'I...'

'Are you any less alone, Ma?'

'Sylvie, I...' Baseema took a step closer to her daughter. But Sylvie backed away.

'Do you remember the cherries dipped in chocolate?'

'The cherries?'

'Sure you do,' Sylvie said. 'We were eating them on the night of the fire. Madame Borja's birthday meal. You brought out a whole big mountain of them. They were Daniel's favourite food.'

'I didn't do that, Sylvie. It wasn't me who was preparing the food here that night. She hired a cook from town, remember?'

And Sylvie looked confused then and she moved to go downstairs.

'Wait,' said Baseema. 'If you had some money, Sylvie. If you suddenly had a lot of money. What would you do?'

'I don't like to torment myself with thoughts of the lottery, Maman, because what is the point in that?'

'I don't mean the lottery. I mean, just if you suddenly had some money. A little bit of disposable money.'

'Have a kennel,' she said. 'Lots of dogs. Why?'

'Well, because your father wants me to contest Lucie Borja's will. Come. Downstairs. Let's have something to eat and then we can talk.'

Sylvie opened her mouth to speak. 'I...'

Baseema ignored her daughter and carried on towards the kitchen. It was when Sylvie had caught up with her and was standing in the doorway that she came out with it. 'You don't need to tell me by the way, Ma. It's just that I... I do know about me and Daniel and Frederic. I've always known that you're Daniel's real mother. I was eleven years old when I figured that out.'

Baseema said nothing.

'Ma?'

'Let's eat,' she said quietly.

Baseema had her food at the kitchen table and tried not to watch her daughter eat. Each mouthful of food she put in her own mouth had a small battle to fight with her simultaneous urge to cry.

'I worked it out. You don't know this. I was a kid. I came home one day from school in the summer. Papa was shouting at you for spending all your weekend preparing a dish for the Borjas when you should have been thinking instead about us, your own... And then you said about how if it wasn't for the Borjas you wouldn't have this house.'

'So, if you knew...?'

'No, I didn't actually *know*. Not – swearing on it – know. I didn't know what that bit meant – and then he said only a woman who loved the Borjas more than her own family would do all the work you did for them...'

And so Sylvie had thought about it and she'd let it work on her until she understood. That was all there was to it. It didn't matter much, she said. What mattered now, she said, was that the boys never knew.

Baseema listened to the oven clock. She took deep, sad breaths. Sylvie had fallen asleep on the sofa worn out by all the crying and the emotion. It was like watching a girl. It was true what she said about herself. That fire had frozen her in time.

When she had finished her tea Baseema rinsed it in the

sink and poured Sylvie a glass of water, which she left beside her on the table. Halfway up the stairs she turned and came back into the kitchen, thinking to move the glass in case Sylvie woke and knocked it over. She found her daughter sitting upright, her left eye wide open and staring, her right eye almost completely closed with salt and sleep.

'I'm going to bed, Sylvie.'

'Thank you, Maman. For coming here. It's good to have you here with me.'

Upstairs, Baseema put the torch on the chest of drawers in Frederic's old room and sat herself on the end of his bed where the dog seemed to have been sleeping in among the piles of clothes Sylvie collected and sorted through for the children at the orphanage in the city. There was a single bed and a chair with the weave fraying in the seat.

Baseema placed her palms on top of Frederic's chest of drawers. She remembered the day they had picked it up cheap at the car boot sale outside town – how pleased they had all been to find it with its shiny brass handles – and the mirror Lollo hung above it.

The light in the room was dim and yellow, the bulb and wicker shade thick with dust. Baseema pushed the shutters open, sitting back on the single bed to take in the view of the chateau and the tower, lit by a streetlamp now, standing tall and proud, like the tower on a toy castle that the boys would have played soldiers in.

When the breeze came the window closed a little, and Baseema's eyes swam forward to the glass where her face was momentarily reflected.

Wearily, she pulled her clothes off and folded them neatly on top of her suitcase. She wondered if Lollo had eaten anything tonight. There was that casserole of pork, tomato and lentils. But she sensed he hadn't even the energy to lift the lid and sniff the contents, let alone strike a match to the stove. Perhaps he would ignore all of it; simply wander in for another beer and leave the food exactly as she left it. We have to eat, she told him, the first night they arrived there. To move forward at all, you have to forget the past, or at least not think back to that same thing all the time. 'What's the point?' she said. 'To think of the roses bobbing, the children growing, the quiet square?' You let things come for a moment and then you let them go.

When Baseema had brushed her teeth and dragged a comb through her hair, she climbed into bed and wrote her list for the morning. She wrote:

> *eye test for Sylvie*
> *dress for Sylvie*
> *can of apricot paint for the front door*
> *floor cleaner, cloths*
> *comb for the dog*
> *some face cream for Sylvie*
> *shampoo*

Again she wondered if Lollo had tasted her casserole. She thought of the cabin with its cosy kitchen, its neat little curtain in the window frame, its reassuring pot on the stove, and its clean slants of morning sunlight carving up the floor. These objects and routines were, she knew, all they had to survive on. And then one day it would all be over; they could fold their lives up, be gone. In the meantime, what they had was days to be filled. And if she'd felt there was anything out there rolling round in the darkness, she would have sent a prayer out for Lollo and Sylvie too, for Daniel and the truth he didn't know, for the souls of Frederic and her parents who had come here from Algeria and left her here, not knowing any of this.

7

For Baseema's last night in the village, Sylvie wore a cotton dress. Before dinner they decided to go for a drink in the square and take the flowers over to the cemetery.

It was early evening as they arrived up at the cemetery and the streetlights had come on, flickering white in the empty streets.

At the gate, Baseema picked up pace and walked through quickly, breaking away from Sylvie so that she could be the one to get there first, to stand with her hands down by her sides as she read the wording on her Frederic's gravestone.

Sylvie came to stand beside her mother. Baseema felt the pain. There was no thought, nothing to say.

'Daniel didn't kill Frederic, Sylvie.'

'No, Ma. I know.'

'Frederic did it to himself. He didn't want to love Daniel the way that he did.'

Sylvie was quiet. The two women sat together, on their knees, side by side. Baseema felt the hard ground seem to give way beneath her, as if it were trying to take her in. In her mind, she saw them clear as day – the big shutters slamming open that afternoon she had come to the chateau when Lucie was sick and Daniel had asked Frederic over to play and the two boys, in from the garden, had appeared on

200

the sun-splashed balcony overlooking the internal court-yard. The boys were larking around; they performed for Baseema looking up cautiously from the ground below. They bowed and hollered and whooped with their hands over their mouths. Then they flopped over the railings. Daniel's hair was thick and black and glossy. In the village they joked that he looked like a girl with his jet-black curls, his long blue eyes. He was so like Baseema. But small too, like a bird. Quick, and imaginative. By comparison, Frederic at that age of five or six was slow and shy and loitered in Daniel's shadow. But Daniel didn't notice these things about his little friend. So delighted was he to have someone to play for the day. The boys ran inside into the cool of the rooms and the balcony was suddenly deserted, the shutters and doors left swinging open and Baseema remained, looking up, her body leaning forward but out of sight on the bench, her hands fingering the pockets of her dress for a tissue to wipe her nose...

'You did do the cherries that night, Ma. You did the dessert. As a favour. I remember because you came to get us from the garden room when you brought them round. You saw us dancing and you went away. Then, later, I went to find my guitar back at the house and you were there, with all the cherries in a bowl in front of you. You were arguing with Dad. I had to take the cherries myself back to the table.'

'It doesn't matter though, Sylvie. You must try to forget...' she said but stopped herself short.

'People get crushed, Ma. In the wheels of living, people get crushed.

'Sylvie?'

'Sometimes you can love people too much. It crushes

the life out of someone when you love them too much. It fucking strangles the life out of them. Don't you think that's right?'

'Yes,' said Baseema, and then she smiled and she turned to her daughter sitting there on the dark earth with her awful unhappy shoulders slumped forward and the irritated skin underneath her chin. But it wasn't Sylvie who felt the need to pick and scratch at her own skin. Baseema knew who it was who was really blemished. She placed her fingers flat on the ground to the sides of her knees and breathed. Still, the tears didn't come.

'You were born cat-like,' she whispered.

'Ma?'

'It's what I want to say to him. You were born cat-like. I have tried to write my thoughts to both of the boys, Sylvie. I don't know what to say. To Frederic, I speak sometimes. At night. Just to tell him what's going on. Nothing special. Just this and that. He didn't want much more. But talking to Daniel, even in my head, is harder. And when I try to write to him I find it's like writing into a void.'

In the kitchen Baseema laid spaghetti on Sylvie's plate. She sprinkled herbs, cracked pepper, forked through a sliver of butter.

'If you have a child, Sylvie,' she said quietly, then pulled herself up. She brought the plates to the table and stood there holding them for a moment, watching the steam curling. 'You see, the thing is. I handed him over. Quite happily!'

Sylvie had both of her knees tucked up in front of her.

'Maman?' she said. 'We could all have done something different… We were smoking. I was drunk already. I thought I was going to be sick. I left them to come here and have some water. I made some coffee, really strong, and then I lay down for a while, till I started to feel better.'

Baseema sat down at the table, and laid a napkin across her lap. She sat with her head held so high it made Sylvie seem like a dwarf beside her. They didn't look at each other when they spoke. Sylvie put her knees down. They twizzled spaghetti on their forks.

Baseema could only manage a mouthful of pasta. She laid her knife and fork together, then collected them up again in her hands, tried to eat a little more. Finally, she wiped the corner of her mouth and laid the napkin on the table.

Sylvie was crying while eating now, shaking her head.

On the oven, the clock read 22.47.

'It should have been me who was burnt, not you, my Sylvie.'

Sylvie looked up, brushed the tears from the swollen lids of her eyes. She sniffed and coughed and pushed the table away from her and slid out, her napkin tucked into the high waist of her skirt.

'One postcard I've had from him,' she said, walking over to the dresser Baseema had polished. She opened the door with trembling fingers, brought the postcard back to the table.'

'It's postmarked from Mexico, and this address is the one I replied to.'

'This is a Mayan ruin,' said Baseema, peering closer at the print on the postcard.

Sylvie took the card and straightened herself to read the words that were written in black ink on it.

> Just as a mother would protect with her life her own son, her only son, so one should cultivate an unbounded mind towards all beings, and loving-kindness towards all the world. One should cultivate an unbounded mind, above and below and across, without obstruction, without enmity, without rivalry.
>
> Standing, or going, or seated, or lying down, as long as one is free from drowsiness, one should practise this mindfulness. This, they say, is the holy state here.
>
> *Sutta Nipata*

'You don't need to be ashamed, Ma. After all, this...'

'I gave him up.'

'You had no choice.'

'Pah! I had choice. We all have some choice, Sylvie.'

'You weren't to know any of this would happen.'

Baseema lifted herself a little higher in the chair and then her body slumped forward. She was beginning to feel so tired.

'Fire was Daniel's means of requesting help. He didn't kill Frederic. Frederic killed himself. You know that, don't you, Sylvie? He loved Daniel with all his heart. He didn't want to be gay. He didn't want to be gay... And Daniel loved Frederic. Daniel needed help himself. Perhaps he still needs help.'

'He's a grown man now, Ma. All this will be so far behind him.'

'He won't want to see me.'

'I think he will come back here, though. I do think he will come back here. Of his own choice.'

'We have to get on, Sylvie. We have to get up, get dressed, build ourselves a day, each day.'

'And the others?'

'Who?'

'The people who get crushed?'

'Who gets crushed?'

'People get crushed, Ma. Like I said. People like me. People like Papa. Daniel's free. He's not crushed. Everyone loves Daniel. And you too, Ma. You're free. Like Kate Glover. But not me. I am one of the people life fucks over. Like Frederic. Like Papa. Like me.'

8

In the Pyrenees, the early-morning air was wet and warm. Baseema drove fast on the road, which wound in a series of tight hairpin bends through the mist. She leant forward over the steering wheel as the wipers slushed back and forth. Her mind was empty, her body felt big and stiff with tiredness. She breathed slowly, then hardly at all.

In the driveway, she pushed the car beneath the dripping pines and drove round behind the guest rooms to the wooden cabin with its lights on in the windows.

She reversed the car into the double space beneath the low hanging boughs that no one had thought to trim. There was another car parked here. A small white van that she hadn't seen before. She looked up the wooden steps to the cabin with its gingham curtain in the window.

She barely noticed the way things had been rearranged: the slight, but only slight sense of disorder: a couple of cups, a stain, smeary fingerprints on the windows, a book on the floor, as if, while she had been away, the cabin had tilted quickly on its side, displacing ornaments, here and there.

It was quiet inside. And calm. He was standing by the stove, a cup of coffee in his hand. But it wasn't her standing there before him. As least, it didn't feel like her. It felt as if she had found herself in another world where hous-

...es flipped over like cards in a breeze, and minds warped without warning, emptying out in an instant while the animal Arnaud had said to her was in us all, was all we were, had finally found its opening and burst forward, eyes rolling, teeth bared, like a horse breaking into the house of its abuser and rearing up, using the last of its strength to take revenge.

Lollo did nothing. He went down like a leaf and lay there to be pummelled. His face was white, his lips slack.

And afterwards they sat across from one another at the small kitchen table and Lollo called his wife a Maghreb cunt. There was a bottle of Russian vodka between them and they took it in turns to drink from the bottle. Baseema's head was empty, eerily so. Lollo sat with a towel wrapped around his hand. He wept. After a while he stopped.

Above their heads a naked bulb burnt low over the table.

'What did you do with the light shade?'

'I binned it.'

'Oh.'

'I moved things.'

'Is the car yours?'

'What car?'

'The car parked outside. A van.'

'There's no car outside.'

Baseema drank vodka from the bottle and swilled it round her mouth. She would have liked to get up and show him the van, but for this strange feeling of exhaustion, this slowly creeping desire to crawl into bed upstairs and give it all up. But still there would be peace here, in this cabin in the mountains. There would still be the lemony light to recover, the quiet rhythm of her days.

She looked at her husband now and the way his lips were moving to try and form some words and she wondered how on earth she had stuck it out so long. How on earth she could have gone on pretending he almost didn't exist.

Still, she didn't know what to do.

After a while she got up and she carried her bag up to the bedroom, noticing the changes now, the few things left off kilter, the dust on the stairs, on the table.

She brought a sponge and a clean towel from upstairs, a T-shirt for him to put on.

'You're a bitch,' he said, as she wiped the blood from his face and under his neck. 'You should leave the blood, but you can't bear to see it, Baseema. Your own violence. You will clean it up as you have always cleaned everything. Trying to make yourself shine. Always thinking you were somehow better than the folk in the village. With your clothes and your privilege. Fancy thinking you would get the chateau; that the nephew would actually give it to you – just like that. But you don't have strength and you don't have courage. You can't even face your own son.'

'Daniel came to see us,' she said, standing with her back to him at the sink, her eyes on the view. 'I think he was seven. He came one Sunday to sit in our kitchen. It was you who answered the door. Don't you remember? It was raining and Daniel was standing there, holding a bag with his toothbrush and a plastic bag with some toys inside. He said he'd come to stay with us for a while. I can stay here? Would it be all right?'

Lollo said nothing. He was winding the towel around his hand.

'We fed him a cream cake and then we turned him away. He was scared. Do you remember?'

'What fucking choice did we have?'

'Right!' shouted Baseema, spinning round now and baring her teeth at him. 'That house we had. That café. Well, God above, we were like royalty. Except it was better than that. We weren't like the Borjas. Were we? We weren't from the city. We were like everyone else, accepted by everyone else. Except for the fact that we had more than them. We had the best of both worlds. Friendship and privilege. Accepted and better off. And well we knew it. Well we knew.'

'So you turned him away.'

'No, Lollo! *We* turned him away. We did it, you and me. We fed him a cream cake and shut the door.'

'He would have burnt us into the ground.'

'He was seven years old.'

'He was damaged.'

'Seven years old!'

Outside, the rain had begun to fall and she walked slowly on the path that was wet beneath her feet. When the first of the snows came, the air would be sharper, all would be white; things would be clear. Her stomach rumbled. She hadn't eaten. And there was an ache at the back of her head where her neck had buckled on her shoulders. She would take long walks in the snow this winter, hire some cross-country skis, even; take refuge in the hills .

In the lobby, she switched the lights on and looked around. There was a tall vase of exotic flowers on the desk, and black and white photographs of mountains on the walls. She was proud of this job of hers in this quiet hotel. How she loved this vase of flowers and the computer that waited for her behind the desk. After her swim she would come in here with her hair washed and dried and ready herself for what was left to salvage of this day. She would make a cup of coffee and sit quietly, sifting through her emails. Things would start to seem better then. After all, what damage had been done? It wasn't a question of pride. She was holding onto what she knew in order to protect him from the pain of their reunion. It was the only thing she could do for him, after all this time.

In the pool room, the lights came on automatically. Beneath the water, there were cones of yellow light from the spots on the sides.

Baseema put her towel on one of the loungers and held onto the bars as she eased her body down into the water. When she sank beneath the surface, the water held her hair up above her head so that it waved like velvety weeds clinging to a rock.

Yes, she was ready for winter. She was ready for the winter that would come and lock the secrets of the summer in. She loved how quickly it came and stripped the trees and flushed the dirt from the roads, how it went over everything with its cold hard brush and then laid the snow down so that everything could be covered over and quietly contained while the earth turned beneath.

—

Rape wasn't right. Because rape wasn't what it was. She'd been fourteen. Only just on her period. Fresh little eggs popping into the bright clean blood of her for the very first time. Lucie had explained everything. She took her through it all. There were diagrams that Lucie sat down at the kitchen table and drew. It wouldn't hurt. Nine months was all it would be. She remembers the hot fondling in that tower room; remembers how quickly Arnaud got to sucking at her breasts. She was still a child. And now, after all this time.

It was a joke, Lucie had said, when she'd gone that evening to get the gun from the cage above the fireplace. She'd wanted to have a baby. She was barren, and too old.

It was a joke and not a joke.

She had clicked the gun and pointed it at Arnaud, who laughed and shook his finger in the air. But Lucie wanted them to do this.

Baseema didn't care for the wine they had given her. But they had made such a fuss of her. Even she was giggling at the strangeness of it all. And when at last it happened, it happened. And after it, life went on, and she was carried forward, living as she always had, under the gaze and direction of the Borjas. It was early evening. Lucie was standing just inside the doorway, with her arms folded and her neck lifted right up like that of a startled bird. No, it wasn't that unpleasant. The shutters were open in the bedroom. It was a beautiful evening. The sky was pink. And she didn't like the wine but she soon got used to it.

Now she held her head up high above the water. When she moved she stretched her arms right out in front of her and propelled herself forward using her strong muscular legs. She made it all the way to the end of the pool and she felt the water rinse and purify her, seeping into her pores.

The white van that was parked under the pines was gone, leaving only a trail of angry tyre marks, like a game of brown dominoes in the mud.

On the table in the kitchen, beneath the bottle of vodka, there was a piece of a paper. It said, 'Bye, bye. I'm going home,' in his writing that was as bad as a child's.

Baseema took the paper out from under the bottle. He had finished the bottle before leaving. And in her mind she saw him hunched behind the wheel, the spray of grey curls, those feeble fingers on the wheel. And she wondered, for a moment, about his intention. It was possible someone would find him in a day or two, the car gone down into a ravine, in between the dripping mountains; and buried in the mist and the forest, he would be fallen, hunched up over the wheel. They might wonder, peering in for a moment, what wild dog had been here for him and pinned him down, tried to rip out an eye. These policemen wouldn't know it wasn't him she had been after but the man in him, the deep stubborn unapologetic French man sunk down and drowning deep inside.

But she didn't want that for her spouse. Of course she didn't want that. She wanted him to be back where he felt safe, in the village, in his house with Sylvie, the house she had readied for his return.

And she knew that the chances were he'd have pulled over and fallen asleep somewhere. Then he'd wake with the first of the light and shake himself and gun the engine so that he could get to Sylvie's in time for coffee, for bread and jam.

He'd shuffle in through the front door as if he'd never been away. He'd seat himself at the kitchen table and grin, looking around. He'd look at the line of Spanish plates falling on the wall, and he might remember, as Baseema couldn't, who from the village it was who had made the gift.

The man would be back in his house then. Across the square he'd see the lights on in the café. He wouldn't see the dark lumps of the chateau behind the wall. He would only see the café, and the women walking through the square with their baskets on their arms. He'd seat himself at his old table in the house that once was and would always be his, and he'd cross himself then and know that he was home.

DANIEL

1

Paris, July 2006

Lollo Pépin didn't say hello. He wasn't smiling. The waitress had disappeared.

He leant forward over the bar. 'I drove here. From the Pyrenees. I stopped and slept in the vehicle. All because my determination was to face you, finally.'

Daniel tried to focus on what the man was saying. On Lollo's head was a black triangle of sweat. It looked as if his crown had been pressed with the tip of an iron. Daniel felt the advantage of his height, the length and breadth of his torso. The simple black T-shirt and jeans that he wore to work were effective by contrast with the stained collar and crumpled beige trousers before him.

'They cut him down,' Lollo said, staring shakily up into Daniel's face. 'I sat with his head for hours. I just sat there like a mug.... and you had disappeared.'

Daniel's eyes filled up with tears very quickly in the shadows behind the bar. 'He was my friend.'

'Yeah,' said Lollo. 'Pisssssssth,' he said. Then he seemed to lose courage and he rocked on his elbows. He looked to the street, drew phlegm from the back of his throat. A coach load of pale staring tourists rumbled past the window.

In a moment, the kitchen door swung open and in

came Suzette with armfuls of napkins. She smiled shyly at Daniel, unaware of his customer. Daniel watched as she settled herself at table 12 and began to fold the napkins. He stared at the brightness in her gleam of blonde hair.

Lollo had walked the entire stretch of the Boulevard St Michel to find the restaurant Daniel was working in. It was a shock for both of them. To come face to face like this, after so many years.

'Who do you think you are?'

Daniel said nothing. He took the bottle of tequila down. Lollo's jacket creaked as he leant over the bar. 'Maghreb,' he said. 'Fucking Maghreb bastard. That is what you are.'

Daniel gave Lollo another drink.

'Your biological mother was from Algeria. And... You know, don't you? You know who I mean.'

'I...'

'Maghreb.'

'I'm sorry.'

'Fucking Maghreb bastard.'

Daniel stared at the clear liquid as it filled his own glass. Maghreb was a word that snagged in the throat. He didn't know much about Algeria. In his mind, it was an area of confusion and unresolved pain. A bartender had told him once that the Algerians were waiting for an apology. Acknowledgement. Recognition. The bully who cut off relatives' hands. But France, like the silent dad, refused to concede the damage done.

Daniel looked at Lollo's face and saw how the years had hollowed him. Where once his eyes were slitty and hard, they now drooped at the corners and seemed pinned into the top of his face. The two men drank. Time had slowed down. Daniel nodded his head in the darkness, and he placed both hands on the bar and experienced some kind of emotion that felt a bit like wind. He hit the flesh on his chest and coughed the alcohol into his stomach.

It didn't come as a surprise to him, what Lollo was telling him, drip by drip, about the truth of his birth. It was clear: Lucie was not his biological mother. His biological mother was the quiet woman with the dark chignon in the square. Lucie had kept him close and tried to keep him warm – he got so warm he nearly died for lack of air. Love to the point of asphyxiation; her timid little fretful voice breathing deep into the drum of his ear. From the balcony railings Baseema was far away; she was Frederic and Sylvie's mother. She was strong, and calm, like lake water.

'Why do you look at me like that, huh?'

'I don't know what to say.'

'Me? I don't give a shit what you say.'

Lollo grunted for more tequila. He wasn't finished. 'Now the chateau is your property, Daniel, and you have a chance to make amends.'

Daniel's gentle nodding was a tiny movement but there, nonetheless. Guilt was his reflex. He had felt it always, without knowing why.

'What do you say?'

'I said the chateau is nothing to do with me. I want nothing to do with it.'

'Ah! Fuck this, fuck that. Don't take responsibility for this or that. It's all the same with your generation. Chiefly the rich cunts like you.'

Daniel turned away and looked again out the window.

'But, see, the chateau at Canas is everything to do with

you. It's all there is. For all of us.'

Daniel swallowed. His stomach lurched. He looked at the man before him and tried to blur his eyes as if to fade him out of the picture.

'What does it matter? I come from the same place as Frederic and Sylvie. I am the same.'

'No.'

Daniel thought about Sylvie and the fire as it had flamed into her hair. She had tried to trace him. He'd received an email from her, to which he had never replied.

'You can think what you like of me,' he said calmly, before stepping out from behind the bar. 'It doesn't matter to me. Nor to anyone. Frederic killed himself. So there is nothing more for us to discuss on this or any other day.'

From the corner of his eye, Daniel saw the old man rise a little from the stool. He tried to tuck his T-shirt into his belt as he went through to the back. He took his apron off and hung it on the pegs outside the staff toilet rather than on the usual ones in the storeroom. Then he opened the door to the cleaning cupboard and closed it again. In the toilets, he looked briefly at his face in the white light. He pumped soap into his palm and closed his fingers around it. He closed his eyes but when he opened them his face was still there – big and startling and huge. He washed his hands and then held his wrists under the stream of cold water. The hand dryer wasn't working so he left the water on his hands and yanked on the fire door and went out into the street.

———

He was carrying a paper bag full of plums when he rapped

on his landlady's door at eleven o'clock and found that she wasn't asleep, but up with the television. He declined the offer of coffee and handed over the plums. Daniel told his landlady that he was leaving Paris for the south at first light in the morning. He would put his rubbish out in advance and if it was all right he would use one of her bins. There was no need to worry about the post and he would hold onto his key. He was going, he told her, to the village that he was born and raised in. First thing in the morning. To sell his father's house. Most of the money he would be giving away to some members of his family who hadn't done so well – he had a biological mother who lived in a hut in the Pyrenees and a half-sister with a burnt face. He would bring back some of the money for her, and he bowed slightly and apologised for falling behind on his rent. Then he said he would never forget her understanding and kindness.

Mrs Orlandini was pleased. She said that it sounded like a good plan. She teased him about all the girls who came to see him. All those skittish little hearts he was breaking, she said. Then she kissed his hands and he stumbled a little and fell into her cooking-smell arms.

––––

Early the next morning, Daniel was the only one on the platform, standing right at the end, very still. The last carriage of the train was empty. He could see that. He smiled to himself in the glass sliding by. He was wearing the same black jeans, with a blue shirt that his girlfriend Carey had chosen because of the way it brought out the blue of his eyes. Daniel was mostly embarrassed by his eyes.

An accident of birth; but a beautiful face was the best disguise in the world. Carey had moved into his flat and tried to love him for who he was. Lovely Carey. With her vegetarian burritos and her healing hands. But that was the problem, in the end. Carey laid her hands on him and tried to heal him and she got too close to the core. 'Sometimes,' she'd said, towards the end, 'I feel like I could put my finger through your skin and find that you're not really there.'

———

The train was air-conditioned and cool inside. There were all the seats in the carriage to choose from and Daniel went straight for the window seat, the second one on the right. He stowed his rucksack away on the overhead rack, and his watch, which was plastic and digital, he removed from his wrist and placed neatly on the table in front of him. Then he took a breath and closed his eyes as the train pulled out of the station. Lucie had said he was a genius. There were many waiters in the world who were geniuses. Lost souls. Into the restaurants they came, looking vaguely around for a peg, and an apron – and some other people with whom to attempt solidarity. He took a breath and opened his eyes. There was a money spider on the window. He glimpsed his own reflection again. It was Daniel, the Daniel he used to be – crunched-up features, shadows around the eyes, tension in the forehead; the one holding a pencil, chewing it, worried, towards the end. Something in his head, he said; like an eerie, open sound, like a rolling feeling – space was the matter – he had tried to tell Frederic about the pressure but

222

found that he couldn't explain.

Outside, the French countryside flattened and changed as the train clattered towards the south. Daniel watched the people leaving the train and new people coming on, settling themselves with their mobile phones, like strange little arm extensions, on the little tables in front of them, with newspapers and books and magazines, with music and food and gadgets and bottles of water and Coke, and he saw how the children did just the same, came armed with phones and games and drinks and sweets and magazines with coloured pens and pencils attached in cellophane packages, and how some of them even came on and sat with small computers with screens on which to watch their films. A little girl shrieked when she dropped her bag of things beside him and he bent down to help her and picked up a pencil case that had slipped under his seat. The little girl sniffed and said thank you, and stared at his hand, which had a cigarette stub in it.

Daniel looked out at the fields and all the hanging greyness and the cows pushing their bums against a five-bar gate. In one field a horse was taking a piss and the steam was rising around its flank. There were towns of houses piled up close to the tracks. Lanes twisting off towards bigger houses full of big families, he imagined. Little girls running about in rubber boots. Women milking cows. You could picture them in spring. Happy boys playing with caterwauls. Raincoats shining. The path to school. Gates. Leaning. Shouting white teeth laughing. Then, nothing. Flat land. For miles.

When he got hungry he ate a roll with a tablet of butter he'd taken from the station café. He ate in small bites, savouring the taste of the bread in his mouth. Then he wiped the knife clean with the wrapper and folded the foil in half, then quarters. Then he slipped his knife through the fold. Then quarters again. Then he popped the tiny book of foil into his mouth and swallowed. From now on there would be no crumbs. There would be no clutter and no remnants. He would leave no trace of himself.

At Béziers, he got off the train. For a long time he sat on a bench in the square, his rucksack strapped to his back, his head moving all around. He saw how the trunk of the big olive tree split and then came together again, two trunks meeting above his head. He watched a small bird peck at the remains of a burger dropped on the ground. A woman walked past pushing an empty pushchair.

He checked himself into a hostel near the train station where the beds were laid out like hospital beds with plastic undersheets. It was four in the afternoon. He had no plan. Lollo had said you must go back and sell the chateau. There was an English bitch sniffing around the place, he said. Some rich cunt from London wanting to take it on. She would pay and when she handed the money over, Daniel would give a third to the mother who had carried him, and the sister whose life he destroyed. Lollo had spread his piece of paper out on the table. It wasn't a contract. The paper had been torn out of an exercise book. But Daniel had said ok. He'd taken the broken bit of biro, and he'd taken the piece of paper, but he hadn't signed. There wasn't any need. He knew the time had come, anyway. Lollo was half soaked on tequila by then, and hanging onto the bar.

Now he sat on the bed in the airless room and waited. The walls were white and had biro marks – swear words and hearts mostly, random scratch marks from a bunch of people who knew not very much about anything. Nothing on the soul, nothing important, nothing that might be a guide. He closed his eyes and saw himself as a boy in shorts and T-shirt, hurrying to buckle his sandals on the steps outside the chateau. It was high summer, early morning. Frederic was coming to play. They had arranged a secret meeting and through the gate the boy came, wearing a gold crown and carrying a plastic gun. He ran towards Daniel, waving the gun as he came. 'Daniel,' he shouted, then again, again, 'Daniel, Daniel.' Daniel was crouching on the steps with a finger to his mouth. 'It's me. It's Frederic, the King!'

There was a thud of a can in the drinks machine. A girl with a shaved head and a sickle tattoo on her neck came in and offered him a piercing. Daniel looked at his watch. He looked at her reddish eyes and her nice smile and he slithered off the bed and went off to join her.

In the corridor he smoked pot with the girl. He watched while she kissed another girl, whose name was Mandy. They spoke softly. They were thinking about going to Morocco. They agreed there wasn't much to believe in. Mandy had a balloon. She kept blowing air in and letting it go. And the girl with the shaved head put a hand on Daniel's cheek and told him that his eyes were beautiful. One of the girls started giggling and kissing him but it tailed off, after a while, and so they sat and looked at the streetlight through the grimy windows, and heard the television blaring in the common room.

In the morning, Daniel got up early and went in search of some food. He tapped on the window of the bakery and bought a loaf from a woman in a dressing gown. She had covered her face in a green cream. She took his money and handed over a crusty baguette in a twist of grey paper. For a moment or two, he stood in the warmth of the shop with the smell of bread in his nostrils, then he went outside and sat down on the bench, eating the bread slowly; he pulled rough chunks from the stick and shook the crumbs out for the birds gathering around his feet. The sun cast a pale orange light on the shop fronts across the square. He thought of Carey and her soft, healing hands. He blinked. 'I feel like I could put my finger through your skin and find that you're not really there.'

He went into the church and stared up ahead at the light coming in through the stained-glass windows and onto the polished head of Christ. It was quiet and orderly in there. He watched an old woman kneeling in the front pew, anxiously tick-tacking the beads of her rosary. Tick tack knock knock are you there tick tack? Daniel sat down in a pew and put his chin on his hands. He looked at the knobbly protrusions of the woman's vertebrae and felt her despair. Lucie rarely went into the church in the village for a moment's respite and reflection but slept with her saints on her bed instead, bent like a stick in a blue-and-white nightdress with a ribbon around the waist. Like a little girl dreaming of martyrdom. That strangely fantastic version of Catholicism she had. Muttering to the Mother Mary and Saint Perpetua while fretfully avoiding

God. And sixty already. That yellow summer, Daniel's footsteps in the corridor, softly moving, one foot after the other, trying not to wake her – he who had become so accustomed to a mother sleeping – when he stopped at the window with his gift of sugared almonds and looked down on the courtyard where the birds were gathering, blackbirds mostly, looking up, their eyes full of rain and the grapes that Arnaud prayed over, season after season.

Daniel had come to think he didn't believe in God. But he liked the fact that Carey believed, and that it brought her comfort, and that when she put her hands on his hot and worried head, she was making some peaceful connection with a higher, holier power and transmitting something that might be able to save him. He had come to understand that, despite what he used to think, comfort wasn't a bad thing, tinged as it was with deception and fear.

On the outskirts of Béziers, Daniel hitched a ride on the road heading north. The truck stopped at the crossroads on the heath above the village. Daniel had nothing to give the man in exchange for the ride, but he raised his fingers in a half-hearted salute and waved the vehicle on its way. A line of dust rose under the wheels as the truck spun on the crossroads and continued on a single-track road into the hills.

The air up on the heath was cooler and clear. He stood for a moment, listening to the sound of the engine as it died away. Then his ears flooded with the sounds of the countryside. He heard the scuttle and nest of insects, the chirrup of a bird. He heard the grass swish as the air moved through it and he bent down to touch it with his fingers. Across the heath was the air hangar. To the left of the hangar some clothing flapped around on a line. There was the turning field, the petrol pump and the runway. There was no one about. Daniel walked slowly towards the hangar to see if there were planes inside but the big doors were closed. The corrugated shelter rattled and ticked in the wind. He ambled quickly across the heath and cut through the line of trees to the hill-path. The ground was white here. He remembered. The heat of summer. The distance fading. Whiteness. Hiss, hiss; the grass that throbbed until nightfall.

From the ground he picked up a stone and rubbed the red earth from it with his thumb. Then he stooped to collect up a leaf, the underside pink as icing; and he put the leaf in his pocket with the stone, with a broken twist of vine, with the silvery leaf of an olive tree, several olives, green and hard. These were the things he had thought of over the years; this the stuff that had danced under his eyelids in the bleach of slow, restless thought.

He knew he wouldn't be recognised in Canas. It'd been twenty years, at least. In his jeans and crisp shirt he was like a man from any city in Europe. He was a man from nowhere. They wouldn't identify him now. Halfway down the hill path he stopped and sat on a rock. From here, he could see the whole village. The windows were all on different levels, like old people's eyes peering out from their stone skins, cranky old shutters, roofs like the soft hats the old men wore in the square. There were fences laid out like teeth around patches of land and doorways – dark little openings – like a hundred chattering mouths.

Daniel closed his eyes for a moment or two. His feet slipped out in front of him, his ankles making grooves in the track. There was dry grass around him, wild asparagus growing, fennel, gorse. He swallowed and looked back down the hill, focusing his eyes on the chateau and the tower rising behind the wall.

He walked down into the village and he stopped in the square. The first thing he saw was the Pépin house. It looked the same. But paler somehow, and smaller. He saw that the door had changed colour. Sylvie would be there. He looked at his watch and walked towards the door, and then he turned halfway across the square and slipped into the café.

Inside, the air was thick with cigarette smoke. Three, maybe four old men sat hunched over the bar top. Daniel went to the bar and said he was going to sit outside and he sat at one of the four zinc tables in front of the fountain. He folded his fingers together on the table, tensed the muscles in his wrists while he waited. From the fountain, water dribbled in greenish strings. Things loomed up. Looked strange. When he half closed his eyes it could all be here, just as it was. There were flowers on the balconies. Buildings were smaller, squatter, things seemed quieter.

Behind him, the church stood as it always had: big, and old and crumbling away. He remembered himself giggling in the shadows and Frederic, standing up in the fountain, his pants sliding down to his knees as the old women of the village appeared through the door from evening Mass. He saw Frederic rubbing his hand up and down and calling to the women to look over at him. But the thought of this boy tugged at Daniel's heart now in a way that made him feel angry, so he closed his eyes and counted while the bad feeling leaked away.

'Does Sylvie Pépin live in that house there?' he said to the bartender, a little more roughly than he'd intended to, and he lifted his arm up and pointed across the square. Daniel felt how rickety and insecure the table was, how flimsy the chair, and he got up out of it and moved to sit in the other one.

'Yes,' said the barman. 'You know Sylvie?'

'I used to,' said Daniel, and he shifted the chair by picking it up by the arms and dragging it onto more even ground. 'I knew her once.'

The bartender's head was marked with a zigzag shaved into the dark bristles of his hair. He hugged the tray against his chest. In a house across the square, a front door banged open and a slim woman in a long green dress tumbled out onto the steps. The dress was crinkled and silky and it swished elegantly around her ankles as she stopped and turned. She bent to sniff the roses outside the house and she tucked her hair behind her ears and then she went back into the house and banged the door behind her. Daniel had forgotten this, how mad people were down here. How they ferried about in their odd little lives doing things that the rest of the world would deem so unimportant with the pomp and ceremony of kings.

He watched as the slim woman in the green dress came back out of her house carrying a bottle of water and a plastic bag. She wasn't wearing shoes. She wasn't from here, after all.

The bartender swung his head and smiled like someone smiling in his sleep.

'Les anglais,' he said. 'Rumour is she's trying to buy the chateau. She came here in winter with her husband. Now she's here on her own. She's crazy, I think.'

'Crazy?'

'In the way that they are. These people.'

They watched her walk on beyond the chateau and turn down the avenue of trees.

The bartender was bored. Daniel was looking over at Sylvie's house.

'You have family here? Friends?'

'No.'

'So how come you know Sylvie Pépin?'

'I knew her from school.'

'You went to school here?'

'Not here. Toulouse.'

'Sylvie didn't go to school in Toulouse, man. Sylvie never went anywhere. I'm not from this village; I come from the next village that way, but my mum said something weird going on with that one. She's nice, though. You know? Gentle.' The bartender shrugged and changed the subject. 'This used to be called the Café Union,' he said. 'Then I took over.'

Daniel nodded to show he understood. The chair was driving him mad. He leant right back in it and looked over to the chateau. The bartender looked over too.

'You like these big old places? So many of these in this region, you know? The tourists like to come and gawp at them like they never seen an old stone.'

Daniel felt the heat of the sun and he curled his shoulders right forward over himself and smoked like a man smoking his last ever cigarette. He felt sick, and he fell silent.

The beer was brought out in a tall glass. Painted circles of lemon and lime tumbled down the sides. Daniel drank it quickly and watched a bird peck around the fountain.

After a while, he wandered inside the café to ask how much he owed. Very quickly he drank another beer and then he bought a packet of cigarettes and the bartender fiddled with the radio. Daniel stood still, in the middle of the room, and thought about what he should do.

At number 6 he knocked and picked a flake of paint off the door. He knocked again. He heard a shuffling noise inside. The smell of the house was coming through the door. It was musty and familiar. He heard a dog whine and scratch a little inside.

Daniel tried the handle and opened the door. Inside, it was murky. There was a single light in an old red shade above the table. Sylvie was there. She was sitting at the table and staring right at him through her glasses, which were steaming up. Her cheeks were bright and puffy and white with scars and glistening with bright starry tears.

Daniel stood in the doorway with his rucksack in his hand and he did nothing. He saw that Sylvie was wearing a grey hooded top, and that her breasts sagged a bit inside it. Under the table he saw a pair of jeans, and pink socks.

She took her glasses off and wiped them, then brushed her hands over her eyes.

'You're here,' she said.

'Shall I go?' he whispered. He put his rucksack down on the floor.

'Look at you!'

'I'm sorry.'

'It's a shock. Why are you here?'

'To sell the chateau.'

'Oh!'

'Lollo came to find me. In Paris.'

'It's business, as usual,' she said. 'You're here on business. Yes, the chateau is up for sale. People got in a fuss about it to start with. Then everyone forgot. Except Dad. He doesn't forget anything. Soon he will come here. To live with me. You seen my dog?'

Daniel smiled. He looked at her chin, holding itself up with all the will in the world. He saw the pale, freckly skin and what the fire had done to her lovely eyes. He saw her hair, how big and thick and familiar it was. Like a dancer. Like a lovely Spanish dancer with all this old love, and feeling, and contempt for him.

'I think I should go,' he said.

'Good,' said Sylvie, and she pointed to the refrigerator. 'You can leave your bag. Just stick it over there beside the fridge. I won't ferret through your things. And no one will come to take it. We don't have burglars here. Not like in the city. We're innocent folk mostly. Nothing changes much.'

'Sylvie?' said Daniel quietly.

'What is it?' she said, flicking her hair back over her shoulder again.

'Look at me.'

'Not on your life.' She sniffed and wiped away another stream of huge sliding tears.

Daniel left his bag there and slipped out into the heat of the square. At the bar, he had another beer or two. There was a hole which slowly started to fill with liquid. After a while, he joined some men for a jug of wine and a round of cards. The afternoon passed into evening, and the shifting purple light got the men moving; things were said but he didn't remember much and they all fell out of the bar and scattered in the square like marbles thrown out. They bantered with him to go find some woman who might take him into her bed for the night. Daniel felt the heat of the night coming down. He laughed, but there wasn't a cash machine for miles around and he had no money to pay for the drinks he'd had. He watched the men stagger home and he placed his hands on either side of the fruit machine, letting his head hang down. He felt his forehead touch the glass and he stared in at all the lights blazing away in there. Then a painted lemon glass, and the glass was full with water. The bartender grabbed Daniel's neck and told him to go sleep and to come back tomorrow and settle up the bill. Then he laughed, and Daniel took the man's hand, and everything seemed all right then. The day was done.

'You can't play the crucified man on me, Daniel Borja,' said Sylvie, opening the front door in her dressing gown a few moments later. Her hair was hanging in a side plait over her shoulder. 'You're no Prodigal Son.' He swayed a little on her doorstep, tried to place his hand on the frame. You're drunk.'

But it made her kind, and she opened the door to take

234

him in. It was a shock seeing him tonight, as it had been this afternoon, but this time she was active with it and it made her tend to him with a bed and coffee, which brewed while she doubled over in the kitchen and made a strange guffawing noise to herself.

2

He didn't think it would be like this. That the memory would be so hazy. That he would feel nothing, like stone. Daniel hadn't meant to go into the chateau yet but he found, two days later, walking along the avenue of trees with his hands in his pockets, that it was easy to scale the boundary wall. He felt a little restored since arriving here; he'd been fed, and he'd slept surprisingly well in the cool, redolent disorder of Sylvie's house.

They hadn't talked much. She'd cooked plate after plate of pasta with butter and cheese. Someone brought tomatoes round in a plastic bag; they had eaten them on the sofa while watching TV. The dog had lolled around with them in the gloom. She had fleas, Sylvie had said. It was too hot to go out. Daniel put bottles of lemonade in the freezer and they had those mixed in tall glasses with beer. She'd been planning to grow some flowers, she said, but she hadn't got around to it yet. One night they'd heard a nightingale and they'd sat in the silence of the kitchen and smoked and listened to it.

It was Sylvie who'd remarked on how much he slept. As if he'd come home from a war, she said, smiling at him after a shower. He looked at her shoulders, which were shiny from the moisture in her hair. She was pale, and her shoulders were soft and round and giving. But her neck was thin, and shrivelled, like chicken skin, with scars. That was the irony. The thing she said about war. Frederic had been the one going off to National Service. Daniel went off to be free.

'I bummed around,' he'd told her. 'And now all I really have is this sense of not going very far.'

'I'm happy you're here, Daniel,' she said, over and over again.

'Don't get used to it,' he'd joked one evening; he hadn't expected it to make her cry. She'd told him how beautiful he was and how much she hated him. She told him about some stuff that had happened to her. And how, one day, she'd gone into Arnaud's vineyard and dug up the little bones they had found as children. 'I had them analysed,' she'd said. 'I found out they were goat bones.'

Then Lollo arrived. It was late in the afternoon. Sylvie brought her father's bag in and said he'd been away, down to the sea. He had a friend in Tossa del Mar.

'He will sniff you here, Daniel. First thing he asked was, had you been here?'

'What did you say?'

'I told him that yes, you were still here. And that you're trying to sell the chateau.'

'I'll go out the back,' suggested Daniel, kicking his bag under the table.

'Yes,' she said, and a portion of her hair had fallen down in front of her face as she looked at her shoes. Then she bent beneath the table and picked up his bag and went upstairs to put it in her room.

———

Daniel couldn't see what lay on the other side but he climbed easily, his limbs remembering the thickness, the strange alliance of hard volcanic rock and the soft limestone, then the flick of his legs over the top, and the lift of his heart as he jumped down the other side. His heart thumped. His body moved slowly, awkwardly, unsure of itself in the nakedness of open space. He walked around the court-yard, keeping close to the wall. At his feet there were tall grasses and weeds, patches of dry scrub that he caught with his shoes. He reached forward through the overhang-ing boughs. There were steps at his feet; he felt for them through the ivy. Then an opening in the wall, a keyhole shape that gave onto the pool. It was smaller than he re-membered, entirely overgrown. It was all here.

Daniel stood for a moment, inhaling the smell of stone. His eyes adjusted quickly, and he saw the garden room and how the garden had grown over, blocking out the light. At the window he tried to pull at the weeds. He heard the blast of fire that had blown out the glass. He leant his body through the opening and pressed his head into the leaves growing in.

They had left it, exactly as it was. Black and char-coaled. The three of them spinning around him now. He had loved and laughed at this simple village boy with the bad reputation. A boy who pulled his pants down at the ladies coming out of church. A boy who sprayed graffiti and smoked all manner of leaves rolled up. A boy who danced on the chateau wall with alcohol in his veins. And a village girl who loved her brother and loved him too. Sylvie and her braces who laughed and laughed. The three of them loved each other, friends from the very beginning. He saw them all sitting out at the table in the courtyard, dragging it out under the olive trees, stopping for breath in the heat. He remembered the Chinese lanterns swinging in the olive trees. Sylvie wearing a dress with flowers on it. She kept leaning in and kissing everybody. Delirious with happiness. She was getting high. What a party... what a lovely party... Sylvie's eyes had once been lively. They were smaller now, and lifeless, like beads in the face of the doll.

Daniel the boy. And Lucie always shutting the window in case the birds came in. Arnaud away as usual. Daniel had rolled up a dry cloth and placed it in the sink. He was seven or eight. He lit the match from the fire and walked very carefully and pressed it into the cloth in the sink. He held it there. Then he lit another. And held it there. The silence was deathly, and quick. No one had come. Lucie was sick, dying, it looked like, in her sleep. Arnaud was always outside. Always working outside. And Lucie was sick. That was the thing. It was dark and quiet and cold in the chateau in winter. And the village children had crept up over the wall with their grubby faces and their big pink grins. He loved those grubby faces. Dark as little buttons they were. And the fire had nothing to hold onto; it raged in the stone sink, and then burnt itself right out.

In the courtyard, Daniel lay down beneath the olive trees and closed his eyes. If there was no soul inside him, and he had no reason to believe in anything, what did it matter if he simply turned himself into the ground and expired? He had come full circle, twenty years; he had been around the world and brought back nothing. He wanted someone to put his arms around. What had he learnt?

He closed his eyes for the sleep coming up from this old ground, snickering upwards, wrapping its hands around his brain. Beneath his eyelids now the kilometres he had travelled to get here, the damp northern weather, rain lashing the train windows. Prodigal Son – he was, wasn't he? – over the mountains, seven towns.

─

When he woke, he looked through the dust in the court-yard and saw the English woman walking about on the steps outside the chateau. He saw the green dress and the way she had her fingers interlocked behind her neck. She was thinking about something, unaware of him.

Daniel sat up. The English woman was walking to-wards him now. She crouched down outside the circle of olive trees. Her face was shiny with sweat. She had her chin in her hand. 'Hello,' she said, in English, and her voice was direct, and bright, and sweet. 'I just wondered. You've been here a long time. Are you all right?'

He smiled lazily. 'It's hot,' he replied, in English.

'Daniel?'

'How do you know my name?'

'Just a guess,' she smiled, and then she frowned and backed away. 'Aren't you feeling the sun?' she asked him, in French.

'What here? In the shade?'

Kate laughed. But she looked a bit serious for games. She stood with her hands on the hips of her silky dress, and turned her head away and sighed, as if she wanted to be somewhere else but couldn't figure out how to get there.

'Are you the one who wants to buy this place?'

Kate shook her head. 'No. Not anymore.'

'No?'

240

'I mean, I was.'

'You were?'

'I left my husband for it,' she said, a bit glibly, even though it was clear she very much wanted him to know that.

Daniel coughed politely, and took a step back. 'Oh! Right.' He smiled then and curled his shoulders forward as he stood up. 'But not any more?'

'No. Not any more. I've sort of lost the heart for it, I think.'

'That's a shame.'

'Is it?'

'Well, yes,' he said, and he laughed.

'I'm Kate,' she said sweetly, and she looked at the ground. It was clear she wanted him to feel something about the fact that she was here, on her own, trying to take the old place on.

'I'm sorry you're not going to be the buyer then,' he whispered, and Kate's dark eyes flashed greedily at him. She was gentle, and fierce. She was in another world. It roused him in a way that surprised him. 'And it's a problem for the guy who runs the bar,' he added, with a shrug of his shoulders, 'because until I have money, I can't pay.'

'You want to sell this house in order to settle your tab?'

'Precisely,' he said, and he laughed while she giggled and he shook out a cigarette and offered her one.

She was eyeing him strangely.

Daniel tried to carry on the joke. Then he stopped very suddenly. 'I'm a fool. I haven't been back here in a long time. I'm walking with ghosts.'

Kate took a deep breath. 'Let's have a drink,' she said. 'I'm staying over there, I can cook you some lunch.'

'Like a date?' he said. It was easy to talk like this. Much easier, he'd found, to be like this with women than it was to be anything else. Particularly with the ones he fancied. But this one was different. She was, and she wasn't, playing his game.

'I beg your pardon?'

'I'm kidding, and a drink would be a good idea because it would give me the chance to talk to you about the price.'

'Honestly. I've really lost the heart for it. It's a fantasy I had. Nothing more.'

'Is it?'

'I've lost my courage,' she said, and they walked together across the courtyard listening to the quiet crunch of their feet.

—

They opened the door to the village house and Daniel stood with his hands in his back pockets. She gave him a glass of red wine and he watched the straps of the green dress stir on the muscles and bones in her back as she stood at the stove waiting for the eggs to boil.

'It's only going to be a salad,' she told him. And Daniel said that was fine. 'It's so hot,' she went on. 'Is it always like this? Suddenly, just absolutely baking?'

'It all goes very hot, and white, all of a sudden. Sometimes it gets so hot that nobody can breathe.'

'It's not unbearable though, is it?'

'Isn't it?'

'Depends on what you can handle, I guess. Dry heat I can bear.'

Daniel drank the wine. He felt hungry. But when they got to it, they found it was too hot to eat even the salad. They drank the wine and they drank glasses of water. They moved from the table and sat, side by side, on the tired sofa that sagged against the wall. Daniel said nothing. He sat with his legs splayed out a bit and he listened to her talk about the death of her mother in March and how losing her had somehow burst the bubble she had been living in down here. Her husband had been so relieved to go back. And Kate had suddenly determined to make her marriage work.

'It was all I cared about. I was so bloody serious about it all of a sudden. Love, I kept saying to myself. It's a question of committing to it. Just love, with all your heart.'

Daniel watched her hands, which fluttered about in front of her face as she talked. Her teeth were very white and very clean. He found that they distracted him, and prevented him from looking into her eyes.

'It was as if I had suddenly absorbed my mother's way of doing things – being the perfect wife, without fuss or self-pity – and surviving by being good at it. The commitment created its own amazing momentum. All that rebellion fell away.'

Kate said that her husband had been so happy to get back to work. He had missed the structure and the routine, and he took up cycling again, which made him feel better. But he was the one who kept talking about the village, and the chateau. He had kept asking her if she didn't miss it.

'I think he worried I was in denial,' she said. 'And then

one morning I woke up and thought, Oh God, what have I done? I thought, this isn't right at all. I heard the water running. Stephen was in the shower. I lay there thinking about how much I wanted out. Stephen came back into the bedroom and started drying himself. I couldn't look. I couldn't bear to look at him any more. He sat beside me on the bed and he took my hand and asked me if I was all right. I said, "No. I don't want to be here any more".'

'Not with him or not in London?'

'Well, both – not with him, and not in the world at all. Isn't that what it feels like when you're stuck? You can't distinguish what it is exactly that is making you feel so stuck because in my case it seemed like such an awful upheaval having to try to untangle everything. So I tried instead to be better at being married. But that only made me want to burst. So being married and being alive had become the same thing.'

'Did you tell him that?'

'We're always saying, I've had enough. I can't take any more. He'd stopped listening to that.'

'So what did you do?'

'I waited till he'd gone downstairs. I heard him put his bread in the toaster. I put some clothes in a bag. Then I walked downstairs, took my coat off the peg where it hangs in the hall, opened the front door and went.'

Daniel leant forward and put his chin in his hands. This was what he always did. He sat and he listened to women talking about their lives. It was all anyone needed. To feel that they were being heard and understood. And Daniel was good at doing it. And he knew the effect it had on them. After the trust, then he could tease. After he'd won them over with kindness, then he could use his brawn. But there was something about Kate that unnerved him. He felt her sophistication was something he needed to reach, and so sitting here just listening to her wasn't enough. He wanted to say something that would hold her attention but he felt that it wouldn't work in the seclusion of this little house where she was in control and they were both taking refuge. If he could get her back outside, then the balance might begin to shift again and the unease he felt would dissipate.

'Did he follow you?'

'He must have come after me, as soon as he heard the door close. He caught up with me at the train station and scared the life out of me by tapping me on the shoulder while I was waiting to get my ticket. He asked me to go into a café with him and have some tea. I just sat there, at this table, crying in my coat. He asked me if I needed to see a doctor. He looked so forlorn and unhappy then. I asked him – could we perhaps just take a little break from each other? I blamed it all on my mother and how I sensed it had made me depressed and I needed to figure some stuff out. Stephen said I should be with him, living with him, while I did that. Then I asked, had he never felt the need to have somewhere else to be? He looked confused. But worse than that. He looked completely and utterly disengaged. Like he had neither heard me nor even begun to try to understand anything that was going on in my head. He just can't do it, I said to myself. He just can't make the leap. After a few minutes of total silence, his stomach rumbled so loudly it almost made me laugh. He was looking vaguely over towards the sandwiches and then he got up to get an egg and bacon one which he brought back to the table and couldn't eat. So he left it with the wrapper flapping open and the smell making him feel queasy. "It stinks," he said. "The egg really stinks." I said to throw it away. I started to feel desperate then. I told him I had to go and find the bathroom. He looked at me sheepishly. "I'll hold onto your bag," he said, and he reached down and clasped the handles and pulled it onto his lap. It was like he was holding onto our child. I said, ok. And then I left him with it and ran away.'

'How did you get out?'

'I just walked across the station concourse, then stopped at the machine and bought an underground ticket. I wasn't even shaking. I was completely and totally calm. It felt like survival. I had my wallet and passport in my coat-pocket and there was nothing else I needed. I left him in that café holding my bag of clothes. I got straight on the Tube and sat down and watched this woman with a cello putting her make-up on. I think I was barely breathing. And by the time I got to the airport, it was almost midday. I bought a plane ticket, withdrew some money from the bank, ate some bananas and some biscuits for lunch, read the paper from cover to cover in the departure lounge, and then I flew.'

'Good feeling,' said Daniel, biting his lip. His left leg was jiggling ever so slightly on the sofa.

'Yes. The plane landed at Montpellier. It was early in the evening...' Kate smiled, showing her teeth.

He had destabilised something in her now. She swam back up to the surface of her experience and tried to reflect.

'In the end, I found I just couldn't do it. That thing people say about finding freedom within constraint. I found couldn't breathe.'

'Many people find that.'

'I felt sick at the thought that the compromise was all it was going to be. The love died.'

Daniel straightened his leg out to reach his cigarettes. On his knee there was a tuft of hair, from Sylvie's dog, which he brushed away with the palm of his hand.

'I couldn't work out how to live with the fact that my love for my husband had died. I sat on the steps outside the chateau and tried to figure out if I could or couldn't live with it. The dead love. It's so subtle.'

Daniel looked at the shine on Kate's perfectly tanned little cheek. There was barely a spot of imperfection on her, and it bored him slightly, the vanity that came with. He looked down into her cleavage. Her breasts were quite small, tucked neatly into a simple cream bra.

Kate got up. She shook the dress out around her legs. 'And now he's getting on with life as usual. He's getting up and going to work by bicycle. He'll be eating, at 7.30am, a bowl of natural yogurt with walnuts, two pieces of granary toast with butter.'

'Don't feel guilty,' said Daniel, getting up to get the ashtray from the table.

'I don't feel guilty.'

'You will.'

'Not now.'

'No. But you will. When you realise you left him to prove you're not getting old.'

'What?'

Daniel was teasing her. 'I'm kidding,' he said.

'How dare you?'

'You're not old, Kate.'

'No,' she said. 'Not yet.'

She looked at him, and he looked kindly into her eyes and saw how the colour rose to her cheeks. Usually, it made him feel powerful to see this. But with this one he was starting to feel vaguely hopeless. He finished his wine.

'I have to go.'

'Where?'

'I'm overstaying my welcome.'

'Please don't go.' She sat back down on the sofa, right on the edge of it, and folded her hands very neatly on her knees. 'I would like it if you stayed and had at least one more glass of wine with me.'

'Ok,' he said quietly, and he grinned.

'I heard this thing,' she told him, staring out ahead of her into the garden now. 'I heard this thing about children, and how if you lose a child on the beach, you must always walk towards the sun to find it because children naturally walk towards the light. Always.'

'Yes. It makes sense. Because they're frightened of the dark. It's human instinct to go for the light. But there will be some kids, very few, who will go towards the dark. Not many, I think.' Daniel took a deep breath through his nose. 'But then the kids grow up, and they start to become interested in things that are daunting. They test themselves against the forbidden, the subversive, and try to embrace it.'

'It's weird, though, isn't it?' she went on, 'when you find you have stopped doing all of that. You become good at working, having a home, maybe family. You haven't run towards the light for a long time, and you don't bother to meddle with the dark either. You know what you know.

You get on. Because what else is there? And so then you begin to feel that the difference between the dark and the light is fading. First in the imagination, and then in reality. And you know there's war and madness out there. But by then you're cocooned. You've done it to yourself. And what you're left with is this sticky sort of grey matter all around you, like some nasty chrysalis of middle age. And so you take up smoking again. Or you find somebody to fall in love with. Or you walk out on your marriage. But it doesn't really matter, because nothing really changes. You'll never feel that intensity of life – that fear as you ran towards the sun on the beach – that what was behind you was big and black and terrifying, or that thrill as you turned and went towards it that what you were doing was choosing the unknown. You've lived long enough to know you know enough to get by. And the challenges start to lessen. And nothing really moves you all that much. I mean it moves you by surprise, but the brain adjusts and you know what you're doing again. Over and again, you just keep figuring out what it is you're doing. The ability you have to adapt surpasses your longing to be surprised. And so there isn't any real fear or wonder any more. Like that thing at the end of Gatsby. And how in the greyness of everything nothing measures up.'

Daniel nodded.

'And we need to be in awe,' said Kate. 'But we've lost our capacity. And so we beat on. Boats against the current, borne back ceaselessly into the past.'

They talked through the afternoon and into the night. When they got hungry from all their talking, Daniel got up to make them both a sandwich. He put the sandwiches down on the table and she said how drunk she was.

'I'm happy, though,' she said. 'Thank you so much for being here.'

Daniel said he was drunk too. He thought it might be a good idea to have some coffee and, because he was tired of talking, and in need of somewhere quiet to be, he went upstairs and sat for a while in the bathroom and stared out of the window at the east wall of the chateau, lit by the streetlamp.

When he came down, she was curled up asleep on the sofa. Daniel stood for a moment or two and looked at the face that had softened and the lips that had opened slightly. Still her little hand was curled up with tension beneath her chin. He left her like that, and he went upstairs and opened up the shutters which gave him a view onto Sylvie's house. Then he stretched himself out on the faintly scented bed and fell asleep.

In the morning Kate was gone. There was a note on the kitchen table.

'Something's changed,' it read. 'Meet me at the bar tonight at 7 o'clock and we can talk some more.'

Daniel sat in the garden. He picked some blades of grass. He went to see Sylvie in the afternoon but he found that she wasn't there.

'It's a challenge,' said Kate, that night at the bar. She bought a bottle of wine for them to share. And then she bought another.

He agreed with her. He said that yes, it was a challenge. 'But one that I think someone like you will thrive on.'

They were drunk by the time they left the bar that night and Daniel took her hand and they carried on walking past the village house and down the road behind the church.

'Let's walk,' he said quietly. 'It's such a beautiful night.' He linked his arm with hers and they walked slowly under the orange streetlamps, taking the road that curled up onto the heath.

'My mother thought birds foretold the future,' said Daniel. 'She was always out feeding them, watching them from the upstairs window, waiting for one of them to fly right in. She saw the women from the village in the birds that gathered in the courtyard. In their scratching and cawing, she said there was gossiping and picking. She thought the gossips had come to pick out her jewels, and to pick out her eyes. Fear made her blind, more blind than anyone. But she wasn't my real mother, of course. My real mother was Frederic's mother, Sylvie's mother. Her name was Baseema. She was my real mother. She was a prisoner in the castle you want me to sell you.'

'The castle that you will sell to me,' said Kate coquettishly, leaning in on his arm.

'Ha, ha,' he said, lifting a hand out to the side. 'Sell to you. And then I'm free!'

Kate stumbled against him. 'Tell me about your mother.'

'I think of her hands.' He stopped on the road. 'I love to watch women's hands.'

Kate turned to him.

'Could you kiss me, do you think?'

Daniel looked at her then. He saw how pretty she was, how elegant her fingers and wrists. Daniel felt as if, in that moment, he saw the whole woman in her. He saw who she had been, and who she would go on to be. He saw the lover, the friend, the wife; and he saw the mother in her. He placed his hands on her shoulders and kissed her very gently on the lips. Kate shivered slightly, and smiled. He looked into her face, and around her shoulders; he looked at her arms. Something was emerging in her; something light and fluttery trying to push its way out. Daniel was drawn to that and also afraid. He stood back a little on the quiet road. Nothing moved in the air tonight. In him there was nothing emerging, he felt. He wanted to make it. He just didn't know how.

'No one told me that losing someone would feel like this,' she said, almost to herself.

'Like what?'

'Empty. And tired. I feel so tired. I feel like I can't do anything. I can't imagine having the energy to go back and do my job and be in my life. I can't imagine doing it all over again.'

'And yet you have the energy for all this,' he said, looking back, as they began to walk again.

'Is this what happens?'

'What?'

'This tired all time. Is this what it's going to be like?'

In silence they walked together to the end of the runway. The land was still swollen from the heat of the day.

Kate was quiet now. He left her with her thoughts for a

while and walked towards the trees. He cleared the gorse around the spot in swift clean strikes. He leapt up into the lower branches of a pine and swung till the branch gave up. Then another, and another branch. They were spindly as an old woman's arms. He held these arms against his thigh and broke them above and below the elbow.

Kate watched him crouch in front of the fire and she saw the way he worked: clean, and precise. She sat silently beside him. Daniel pressed his lighter into the mound of gorse and watched the dry twigs take flame.

She took her clothes off over her head. He looked up, stood a little to receive them.

Then she sat down, her knees clicking quietly. Daniel looked at her and he thought about how he could love her.

He left the fire then and he moved slowly towards her. They held each other for a long time and then he lay her down on the ground. Beneath him she turned her head to the side and watched the flames burn through the branches. Behind the fire the last of the light was leaving the sky. The silence was filled with the sounds of the fire. It crackled and spat. He could feel her lift up beneath him. He put his fingers to the softness of her hair and he closed his eyes.

They dozed and then woke feeling cold and stiff, and so they dressed and walked back to the village without saying a word.

It was four o'clock in the morning. When they got to her place Daniel asked Kate if she was all right about what had happened up on the heath. It made her laugh, a bit; but she was too tired to deal with it now. She started to make some coffee for them both and then turned the gas off and went upstairs to sleep. Daniel came up and got in beside her. Just before he nodded off, he rolled towards her and whispered into her ear.

'We did it, Kate.'

'Yes,' she said. 'We did.'

Daniel closed his eyes then. Whatever was to come, and he sensed the darkness already, he knew that in that moment at least, up there with this woman in his arms up on the heath, he had been blessed.

—

When he woke it was almost midday. Kate was sitting outside the house in nothing but a long white shirt. Her face was unwashed, her hair unbrushed. She was straddling a chair and spooning yogurt out of a pot.

'Hi,' he called shyly, and she looked up to see him standing in the doorway in his jeans. She gazed at his torso and grinned. 'I can't quite believe this,' she said happily, and she pushed him back indoors so that she could put the coffee on to brew. She chucked him the pack of cigarettes so that he could come sit outside and join her on the steps in the sunshine.

'I don't want to sit outside, though,' he told her, frowning slightly. Then he took a cigarette and lit it and stood for a moment or two rubbing his hand through the back of his hair.

'Ok,' she said, and she leant up and kissed his neck in a light and silly way.

'Any minute now, you'll be asking to borrow my T-shirt.'

But Kate hadn't heard him properly. She was busy humming to herself as she ripped a bag of coffee open with her teeth.

'My T-shirt, it's... upstairs,' he muttered, drawing heavily on the cigarette and watching the ash fall to the tiles on the floor.

'What's that?' asked Kate happily.

He didn't look at her. He walked towards the window and stared out onto the garden. He could feel Kate watching him. She was beginning to notice his mood. After a while, she came up behind him and wrapped her arms around his stomach. She breathed into the warm skin on his back and placed a very gentle kiss between the shoulder bones. He felt the tension ease a little in his shoulders. He felt the sunlight on his face and he watched the garden for signs of life.

'It was lovely, wasn't it?' she murmured into the skin on his back.

He nodded, and then he disentangled himself from her in order to find somewhere to put out his cigarette.

'I could do with a washing machine, to be honest. I've been here several days – since Monday – and I haven't yet had a chance to wash my clothes.'

'You've been here since Monday?'

'Yes. My stuff's at Sylvie's.'

'I guess it just goes to show,' she said politely.

'What's that then?' His eyes were a little narrow now. Something had changed in him. There was this tension in his shoulders, a stiffness in his neck. It was the thought of Frederic that he had woken with; a split second of something deeply uncomfortable that he had pushed out of his mind as he got out of this pretty woman's bed. Her bedroom, her sheets were full of the scent of her. He was tired, perhaps. Now Kate was moving about her kitchen, throwing her hair around in a smug way that made him feel embarrassed. It exposed her conservative side; this slightly pathetic bid for freedom she was making. It was just a fuck. That was all it was. Just a quick fuck up on the heath.

She started to fiddle about in her bag for something. She found a pot of balm and began to apply it to her lips so that they looked a bit greasy. 'Want some?' she asked, for want of something else to say, at which point Daniel began to think it was time to go.

'No, I don't want some. And I have to go now.'

'To get the key to the chateau?'

'Yes. To get the key.'

'I'm feeling really good about it all today,' she said. 'I think I might have the strength for it, after all.'

'Oh!'

'You don't seem pleased.'

'It's so strange, though, isn't it? The world we live in. That you can just make this decision all on your own, Kate. And the only thing it depends on is whether you have the strength for it, or not.'

'That's life, though.'

'Modern life,' he said. 'It depends on nothing but how depressed we are or aren't. And if we aren't then we can get on. And if we are then we can't.'

Kate raised her eyes a little. 'Sorry. Was it something I did?'

'No.'

'Oh,' she said, a little awkwardly.

'Shall I.... shall I come back later?'

'Stay now,' she pleaded, suddenly feeling panicky. 'I don't want you to leave.'

'I think I have to.'

'Why?'

'Because of what happened. Last night. I think that perhaps we did the wrong thing.'

'Why?'

'I don't know. I feel uneasy. I feel like it was exactly what I shouldn't have done, in fact.'

'Oh come on,' she smiled. 'It's not as if I wasn't a consenting adult.'

'No.'

'And it's because of last night that I want you to stay. You see, if you go, then I might start thinking about my husband and I would feel guilty then and that would be terrible.'

Daniel smiled. 'So you want me to stay so we can use each other to not think about everything else.'

Kate laughed. 'It's human.'

'It stinks,' said Daniel.

'But please stay?'

He drew in a breath as she came closer and stood in front of him looking up into his pale eyes.

'Come upstairs,' she whispered sweetly, and her eyes were full of longing. He looked deep into the gold flecks in her brown eyes and he saw all her age and her hope and her desperate need to be someone else, quickly, again, today, before her old life came, and he loved her for that, and he put his arms around her lovely shoulders. He drew her to him and buried his face in the softness of her hair before taking her hand and walking upstairs with her into the roof.

Daniel knew, when he left an hour or two later, that Kate was sound asleep on the bed and she would not have heard the door shutting behind him. He was hungry now and he needed food; he needed a clean change of clothes and somewhere quiet to be by himself for a while.

It was hot in the square. Daniel stood and stared down into the water and tried to focus on that for a while instead of the pain at the back of his head and the dry, tight feeling in his eyes

He took a deep breath and held his head up as he crossed the square to the Mayor's office. Surely it wasn't going to be difficult to get the key to his own house? He opened the front door. The hall smelt of old wood and cleaning fluid. The floor had been mopped. Daniel sat down beneath a ceiling fan that wasn't working and he waited his turn to be seen. His eyes scanned the curling selection of brochures on the local area. Resident, or tourist, he knew that he had just as much right to be here as anyone else. The myth of him prejudiced their judgment and that filled him with dread. He knew that the people who lived in these villages were warm-looking, and appeared vibrant, but that – like old-fashioned teddy bears – their stuffing was a tight, close-knit weave of tradition, convention and a skewed, unexamined morality. Daniel Borja was a complicated tale of unstable mental health – uncertain origins and subversive behaviour. His dark face and mysterious disappearance were exotic enough to have him pop into all their minds when they needed a scapegoat. The fact that he may or may not have been gay, and may or not have murdered his best friend, who was also his half-brother, didn't even come into it. He was Daniel Borja. And the folk of these villages didn't let go of myth any sooner than they let go of the parking space they'd been allocated or the food they'd been eating for the past hundred years. Holding onto what they knew was a way of life. In order to survive, the scapegoat had no choice but to cut himself out of the weave, and run.

The door opened and a woman came out with red-rimmed eyes. Daniel stood up and held the door open for her before going in himself to stand at the secretary's desk.

'I am Daniel Borja,' he said to the secretary, who paused over what she was writing and nodded her head a little before carrying on. She whispered his name to herself as she wrote.

'I'm here to get the key,' he went on.

And still the woman ignored him, and turned her piece of paper over, scanning what boxes on the other side needed to be filled. She flipped open a stamp box and pressed the stamp into its pad of black ink. It made a sticky noise as it pressed down on the paper. She looked up briefly at Daniel as she lifted the stamped form and then averted her eyes again to blow on the ink.

She called through to the Mayor, who had been standing inside the door to his office photocopying something.

'The key for the chateau,' she said. 'It's him.'

Daniel went in and sat down opposite the Mayor, who was wearing a thin grey cheesecloth shirt. He was given a form to fill in. He wrote carefully, and the Mayor watched him, sitting behind his desk with one finger pressed to his nose.

'We were sorry to hear that Madame Borja died,' said the Mayor. Then he coughed to clear his throat and tilted his head to one side as if preparing himself for something that would require a little extra effort or sympathy.

'I was born here,' Daniel said, handing the form over the desk. 'While I'm here it would be good to collect my birth certificate.'

The Mayor nodded. He wrote with his left hand curled backwards around the pen.

'I remember when you were born.'

Daniel stiffened.

'Your father came into the office after you were born to make a declaration of birth. I remember we were all so pleased for your parents. They had wanted a child for so long. You were a miracle, we all said. And particularly with your mother being so much older by then. I remember that they struggled to choose the name. Madame Borja had a list of many many names, she said.' The Mayor paused, and smiled. 'And we were waiting for Monsieur Borja to return the birth certificate so that your name could be entered onto it.'

'And did he?'

'Yes, he did. We have it here. Of course. They went for Daniel.'

'Yes.'

'Which is an odd choice really. Such a Jewish name. Hebrew. I think, if I'm right,' he added, pausing to look carefully into Daniel's eyes.

'Yes,' said Daniel and the two men looked at each other to see who would take the conversation on.

260

'You must find the area quite different?'

'Not at all. It's exactly the same.'

'Exactly.'

'Nothing's changed.'

'And yet, politically,' said the Mayor, leaning back in his chair and teasing a button on his shirt between fore-finger and thumb, 'it could not be more different.'

'The far right's a big fucking problem everywhere. Not just here.'

The Mayor shrugged. 'People are worried. Understand-ably so. About unemployment.'

'The world is changing,'

'And so,' said the Mayor, 'is France. But many people don't like it.'

Daniel shrugged. 'It's life. Many people don't like many things. There's not a lot we can do to change things. Either we get used to it, and adapt. Or...'

'Or...?'

'Or we don't.'

'And then?'

'Well, then, we die.'

And the Mayor laughed then – they both laughed – hard and fast and into each other's faces, as if they were trying to simultaneously catch and repel the air from each other's mouths.

After a while they backed off and they sat in the quiet, hearing the noise of the fan. It seemed that the Mayor was waiting for Daniel to speak, to reveal something about himself. After a while, he shrugged and got out of his chair. 'Who knows?' he said. 'And the question now, of course, Monsieur Borja, is what you intend to do with the chateau.'

'I'm going to sell it. And get out of here.'

'To the English woman?' asked the Mayor, turning from his filing cabinet with a twinkle in his eye.

'If she'll buy it.'

'Will she?'

Daniel shrugged and stood up. 'Who knows?' he said, impatiently and he could feel the tension around his chin and around his mouth. 'Who knows?'

'And then you will leave the village, already, after such a short time?'

The Mayor was speaking quietly. From his filing cabinet he took out a white envelope with some keys inside. 'There are two sets here. One of which I can give to you but first I will have to double-check with the agent,' he said, pulling out a sheet of paper from the envelope on which, Daniel presumed, the estate agent's number was written.

'No,' said Daniel, firmly, and the Mayor flinched. 'I don't think you need to double-check with anyone. The house is mine and the key to the house is mine.'

The Mayor shook his head. 'I'm sorry. But there are rules that...'

Daniel had begun to shake a little. He reached across the table and took the envelope from the Mayor's hand. The way in which he did it was forceful. He took a key from the envelope and then dropped the envelope onto the desk.

The Mayor smiled then and his whole being seemed to give up the smile, which Daniel understood to be a sign of relief, on his part, that the conversation was coming to an end, and the door would soon be closed. Somewhere, between the snatch and the smile, the myth that was Daniel had done its work on the Mayor, and this time, had worked in his favour.

The Mayor wiped the sweat from under his chin with the back of his hand.

'Good luck,' he whispered, and Daniel thanked him and turned to go. 'But wait,' said the Mayor smiling. 'Before you go, please tell me one thing. Who are you voting for?'

Daniel paused and smiled. 'No one,' he said. 'People like me don't hold on to anything or anyone. It's not that there isn't any point. It's just that there isn't anything strong enough to believe in.'

'Strong?'

'Hard enough.'

'Hard?'

'Solid. Real. Tangible.'

'In politics?'

'Yes,' said Daniel. 'Everything's in flux and nobody speaks the truth – nothing lasts.'

'Which is so easy to say,' said the Mayor, with a slight lisp.

But Daniel had turned and walked out of the office then. He said goodbye to the woman who was blushing slightly behind the desk. In fact, it had been hard, he realised as he stepped out into the heat on the square, to get his key, despite the fact that the Mayor had been neither friendly nor surprised to see him, nor rude. Daniel the person was nothing to them at all. But Daniel the myth was already there, sitting down and waiting, in every room.

Across the square he stopped at the bar for a cold beer, and he told Cederic's friend behind the bar that it wouldn't be long before he could settle his tab. It was just a question of finding a way to get to a cash machine, and then he would be able to do it. The girl was picking her hand. She said he could go to the village shop.

'You can use your card there and get some money back.'

Daniel said that was good to know, and he drank the beer back, thanked her for this information and walked quickly in the direction of the shop.

He got there just before it closed for the afternoon and he bought himself some bread and cheese, and a big bright tomato as well as two cans of beer. The woman in the shop came from the north. She had no idea at all who he was. She took his card and she nodded her head and said that, yes, of course, he could have some cash back. There were flies in the shop. She scratched a bite under her arm and looked out of the window while waiting for the payment to go through. Then she pulled the card receipt out and shook her head, saying '*Non,*' because his card had been declined.

Daniel put the food back and returned the cans of beer to the fridge without saying a word.

'You got no other card?' she asked loudly.

Daniel said thank you, but no.

'No cash?'

But Daniel had already left the shop by then and was striding angrily back across the square.

He didn't knock at Sylvie's house, but simply turned the door handle with the intention of leaning his head in to call for her.

It was murky in the front room with the curtains drawn against the sun and the air in there was bad with the smell of old shoes and old dog and old stale cigarette smoke. Daniel went in and found Sylvie lying down on the sofa watching TV. Her hair was wet, again, tucked up under her head, and her white towel was thin and old.

Daniel sat down on the floor beside the sofa and bent his forehead to the side of her waist and nudged it so that she had no choice but to place her hand on his head and play with a curl of his hair while she carried on watching TV.

'What happened?' he asked, quietly, and he felt the energy draining out of him and into the floor.

Sylvie carried on playing with Daniel's hair. He felt his body relax, limb by limb. Then she began to run her fingers up and down the back of his neck. Daniel leant back on the sofa and she kissed his head. They went up into Sylvie's bedroom. She lay back on the bed and took away the towel. She was soft, and white, and innocent. It was slow and gentle. Daniel buried his nose in Sylvie's hair. It was the deepest human comfort he had ever known.

3

Kate wasn't at her house when Daniel returned at dusk. He walked very slowly towards the chateau to find her sitting, once again, on the steps. For a long time he stood in the gateway watching her.

He took in a breath of air and looked around him slowly. The world was bright and suddenly full of colour. Daniel's heart was still.

Kate stood up quickly and backed up against the wall. She was still wearing a white shirt, but she had put shorts on. Her hair was dried so that it shone, immaculate, around the tanned nut of her little face.

Daniel put a hand up to wave. In the village, the dogs were barking.

'Well, you're too late,' she shouted. She waved him backwards. 'I don't know what on earth got into you.'

He walked towards her with his arms outstretched. His heart had begun to thump now but outwardly he was calm and contained. The stakes of his life had been altered this afternoon; the balance tipped in his brain, and now the ground on which he walked had loosened its hold on him. The walls to which he now looked were faded somehow, lesser in height, and stature and impact.

'Come on what?'

'It's me!' he said quietly, and he laughed, feeling the

foolishness in what he had said. She didn't know him at all. He looked at the elegant bones in her face, her teeth.

'So, what do we do?'

'We do nothing. My husband is coming here. He called me. He's coming for the weekend. He'll be here on Saturday. That's two days away. He wants to see me. To talk.'

'Ok.'

'Ok, what? What it's got to do with you?'

Daniel looked up to the windows on the second floor of the chateau. 'It's my house. Does he know that you want to buy this house?'

'I don't want to buy it. I told you. I've changed my mind.'

'But the note you left. You said something had changed.'

'It had. But then we forgot all about it, didn't we? And so now I've changed my mind again. I'd be a bloody fool. I'm sad because my mum died. I'm sad because my marriage didn't work out. Buying a place like this won't change that. I won't feel better.'

Daniel sighed and turned. He could barely hear what she was saying, let alone find the energy to listen. It had been a strange, sad day.

'What do we do then?' she called from the top of the steps.

'With all this longing?' Daniel whispered to himself and he kicked the dead white grass at his feet. The cicada hissed.

Daniel carried on kicking the grass and, because it was painful to be here, because the sadness was all around and through and underneath him suddenly, and there was this bright lovely woman on the steps, and his friend Sylvie was sitting at home curled on her bed in a towel. He walked away and lay himself down beneath the trees and turned his body over so that his face lay pressed against the ground. He heard Kate wandering off and he gave himself up then. Sleep came and overtook him and life carried on without him for a while.

When Daniel woke up, Kate had gone. The courtyard was quiet. The village was quiet. The air was warm, and he felt neither hungry nor thirsty nor anything at all. He lay there and soon he drifted off back to sleep. Just before midnight, he woke again and heard the creak of the gate being opened. There was enough moon to see the spray of her long wild hair and the skirt with bells that tinkled around her ankles as she walked.

Sylvie walked to the middle of the courtyard and she stood for a long time with her hands very straight at her sides. Daniel folded his hands on his chest, lying there like a dead man, praying that she wouldn't see him. What had happened between them this afternoon had happened and there was no going back from that. But the last thing he could bear to do now was talk to her. It was time for him to take his leave, to do the right thing, and go. But his heart, as he lay beneath the trees, was knocking against his ribcage with a new kind of fear that was deep and profound, and about that, and the future, there was nothing at all that he could do.

Sylvie stood in the courtyard for almost half an hour. It was as if she was sniffing the air, knowing he was there, waiting for him to make the first move. After a while, she took something small and wooden, like a large pencil, out of her pocket. She looked about a bit. He saw the scars and the awful swelling and the ghostly whiteness of her face. She smoked a joint, for old time's sake. And then she left.

———

Daniel didn't go back to sleep. For several hours, he lay there with his head spinning in a thousand directions before getting up, rubbing his hands over his face and running across the courtyard, clearing the low wall in a single leap. The morning sky was red.

There up ahead was his father's vineyard and the red rose bush planted to protect the vineyard from disease. There was a rose bush in every vineyard because if something got into the soil it would kill the rose before it killed the vine and then the disease would be known about and something could be done. When they were children, they had talked about this. And they had gone for a walk to see the rose that died to protect Arnaud's vineyard and there beneath the rose bush was where they had found the small white bones.

What happened then was a game they made up, called 'guessing where the bones came from'.

In Daniel's mind, there was a child here before him and this child, born to Arnaud and Lucie when they were young, had died, and that's why Lucie was sad and lay down all the time. 'It's haunted,' he'd told his friends. 'Those bones are the child's bones. They buried it here when it died.'

'Little pile of bones,' he used to sing, skipping up and down.

'The chateau is haunted,' he'd insisted, at seven, eight years old. It was his favourite word. 'There was a child here. It's still here. It talks to me. There's a child in there. Just like me. The same age as me. They brought it here with them. From Paris. She has blotted it out of her mind. But there are clues. Everywhere. A room with a crib in it. Clues. I know. And they came out here, in the middle of the night, buried it by the rose. It died one night in a storm and no one knew. I've seen the actual bones!'

And years later, at the party, on the night that Frederic died, the bones had come up again. No one knew what Daniel and Frederic were doing out in the garden room, a little drunk by then, a little stoned. They were arguing over the bones. Arguing over whose story it was in the first place. Years had passed. Suddenly it seemed imperative to remember things. Frederic was leaving. They were raking over the old times. A way of pretending the body wasn't feeling the tingling. A way of doing away for a moment with the desire. Imperative that they remembered everything. Now. Before they parted. Clutching hold of each other. The others were out in the courtyard, eating, everyone quietly pressing food into their mouths; it was hot that night, so deadly hot and no one knew. Who could know? What could they do? And the little bones, whose story was it? Their lives had been so entwined.

Then yesterday, lying on her bed, Sylvie had said she'd gone to find the bones one day. She'd taken them back to the house and got them analysed. 'They're goat bones,' she said.

Now Daniel flattened his body, pulled himself forward, and felt around on the ground. The small wooden cross that Frederic made was still there, it had fallen on its side. He felt it, ran his finger on the old, soft wood. The tears sprang forward and he pulled himself back, horrified; he stood, used the front of his shirt to wipe the tears away. The mound of earth was still there. The bones would be there beneath it. If there were no bones then there was no reason for the sadness that lived in his childhood home. If there were no bones there was no haunting – Lucie, Arnaud, him. If there was no reason for anything... He messed the earth around with his hands and cut his fingers and grabbed handfuls of dry, dusty soil, but his hands would not clasp the bones.

—

Up on the heath, he cut under low-hanging foliage, pulling back branches of eucalyptus and fern. There were dead leaves, white stones underfoot. The ground was hard and dry. Daniel was hungry and dehydrated but his head was clear. In the trees around the heath, he fell and scraped his leg on a tree. The leaves were black and spun around his head. He laughed because this was all there was, it seemed, left to do. He had done it to Sylvie because that was what she wanted. Not just that afternoon because she was standing in her old bedroom in a small white towel, but because it was what she had always wanted. There was nothing else. Just her on her single bed, sitting herself gingerly down. All she needed was for him to put it in and hold it there. Over and over. That was all she wanted. Then she pulled away, leaving him sore, holding himself. In her little bedroom, which was the same bedroom she had as a child, she had lit a cigarette and asked him to leave. Now he lay on the ground and the leaves spun in dazzling colours and a hawk circled far above the trees and he laughed as if she had knocked the wind and the sense from him.

For lying down with Sylvie was the music of his life. He had felt the smooth white softness of skin around her hips. He had held onto her small dancer's body and cried. They had rocked each other, backwards and forwards, and nothing would have stopped them for all the dark and light in the world.

When he woke, the sun was winking in the trees, warming his face in the clearing. In the village, dogs were barking. The sun picked up flecks of black quartz in the rock. He heard the drill of a woodpecker, his eyes shut. What did he feel? He felt nothing. What Kate wanted from him he had absolutely no idea. He couldn't see the point of her; she could only see what was right in front of her face: him, his face, his pebble-blue eyes, the steps white in the morning, a packet of cigarettes, the silky green of her dress. There was nothing there. Not like the weight of water, memory and fire.

The woodpecker stopped. There was silence in the clearing. Daniel watched the sun move, slide along a spider line of silk

'*Keep going. Keep away.*'

He had promised. To live the life. He had promised, pressing the feet hanging, swinging, towards his mouth, that Frederic's death would not be in vain, that when he got out there, into the world, he would take in everything, and not look back. He stood. 'I didn't kill him.' Sylvie had been laughing; he was hard in her, she was asking him to say something that would help her. A surprise, she wanted. Her hand was pressing into his back as she gasped and cried and the dim, distant untrod pathways of her life came to fruition, and burst.

He had looked down at her face which was wet with tears, and her breasts were loose, a towel removed, the blankets of her childhood old and soft beneath them. Sylvie had asked him to move. After a while, she begged him to move; her face was small, and creased with all the years of pain. When he came, she did nothing. Her life felt complete. She closed her eyes.

———

Kate was wearing a black dress. She had put red lipstick on because, she told him, 'one had to make the effort sometimes'. She was sitting at one of the tables, beside the fountain. She smiled politely at him. Her hair was a little wet still; it curled softly around her face. She looked young and happy and full of life.

'Hello, stranger. Where on earth have you been?'

'I had to get away for a while,' he said.

'Oh,' she said glibly. 'Well, Stephen got held up so he's not coming till tomorrow now. And I'm celebrating by drinking vodka all on my own here – it being a Saturday night, of course.'

'Can I join you?' asked Daniel, tucking his T-shirt into the belt of his jeans.

'*Bien sûr*,' she replied, and she inclined her head to encourage him to sit down.

'You look a little rough. Are you all right?'

Daniel smiled and tried to wipe the dust from his face. He looked around the square and took in the tables where a few tourists were sitting with glasses of beer, chatting quietly and leaning back in their chairs after long days in the sun.

'I guess I need a shower. I camped out. I'm starving. How've you been?'

'Pretty well. I spent most of the morning in the garden, actually. Then I had a siesta, and then did some drawing. And now I'm here…'

'Looking lovely,' he said, and he smiled at her. He was starting to feel a little more like himself. Sip by sip, outside a bar with a beautiful woman, he would become more like himself. The night was warm and starry and full of the smell of summer in the country, but this was the kind of urban chat he knew. It was who he was now. There was no time to change.

'So I wonder if anyone lost their kid on the beach to-day,' he said calmly, indicating for the bartender to come over.

Kate leant down for her handbag and opened it. She took her purse out and uncurled a cheque which she handed across the table.

'Half,' she said. 'Half on signature of contract.'

Daniel studied the cheque. He sat back and put his hands up above his head. He took a long and very deep breath.

'What contract?'

'The one we're going to draw up,' said Kate. 'I don't think we need to bother with agents and lawyers and so on. Do you?'

'Er…'

'I mean it's not as if I feel you're in any way inclined to come back here, Daniel Borja,' she said, in English.

Daniel looked at the cheque sitting on the table. When the bartender came he placed his palm over it. Then he drank the vodka.

'How do you feel?' he asked quietly.

'Fantastic!' said Kate. 'I've gone and damn well done it.'

'Half of it. You've gone and done half of it.'

'Which is a start.' And she grinned then, showing him her startling white teeth. 'I thought it through. And then I thought it through again. And then last night I tried to find you to talk about it a bit more but I couldn't find you anywhere. So I had to just sit and figure it out on my own. And that's what I did. And it needed to be done. Before Stephen gets here. But he's bought me a little more time. He got held up.'

'Yes, so you said.'

'What?'

'About the new start,' he said, frowning slightly, because he sensed the tension that the cheque, and the sale, had now created between them.

'Are you all right?'

'Why?'

'Well, because you're talking in riddles. I didn't say anything to you about a new start.'

275

'I know,' he said. 'Ignore me. I'm thinking about some-one else.'

'Who?' said Kate. 'What's wrong?'

'Sylvie,' said Daniel, and he leant back in his chair and breathed and he looked over the square to Sylvie's house.

'Sylvie?'

'I'm worried about her,' he said. 'I'm worried about what will happen to her if I leave.'

'Oh, Sylvie will be fine. I've already spoken to her about it all. When I went to find you last night and couldn't, she said she didn't know where you were and so she invited me in for a drink and I told her I'd made my decision and that I was going to buy and would she consider helping me when I moved in, finally, to get the place going again.'

Daniel nodded. He said nothing. Kate was drinking fast. There was a high, manic energy about her that un-nerved him.

'Her father was there. Lollo? Strange man. But he seemed pleased that the chateau was being sold. In fact, he was delighted. Kept saying it.'

'Kept saying what?'

'How delighted he was.'

'Oh,' said Daniel. 'I try to avoid him.' He looked around the square again.

'You ok, Daniel?'

He shrugged, and turned his attention to the chateau wall.

'Look,' she said impatiently. 'I know you think I'm crazy. I'm obsessing about it to make up for the lack in my life. But it's not my fantasy, you know. There are far more glamorous locations in this world. Like an island, for example. A beach house somewhere. I love it. But my love is far more practical than you think. I am going to *do* things with it, Daniel.'

'But it is your fantasy.'

'I'm forty,' she murmured.

Daniel looked at the pulse of light in her eyes. Then he tried to reach across the table for her hand and he took her wrist by mistake. He shook the wrist a little.

'We are lucky, though,' he said, looking at her hands. 'To have this, don't you think? This human skin, and lovely eyes. To have loved, to be able to love again.' He let her hand go then. 'I will be going back to Paris in a few days.'

Kate was quiet. 'I was joking. About your not coming here again.'

'I can't stay here. There's too much of my past to contend with. Being here again is a little like standing in a great big hole. It terrifies me. And I need to get away.'

'It's so still.'

'What?'

'The night. The air here.' She lifted her drink. 'So what do we do now?'

'Now?' he asked, lifting his drink. She lifted hers. 'Now, we drink.'

'And then...?'

'Then?'

Kate smiled. After a while, she stopped. She reached across the table and took his hand. She held onto it, cradled it in her own.

'It was nice though, wasn't it? It was more than nice. I mean, it wasn't absolutely amazing, but it was a start. We could love each other, couldn't we, Daniel? We could learn to do it, I think. And try and make something of this. I mean, here we are, two people, similar, free, looking for something to do.'

Ha laughed and his eyes were bright and radiantly blue. 'Speak for yourself,' he said. 'Me? I have a life back in Paris. I have a job and a home and a life...'

'And yet, to me, you make it all sound so temporary. As if you've built your whole life on not being attached to anything, not being stuck anywhere.'

'I'm standing in a hole, Kate.'

'Me too,' she said, and laughed. 'Which is why we should do something to help each other get out.'

'You don't need my help. Not you. I suspect you don't need anyone's help.'

'Women need reassurance.'

'So do men.'

'We all do. All the time. Isn't that sad?'

Up above them the leaves began to rustle quietly in the dark. Daniel thought of the feet hanging from the ceiling. Of the grubby children whose faces had first peered over the wall. Those faces were all he had.

'It's not worth the money,' he said suddenly. 'It's less than what you imagine it to be. When it happens, when you have the key in your hand, then you will feel the disappointment. And the disappointment will be the thing that destroys you.'

'You think I'm just one of those women that run from one thing to the next as and when the feeling takes me. But I'm not like that at all. I stay, I fight. I try to endure. But society doesn't trust women who strike out on their own. It upsets everything they hold dear in their innermost hearts. So they all try to stop it.'

—

Around her neck she had tied a necklace of tiny colourful beads. It was a small attempt at lightness, at some kind of happiness, and the necklace against her skin and her black dress and collarbones looked forced and hopelessly out of place.

'I'm sorry, Kate,' he said.

'Don't be sorry…. It was so hot today. Wasn't it? Stephen says he can't manage without me. Which is why he wants to come and get me. To take me back to the city. And while I was thinking about how really awful that was, it occurred to me that I might as well get on with things. That life – the one I had with him – is over. I need to start again. And so we should just be terribly adult about it, I think. Make each other a proposition. Discuss what we want.'

'I need my solitude, Kate.'

'Come on, Daniel. You've got the cheque,' she said, and she took her hands away from his then, which encouraged him to take it and put it in his pocket.

'I have to go,' he said.

'You can stay with me tonight. We'll have some breakfast together. Then we can go in and take a look.'

'A look?'

'And think about how we're going to do it.'

Daniel was starting to feel a bit panicky. Kate was talking fast.

'You're not listening to me,' she persisted, a little aggressively. 'We could just give all the rooms upstairs a lick of white paint and stick a double bed, a couple of chairs, an old wardrobe in each. In town, there are these bric-a-brac places where you can pick up tatty old furniture, but proper wooden furniture, for next to nothing, aren't there? And the point is, we would then be able to keep it feeling rustic, a bit shabby, which is what people love, it's what they need when they want to stretch out a bit.'

'Kate, listen to me...'

'No. Look. I've been making plans. I've done all these drawings. You should come and see. I want to create a space that is beautiful and tranquil, and simple. More than anything else, it's about simplicity. I want to provide people with an empty canvas, somewhere they can come and be, and drift around the overgrown garden and create things, paint if they feel like it, or not, if they don't, and do nothing maybe for a few days. It's going to be whatever they want it to be. So long as they can have the space and the time. And the peace and quiet. To find out what it is they want to make of it... I think a bed and breakfast basically, with a café downstairs that has pictures on the walls from the summer art school.'

'A school?'

'Or a music school. We could make things work, you know. You and me. I think it's fine. We could take it on and fill it with life. With new life. We could have a baby, Daniel. Couldn't we? Isn't that what you want? For us to be together and have a nice time?'

'It's not so simple as that.'

'Oh God, I know. But maybe it could be. What's the point in having things all complicated?'

'I'm not ready,' he said, but she didn't seem to have heard him.

She continued: 'Because what's the point? After all the thinking. It's just you and me, feeling a bit lost. I think we join forces on that. Take two lost people and put them together to make two not-so-lost people. And I could have a baby and we could work on the chateau – work so hard together – all through the winter, making it brilliant. There would be enough money left from the money Mum left me. We could do it, Daniel. Don't you see?'

'No,' he said, and he stood up from the table, and knocked into it then. 'I have to go. I'll see you tomorrow.' And then he walked briskly across the square. Daniel walked on past the chateau and he kept going down the avenue of trees. He walked faster and he took the wallet out of his back pocket, pulling the cheque out to see it again and remind himself that it was real, and then he started to run.

SYLVIE

10th January 2007
From: sylviepépin@aol.fr
To: Baseemapépin@aol.fr
Subject: It's going to be ok!

Dear Ma
Yes, of course, I understand your concerns but
please, be reassured, this is a responsibility I feel
I can deal with. If I know anything, Ma, then I
do know this: I want to have this child. I know
that it will be harder to go it alone but there are
many more single mothers in this world than there
used to be and, to answer your question about the
father, it is quite impossible to contact him since I
don't even know where he lives. There is nothing
I can say except that last summer was a strange
one for many people. There was a lot going on
in the village (for a change) and there were many
foreigners here. They make it feel as if the
holidays will never end. And then there's the
heat, and it makes people crazy. After all that
had happened with the chateau, and Daniel
coming and going like that, and then Kate and
Stephen hightailing it back to London with no ex-
planation. It meant that those of us who were left
here had to rouse ourselves. Me, and Dad,

and Coco even, we went out a bit more and we sat
for the very end of the summer out in the square,
and we talked a bit about all the stuff that had
happened and then we met these nice people from
Europe – Switzerland, I think – and one of the
men was about my age and he was quite nice and
shy at the same time and one thing led to another.
No, of course, I had no idea that I would be left
with child. But Ma, I have never felt so alive.
Please try to understand this.

 Love,
 Sylvie xx

      ——

10th January 2007
From: Baseemapépin@aol.fr
To: sylviepépin@aol.fr
Subject: Re: It's going to be ok!

Dear Sylvie
Having a child is a wonderful thing and I
would not want you to think that I don't support
you in whatever you choose to do. I think you
are brave to go it alone. Things are improving
in this country for single mothers. More than
anything, though, you live in a wonderful village
and have many friends who will always be there
to help you.

 My main concern, I think, is that your father
will become an extra burden to you and that the
last thing you will want to be doing is

caring for him, while trying to raise a child. I wish that men were better able to care for themselves but they aren't, and I feel that I must at least offer to take him off your hands. God knows how I am loving my solitude at last in these mountains. The cabin has been repainted and I have hung new curtains. How blissful and quiet and clean it all is. And yet…

But I do understand how motherhood can be for the first time, Sylvie. Perhaps, it would be helpful for me to start thinking about taking some time off work in order to be able to come and stay with you around the time of the birth.

Let me know your thoughts.

xMa

13th February 2007
From: sylviepépin@aol.fr
To: Baseemapépin@aol.fr
Subject: Re: It's going to be ok!

Dear Ma
Thank you for your email. But please don't worry. There is a plan coming into action here but I need another week or two before I can confirm.

Sylvie xx

20th February 2007
From: sylviepépin@aol.fr
To: Baseemapépin@aol.fr
Subject: Re: It's going to be ok!

Dear Ma

At last I can tell the news, which is that Kate
Glover has arrived in the village and has begun her
work renovating the chateau.

We had heard rumours that she was set to come
back in December but it seemed she was waiting for the weather to improve. Of course, I was
waiting for her the day she arrived. Lollo said that
I shouldn't make such a fuss but I wanted to be
there in the courtyard to welcome her and I made
sure that she had some provisions inside. In the
end, she came quite late and she was so tired. It
was a shock to see her, to discover the condition
she was in – quite frail, she was, and seemingly
depressed. I offered to stay for a bit and help her.
I told her it was actually quite convenient, in fact,
what with Dad and all his smoking going on at
mine.

She told me what had happened in very plain
and simple terms. How, back in August, when her
husband came down for the weekend, they had
this terrible row. They were trying to eat a meal in
a restaurant. It went from bad to worse. She said
she had never seen him like that. He was like a
maniac. They were both drunk. He strapped her
into the car and locked all the doors. He didn't
drive back to the village. He simply turned for the

motorway and drove north.

They got back to England and Kate became depressed. Suddenly she didn't have the energy for anything, let alone leaving him. It took her six months, she said, to find it in herself to leave again.

But the good news is ...She's here, and she was so excited to see the bump. And she has asked me to think about setting up home here – we both agreed that we'd like the company and there is more than enough space.

I tell you, we got our work cut out! We've hired a skip and we've been putting all the old odds and ends in there as we go. First of all I found some stuff in the roof and this was a surprise to everyone because the general assumption was that old Arnaud Borja hadn't kept hold of a thing. Completely empty was what we all thought of the place. And how wrong we were!

I found all manner of things up in the roof. There were two lumpy old mattresses that were thin and good for nothing but the skip. There were books up there, and magazines like from the fifties! Some of them were really hilarious and Kate was quite fascinated when I brought them all down for her to see. We made coffee and went through all the pictures. How we laughed to look at those women with their pointy breasts and swinging skirts, and then we talked about you, and she, and I – all of us – getting on, not wearing things to make us look more feminine just to

please men but doing exactly as we pleased when
we wanted to and how brilliant and bold we were.
We drank to that, Ma, and we put this lovely old
red ceramic hen out on the table in the kitchen,
with a couple of the olive jars and sugar and salt
jars I found up in the roof. Anyway, we're keeping
our matches in the hen for the time being and it's
fun to have a special place for things that we've
picked together. It does mean such a lot to me, to
be setting up house with her. Which may sound
weird to you but it isn't, Ma. It really isn't. You
see, from my experience of Arnaud and Lucie and
you and Dad and now my experience of Kate and
Stephen, it seems to be that marriage is doomed.
How can anything retain its dignity beneath the
barrage of bills and worries and regrets and just
plain old bad luck that comes and rolls over a marriage day after day?

Well, it's like the Berlin Wall's come down or
something. Now anyone can come on in and
wander round the courtyard. And though they
don't really come in and do anything, it's still
nice for everyone to think that they can. Like old
Mr Surte who came in this morning and
just walked to the pine tree, turned round and
went back again to sit on his bench by the
church.

Of course we haven't done an awful lot. And
there was so much cleaning and sweeping that
needed to be done at first. You have never SEEN
so much DUST!

I have already started work on a nursery and I

have painted the shutters in the room right up at the top a lovely pale blue. I just love to sit in that room and look out at the view and run my fingers over the lettering in the wall where you carved your name when you were waiting in there to have Daniel. I feel so completely and deeply at peace in that room, and I think it has been a great comfort for Kate to have me around. It really is an enormous amount of work that she needs to get through with the place and she barely stops working from the minute she wakes up until she goes to sleep at night. You can imagine how slow she's going to be, climbing on and off ladders while painting. There's no question she needs me there – not just to clean as she works but also to make a little food to keep us going, to get provisions from the shop and also to provide her with the company and the healing that she needs.

I told her all about trauma and how I believe it creates its own energy field and she seemed quite interested in that and so we have been working together on the visualisation techniques they taught me at the burns hospital in Toulouse. You see, I also know that pain is all there is sometimes. But I think, you know, that this is fine. I am here and am able to do all the errands that she needs me to do for her.

Love,
xSylvie

2nd March 2007
From: Baseemapépin@aol.fr
To: sylviepépin@aol.fr
Subject:

Dear Sylvie

This morning I received a cheque in the post. It
was for 12,000 euros. There was a note with it.
From Daniel. The postmark on the envelope was
Paris. It said, simply, that he had managed to sell
the chateau back in August as I might have heard.
He said he was sorry that this amount of money
wasn't what he was hoping to send me but that
he'd had to pay off some other stuff and attend
to things in Paris. Things were a bit complicated.
He said he was going abroad on Monday but that
he intended to be in touch when he got back in a
few weeks in order to meet up. Maybe, he said,
we could meet in Paris. He signed off with just his
name, and that was that.

I have decided to give you the money, Sylvie.
Tomorrow afternoon I will go down into town as
I have some errands to run, and then I will talk to
the bank about transferring the money to you. I
know that, in time, you will need this money more
than I. As for the note, well... I don't quite know
what to make of it. I guess I will keep it though,
nonetheless. It was written on a piece of old air-
mail paper.

Did the bedspread arrive ok? Does it work with
the cushions? Is your dad all right?

Ma xx

—

8th March 2007
From: sylviepépin@aol.fr
To: Baseemapépin@aol.fr
Subject: Thanks

Hi Ma
The money has arrived in my account. I don't
know what else to say.
Sylvie

—

8th March 2007
To: Baseemapépin@aol.fr
From: sylviepépin@aol.fr
Subject: Re: Thanks

Dear Sylvie,
Are you ok?
    Ma

—

8th March 2007
From: sylviepépin@aol.fr
To: db3985@aol.fr
Subject: some money has arrived

Dear Daniel
You sent a cheque to Baseema, which she has now

sent to me. I just wanted to say... well, thank you
for thinking of us.

    xSylvie

9th March 2007
From: sylviepépin@aol.fr
To: db3985@aol.fr
Subject: hello!

Hi Daniel

It was a bit of a shock to get this news from you.
I don't think we ever expected to hear from you
again. Let alone receive any money. How are you
doing? This is what I forgot to actually ask you
when I emailed you yesterday. Are you ok? That's
all I really wanted to say. We never found out what
happened to you. As with before, one minute you
were there, and the next you were gone.
But I guess you went back to Paris?
xSylvie

12th March 2007
From: sylviepépin@aol.fr
To: db3985@aol.fr
Subject: hello!

Hi Daniel
It's nice now in the village. You get the sense

that spring is in the air. There's so much going on here, and we're all terribly busy with one thing or another. But it would be great to hear from you if you're not too busy and you get a chance to reply. Your note said that things were complicated…

Hope all's going well with you. It would be really great to just hear a few words from you.

—

13th March 2007
From: sylviepépin@aol.fr
To: db3985@aol.fr
Subject: hello!

Daniel? Can't you even reply to me? S

—

29th March 2007
From: sylviepépin@aol.fr
To: db3985@aol.fr
Subject: important

Dear Daniel
There is something that I feel you should know.
Please be in touch with me. It's important.
xSylvie

—

29th March 2007
From: sylviepépin@aol.fr

To: db3985@aol.fr
Subject: important

Dear Daniel
I can't do this on email. Please be in contact with a
number so that I can ring you.
xSylvie

—

17th April 2007
From: Baseemapépin@aol.fr
To: sylviepépin@aol.fr
Subject: Daniel

Dear Sylvie
Just to let you know that I haven't heard again
from Daniel since he was supposed to have returned from his trip abroad. I never thought that
things would change since his return to the village
in the summer but then one day I found myself
thinking that it might be nice to get together with
him for Christmas or something. How foolish to
be so wanting... much better, I know, to learn to
be self-sufficient, which you must do with your
child... I always hoped that when he knew the
truth about his birth he would want to see
me. But I suspect he feels it's too late for
reconciliation.
   Did you spend any of the money yet? Don't let
your dad squander all of it. Make sure that you
hold enough back for yourself, Sylvie. And do

something with it that makes you feel happy.

I think of you and know what it is you are going through and I know how calm it can make you feel to be carrying a child.

Keep me posted.

Ma xxx

—

18th April 2007
From: sylviepépin@aol.fr
To: Baseemapépin@aol.fr
Subject: Daniel

I have loved Daniel Borja for almost all of my life, Ma. I know who he is and what he is like. He may have been around the world and seen all kinds of things and he seems, when you talk to him now, like the most easy-going man on earth, but in his heart he's a flaker. He won't be tied down because in his heart he doesn't believe in anything. He'll never commit himself; he won't sign up. He doesn't trust.

I knew that he would simply up and run for the hills. That's life, Ma. We can't change.

And sometimes I think how strange it is that everyone – you, me, Frederic, Lucie, Arnaud Borja, even Kate Glover – we have all loved him so much, and we still love him, yet he is like the empty heart at the centre of us all. He is what binds us together. And yet who is he? What does he do for us? Into him we have all thrown so much of ourselves.

And then sat in the silence that follows when nothing comes back to us. We shout; he doesn't echo.
He is already gone. He runs and runs and yet he is
carried by all of us.

Sylvie x

P.S. Yes, I have spent some of the money. I have
bought all that I need for the nursery and I spared
no expense. It is like a dream in that room now.
A brand-new cot and a brand-new mobile, and
beautiful curtains and sheets and a desk of drawers which is handpainted with little white butter-
flies. Kate is thrilled with it too. Almost all of her
rooms are painted white like this. And we keep all
the shutters open and all the internal doors shut
so that each and every time when you come into a
room you are almost blinded.

—

29th April 2007
From: sylviepépin@aol.fr
To: Baseemapépin@aol.fr
Subject: Hi Ma

I'm sorry to hear about Paul Borja having died.
Was it cancer? Had he had it for a while?

And thanks for sending Lucie's journal. I know
that Kate is keen to read it, though I did tell her
that you found it mostly unreadable. I can't see
what there would be of interest in it, anyway.
Didn't you say that all she did all those years was

sit up there in an annexe room above Paul's flat going on and on about the past?

Ma, what a time it's been. Aside from the impending birth, there is so much to do in preparation for our first guests in August. Two of the rooms are booked already and the first of the landscape courses has already got five students booked in for the second week in August. Kate and I will take it in turns to go to the classes I expect – though, as you can imagine, there will be a huge amount to do back at the ranch. It's getting warmer up on the heath in the day now and the light is good, still clear. I will remember this for when it comes to the painting class for next year. Kate is really obsessed with it all. For now, though, she is only expected to draw.

(Did I tell you I cut a lovely thick fringe? Should have done it years ago!)

But I'm far too busy for idle chit-chat these days! I've set up an office in a corner of the chateau kitchen and brought the PC over. We've got a faster internet connection too, which is excellent for our marketing.

As for the bump, well goodness me! I had no idea at all that I would feel this enormous and there's no question that it will be a relief when this baby is at last born and I have my body back to myself again! I'll keep you posted.

xSylvie

29th June 2007
From: sylviepépin@aol.fr
To: Baseemapépin@aol.fr
Subject: pictures of Ruby

Dear Ma
I thought you would like to see these pictures Kate
took out in the garden this morning.
Everyone in the village thinks that she is the most
beautiful baby anyone has ever seen. The doctor
tells me that the birthmark will just fade in time so
we don't need to worry too much.

I am absolutely flat out, Ma, what with this
and the business. But thanks so much for your help
and for your kind words.

Love

xSylvie

P.S. Kate read the journal. She said it was really
interesting.

16th August 2007
From: sylviepépin@aol.fr
To: Baseemapépin@aol.fr
Subject: Re: pictures of Ruby

Dear Ma
Here are some more pictures of Ruby that Kate
took in her nursery. Doesn't she look so sweet
when she is sleeping? You will see that I moved
things around a little in her room. I think it looks

better with the wardrobe against the back wall now.

It has been a strange time with this very hot weather. At the beginning of August the temperature began to soar and the leaves dried out around the fountain. Kindly, Sandrine from the shop was able to take Ruby out in the pushchair for a few afternoons walking up and down the avenue of trees, which allowed me to take a break from her and from the guests and just lie on my bed upstairs and listen to the cicada throbbing in the trees, not stopping until nine or ten at night – such a sound that I have wondered, lying awake in siesta time, how the visitors would ever concentrate on their painting. Yes, it has been so hot... I have cooked and cleaned and organised picnic lunches. And I have noticed all the time Kate spends sitting out in the courtyard chatting to the guests, and carrying on with that old tutor the way she does. I wouldn't be surprised if he doesn't jump her, the way she carries on. It's a relief to think that the courses will soon be at an end and then she will be able to spend a bit more time with me and with Ruby.

But all in all we are well. This morning I was wearing the long black linen dress you sent me. I had to change after lunch because I got so much milk on me but it was nice to see that it does fit! Everything else in my wardrobe is way too small.

This afternoon I wanted to take Ruby for a walk and photograph the houses in the square with the doorways and the paint peeling off the shutters and the roses bobbing gently on the balcony. The brochures we are putting together had come out very expensive on the first quote but I decided to take this aspect of the business into my own hands and spend some more of the money that Daniel sent on marketing.

How very clear and uncomplicated is this way of life, Kate said to me when we first started work on the chateau. And how very real. How lucky, she said, that we were born here where things were so much clearer – clear from the beginning. I thought she was being horribly patronising when she said this. So then we had this big debate about how people like her romanticise life in these villages when in reality it's not romantic at all. But the thing is, Ma, I begin to know what she means as I walk about in the streets here with Ruby and sit outside the café in the square where everyone stops to lean into the pushchair and talk to me and my baby and asks how we are.

I breathed very deep here this afternoon. Of the air and the roses and the dusty smell of these houses, of the people sleeping back to the beginning of time, their hearts full of the sun and human kindness. And I wrote this down in my notes for the brochures, Ma. Because it just seemed so right. 'Full of the sun and human kindness.'

2nd October 2007
From: sylviepépin@aol.fr

To: Baseemapépin@aol.fr
Subject: Re: pictures of Ruby

Dear Ma

October now and the square is deserted. The fountain is working properly again but the pool is full
of leaves. The shop hasn't changed hands, but they
have got rid of the old people's clothes and started
selling other things like towels and bath mats at
the front of the shop. I suggested to Kate that we
bought some for the chateau bathrooms but she
didn't like the quality and so she decided to buy
them from England online. For the New Year they
will have a box of fireworks on the counter in the
shop. This morning we heard that an old wine-
maker from the next village died falling under the
wheels of his tractor, and there will be a funeral
on Tuesday.

The grapes have just about been gathered now
and the Spanish kids who came for the harvest
have gone back home, which, as always, is a relief
to all the residents because they were more noisy
than ever this year and no one liked them hanging
about in the square. It's mostly the old people here
who are not very tolerant. I was discussing this
with Kate, you know, and she said, well, whose
world is it anyway? It's not about land, though,
is it? It's just humans getting irritable with each
other and trying to survive with the old problems
of weather and money. But still, there is this tolerance issue. The Mayor told me that things are only
going to get worse and worse with the suburb

situation in Paris. There are not simply not enough jobs.

But dad is getting a shift or two in the café. And I am cleaning as much as I can.

It was a hot summer, this year, people said. But not too bad.

Some new parking spaces have been marked up outside the church. A baby has been born to Marie and Guy's daughter who has come to live in no. 15 on the square. I hope that she and Ruby will be friends.

Nothing else has changed. Nothing anyone could write to anyone about. The village is quiet, with that blue in the mornings and that air of tranquility that Kate tells me she first fell in love with. Just wait till she finds all the mice coming in off the fields…

EPILOGUE

3rd March 2011
From: sylviepépin@aol.fr
To: db3985@aol.fr
Subject: Hi!

Dear Daniel
Thanks for your message. You're too late, I'm afraid. Kate isn't here.

She sold the chateau because she couldn't afford to keep it on. We were ok for a couple of years and we ran some art courses. We had a bed and breakfast, of sorts, with six excellent rooms. People really loved it here. They came once and then they came again.

We painted the whole thing white. It was really beautiful – so clean and bright. And then we started working in the garden. Kate was like a demon about it all.

But there were problems always with the roof and the damp and the wiring in the chateau and our third winter was terrible. Kate got heavily into debt and there was nothing any of us could do. We tried our best to patch the place up but, quite honestly, it felt like we were putting the smallest of plasters over the largest of lesions and in the end, the cracks became too great; the roof caved in.

Kate left six months ago. She had a brief relationship with an art tutor but she couldn't bear another winter here. So she decided to go back to her husband. As it turned out, she had really begun to miss him. I think she found that life was easier with the compromises of marriage, after all. I'm sorry to learn that you've been thinking of her in that way, which your letter makes absolutely plain.

The village is back to normal. And the new people who bought the chateau haven't arrived yet. They might come next summer but probably not this one. At least, that's what people in the village are saying. They're not from America. They're just European. No one really knows where they live.

So the chateau just sits there now, as before, quietly rotting away.

I have moved back into my old house with my daughter, Ruby. Her father is Swiss but we have no contact. Lollo lives with us too. But his health isn't great. I'm not sure how much longer he will be around.

I wonder if you have found a way to make it all work for yourself, wherever you are. Perhaps you have found a way of keeping yourself aloof. The joy of work, as our mother would say. Perhaps that's the only way. She's content. Then again, in his own way, so is Dad – now that he lives here again, with the only life he ever knew. I don't know about the rest of us. The next generation. What a muddle we seem to have got ourselves in. I

have tried to visualise clearing the muddle in order
to gain some control and sometimes I have felt
rather close to it all.

As for Kate, well, I thought we were friends
but I haven't heard a peep from her. It's mostly a
shame for Ruby, who misses her too.

But, honestly, we are fine. Life just goes on.
I don't think that, if I were you, I would think
of coming back here, though. You won't find
anything here for you, Daniel. It is as it was and
always will be. Not your world, certainly. As you
said to me when you came back here, there's so
little here. It made you feel empty. But where you
are isn't what it's about, I don't think. Before I had
Ruby I was hollow too. Perhaps that's the same for
everyone. But the beauty of living in a place like
this is that no one will let you feel lonely. We sit
and we watch each other's children run round the
fountain. And that, I think, in the end, is all we
really need.

xSylvie

P.S – A few years ago, Ma sent me Lucie's journal.
It seems that Lucie's nephew Paul sent it to her
from Paris. It was mostly unreadable – inane and
deluded mutterings from a woman going mad. But
inside one of the pages was a letter gone a bit yellow. It was written the night you left and Frederic
died. She must have written it when she went up
to bed and we three were in the garden room. It's
strange to think that she might have been up there
writing it while you and I were passed out and

Frederic was quickly dying.

I thought it was quite beautiful when I read it.
I don't think anyone knew she could feel or write
like that. There's something in it about the house
and the bird that really stuck in my mind. And it
just goes to show how there are, in all of us, these
moments of real brilliance, Daniel. And the rest so
murky, so misunderstood.

The heat of the day has gone now. It's lovely and cool up here. And I am cool, my blood is quiet, so still; there is hardly a heartbeat. I am almost asleep. You've nothing to fear.

After everyone left, I came upstairs and went through all the rooms, opening doors and opening up the shutters; feeling the air at last. How the chateau seems to love having the air blow through it. You can almost hear it sigh. This summer has been so hot. It's no wonder things have got so bad.

Sometimes, in my dreams, I see this old house and I see myself as a young woman, newly married, and arriving here, stepping round to look in at the windows, drawing closer to peer in. I go backwards and forwards. In my sleep I feel the rocking motion as I step closer and then back away from the walls, and I never get to seeing what's actually inside before I find I am sitting upright and wide awake. It is always just the outside, and all the doors and the windows blowing open, leaves drifting in.

I've been watching you from the balcony, moving around in the courtyard, night after night, kicking up stones. I cannot imagine what hurts you, Daniel. Always, you seem to be fighting with someone. Fighting with Frederic and Sylvie, fighting with your father, fighting with me.

Come inside. Come sit with me for a while. We don't

have to think about anything. Not necessarily. Not here,
not now. We'll sit in our chairs by the window, looking
out on the garden, hearing the cicada beating themselves
in the trees. Just as it used to be. Summer nights. When
you were young. We'll talk about things. Nothing heavy.
Only things that are separate to us, like the lines of
basalt etched on the moon, or the distance between us
and the stars. We used to consider how long it would
take a car to get us to the nearest star… if you could picture the road. Remember? And politics. You always liked
to talk of politics. The things occurring in Paris,
the problem of immigrants.

The hours will pass and we will be happy enough
together, as we always were, content in the silence,
feeling the comfort of having each other near… Then
it will be time to sleep and maybe, after all the wine
and the party, we'll not bother to go to bed but drift
off to sleep in our comfortable chairs. And I'll thank
you, before I go, for the table you carried out into
the courtyard, and for the lanterns you hung in the
olive trees, such lovely Chinese lanterns, gold and
green, the colours I love, for my birthday.

You'll ask me to tell you again the story of when
we came here, your father and I, and there was nothing
here but the birds and a big empty house. And how for
months we lived only in the kitchen, eating whatever the
garden would provide. We were all scavengers after the
war, Daniel. We were all so hungry, even the birds.

You'll ask me again about the day the crow came in
and flew at me while I was making the lunch, and I'll tell
you again, as I did before, about the parable of the bird
and the human soul, which is from St Augustine, about

314

*how the soul is like a bird that flaps around in a big
house for a while, then finds an exit and disappears.*

*But your concentration will have gone by now,
Daniel, and you'll be back to the things you know about,
the things you know you believe: the earth, the vineyards, the soil, rubbing the smooth surface of a stone
beneath your thumb, and you'll ask me, as you did when
you were five or six, what it would be like to be a stone,
standing still in a wall like this for five hundred years.
You looked down at your hands then, my darling boy,
at your fingernails, your skin, and you turned very pale
then as if you had seen a ghost, as if you had passed
through some tunnel of knowledge about yourself that
answered to a truth that was too painful to bear. You
looked up at me then, Daniel, and you burst into my
arms.*

Acknowledgments

For their love, support and encouragement, I would like to thank the following people:

Fae Brauer, Lara Brauer, Hamish Burton, Ollie Burton, Aurea Carpenter, Jessica Carsen, Karen Cooper, Marie-Hélène Dupré, Alex Elam, Danny Finkelstein, Justin Fleming, Frances Gayton, James Harding, Barbara Heide, Andy Hine, Mercy Hooper, Clemmie Jackson-Stops.

Oliver Kamm, thank you.

Lottie Moggach, Paul Myners, Rebecca Nicolson, Alex O'Connell, Lucy Parrish, Richard Pohle, Rozanne Rees.

Louis and George, I love you.

Peter Sandison, Eleanor Scharer, Sally Sole, Tara Stewart, Caroline Sullivan, Emma Tucker, Alice Van Wart, Erica Wagner, Vanessa Webb, Laura Westcott.

Rhian Williams, thank you.

Hattie Young, for the first book, James Young, and Nicola Young.

And thank you to my parents, Michael and Daphne Young..

Natalie Young has worked for *The Times* for several years. She has two children and lives in London. This is her first novel.